"I . . . I'M NOT MARRIED."

He had to remember she was different from him. She lived her faith in a community secluded and insulated from the world's evil. "I shouldn't pry."

"I'm sure you have lots of questions."

That he did, starting with his own name and his past, his life, the bullet wound in his side. The nagging headache. How could he remember things about Amish people but not his own life?

"Abigail?"

"*Ja?*"

"Thank you for pulling me out of the lake."

<u>BOOK YOUR PLACE ON OUR WEBSITE</u>
<u>AND MAKE THE</u>
<u>READING CONNECTION!</u>

We've created a customized website just for our very special readers, where you can get the inside scoop on everything that's going on with Zebra, Pinnacle and Kensington books.

When you come online, you'll have the exciting opportunity to:

• View covers of upcoming books

• Read sample chapters

• Learn about our future publishing schedule
  (listed by publication month and author)

• Find out when your favorite authors will be visiting
  a city near you

• Search for and order backlist books from our
  online catalog

• Check out author bios and background information

• Send e-mail to your favorite authors

• Meet the Kensington staff online

• Join us in weekly chats with authors, readers and
  other guests

• Get writing guidelines

• AND MUCH MORE!

Visit our website at
http://www.kensingtonbooks.com

The MEMORY QUILT

LENORA WORTH

ZEBRA BOOKS
KENSINGTON PUBLISHING CORP.

www.kensingtonbooks.com

ZEBRA BOOKS are published by

Kensington Publishing Corp.
119 West 40th Street
New York, NY 10018

All Kensington titles, imprints, and distributed lines are available at special quantity discounts for bulk purchases for sales promotion, premiums, fund-raising, educational, or institutional use.

Special book excerpts or customized printings can also be created to fit specific needs. For details, write or phone the office of the Kensington Sales Manager: Attn.: Sales Department. Kensington Publishing Corp., 119 West 40th Street, New York, NY 10018. Phone: 1-800-221-2647.

Zebra and the Z logo Reg. U.S. Pat. & TM Off.
BOUQUET Reg. U.S. Pat. & TM Off.

First Printing: December 2021
ISBN-13: 978-1-4201-5245-6
ISBN-13: 978-1-4201-5246-3 (eBook)

10 9 8 7 6 5 4 3 2 1

Printed in the United States of America

CHAPTER ONE

The wind hit her with a cold, uncaring slap, reminding her March could be a brutal month. A few more days and then April would be here. The sun came to her rescue with a reluctant stroll over the choppy lake waters, its early morning rays timid but steady as they lifted to the sky.

Abigail King loved this time of day, her time to walk the shores near Lake Erie. Glancing back up the bluffs toward the Shadow Lake Inn, she hoped her two sisters would leave her be so she could think. She always talked to God on these early morning walks and rarely missed one unless the weather became too harsh.

Shadow Lake Township was a sleepy little place near Lake City, Pennsylvania, where the small, secluded Amish community got up before dawn and closed down as soon as the sun went away. This steady, sensible routine was comforting and familiar, but Abigail sometimes wished she could travel far away and see some of the world outside these Western Pennsylvania bluffs and valleys. She belonged here and she accepted that. Right here, running the old inn, taking over for her parents. Daed had suffered a heart attack a few years ago, and

Mamm had a bad back and worried about him all the time. Who would take care of them and her younger sisters, Eliza and Colette, if she up and left the place?

Perhaps one day she would venture out of this insular world. Maybe one day she'd meet someone to share her life with, the way Mamm and Daed shared every moment with each other as if it were the best treasure in the world. Years had passed since her Rumspringa. Too many years. But Abigail remained hopeful she'd find that kind of love.

But not today. She'd have to save her daydreams for later. They had guests checking in this afternoon, and that meant cleaning and baking and making sure the bridal suite shone with a sweet warmth any newly married couple would enjoy. The honeymooners were traveling from New York to California, meandering and taking whatever paths they found.

They had discovered Shadow Lake Inn, so named because it stood on a high bluff near a small cove and a waterfall that flowed through a tributary near Elk Creek, down to the main lake. Shadow Lake was not nearly as massive as Lake Erie, but close enough that Abigail could hurry down the rock steps on one side of the inn's vast property for a walk that took her toward the lapping waves of the much bigger lake.

Abigail wanted that for herself, too. Someone to meander with, someone to love and cherish the way her *daed* and *mamm* loved each other. Someone to take her out on the big lake every now and then and speak pretty words into her ear.

She lifted her head and pulled her shawl closer as the wind played with the strings of her black winter *kapp*. Something in the distance caught her attention. A shape on the bronze sand. All kinds of things washed up on these secluded beaches, but this bundle of color looked different.

She squinted and then hurried closer. When she saw a hand touching the muddy brown sand, Abigail let out a gasp. A man floated facedown in the shallows, his upper torso and head out of the freezing water while his legs swayed and bobbed with the crashing surf.

Abigail glanced at the shore, wondering how he'd gotten here. No one was around. This particular stretch of beach was private and usually deserted unless the inn had a lot of guests. But today, in the chilly, blustering wind, Abigail wished someone *would* walk by.

She was all alone.

With an unconscious man lying at her feet.

Kneeling, she glanced at his wet black sweater and dirty jeans, then tentatively felt for his pulse. Alive but weak. He had to be so cold. "Mister? Can you hear me?"

A soft moan.

Abigail ignored the icy water lapping at her boots and the skirts of her wool dress and tried with a rough tug to drag him and flip him over. Her first attempts didn't work, but when she changed her position and bent over him, she managed to get him onto his back and drag him a few more inches out of the cold water.

Gripping his sweater, she began checking him for wounds. As her fingers moved down his torso, her hands came away bloody. He had an injury.

She searched the soggy black sweater and saw a dark stain underneath his left rib cage. A small hole oozed blood.

He'd been shot!

Grabbing for the business phone she usually kept in a pocket, she remembered she'd left it charging in the inn's kitchen. No help there. Abigail went to work, using the CPR method she'd been trained in. *Gut* to know, her *daed* had always said, especially because she ran an inn and dealt with all kinds of people.

Her attempts to revive the man made her blush. She had to put her mouth to his to breathe air into his lungs, which gave her a good view of his dark, handsome face. A hard face, stony and world-weary, dented and scarred, but intriguing. His silky brown hair needed a good trim. His jaw bristled from missing several shaves.

Englisch. But how and why did he wind up here, shot and almost dead?

Abigail kept up the breathing and the chest pumps.

Taking in air, she glanced around for a boat or another human. No one nearby or around the stretch of shoreline toward the cove.

She leaned down to try again, but just as she brought her face to his, the man's eyes came open and his hand lifted to grip her arm. "Who are you?"

Abigail jumped back. She'd never seen such blue eyes. Deep and wild, cobalt mixed with a darkness that startled her and warmed her with an intense heat.

"I'm . . . I was walking on the shore and found you. You're hurt."

He studied her for a moment, distrust in his eyes. "Can you help me?"

"I'm trying," she said. "I'll find help, I promise. Try to relax."

His head drooped, whether from relief or pain, she couldn't be sure. He needed tending, so she struggled to bring him further out of the water. Well-built and solid, his body was heavy.

"Abigail?"

She whirled to see her sister, Eliza, standing on the stone steps leading down from the inn's gardens to the shore. Had her sister been following her all this way? Never any peace around here.

But she was thankful for some help.

Abigail stood and called, "Eliza, *kumm* quickly."

Eliza hurried down the steps, her cloak flowing behind her. "*Was der schinner is letz?*"

What in the world is wrong?

"He's hurt. I found him in the water. I mean, on the shore," Abigail said, frantic now. "He's been shot and needs our help."

Eliza rushed toward her and then stopped. "He's not one of us."

"*Neh,* but he's cold and injured."

Eliza stared at the man as if he were a nasty bug. "He could be dangerous. We should call the Township police."

The man moaned and Eliza stepped back. "Abigail, do you hear me? Police."

"Then hand me your phone," Abigail said, knowing Eliza sneaked out her own business phone a lot so she could call a boy she'd been walking out with.

Eliza's eyes went wide as she hesitated, and then, with a sigh, dug into her hidden pocket to retrieve her phone. "Call the police, Abigail."

The man's head came up and Abigail leaned away, but he grabbed her arm again. "No police."

Eliza tugged at Abigail's arm while the man tightly gripped her other hand. "He might be hurt, but he needs someone to tend him. No police—that means he's *druwwel.*"

Abigail stared down at the man. "He might be *in* trouble, but we don't know that he's trouble. I can't leave him here."

"Well, you can't keep him either," Eliza replied, digging in her dark boots. "Daed will not approve."

"We will keep this between us," Abigail decided, breaking so many rules. "I won't leave him and I'm not calling the police until I can talk to him."

"*Denk,*" her sister said. "*Denk* about what you're doing."

"I have thought about it. You're to go and get Samson and the hauling wagon and drive it around over the bridge and down to the beach. Hurry now. And bring blankets."

Eliza glanced up toward the towering, Colonial-style white mansion that now served as an inn, then waved her hands in the air, her hazel eyes wide with uncertainty. "And where do you plan to put this man?"

"The carriage *haus* apartment. Daed never goes out there anymore."

What had once been the carriage *haus* was now used mostly for storage. It sat attached to the main *haus* by a long, wide, covered walkway that had once been a drive-through for fancy carriages; Amish delivery buggies used it now.

They only opened the apartment, located on the far side, when help had to stay over for a big event. Neat and clean but sparse, it had a small bed and a bath, plus a galley kitchen. He'd need cleaning up and he'd need to rest. That would be the best place, once she had all the supplies she'd need to tend to him.

"This is *dummkopp*," Eliza replied.

"It might seem stupid, but we have to help. Now go."

Eliza pushed at her bonnet and rolled her eyes, but she scurried back up the steps and headed toward the stable located at the back of the property. A long walk. She'd have to sneak Samson and the buggy out, or make up an excuse.

The man moaned again. "Help."

"I'm going to help you," Abigail said. She took his hand and tried to warm him, then tugged at her wool shawl and covered his chest. He began shivering and coughing. She'd need to tend to his wound. She prayed the bullet had gone through without hurting any of his internal organs.

While she waited for Eliza, Abigail prayed for the man who held her hand. The sun warmed her skin now. Past time for her to get back up to the inn, but here she sat, staring down at a stranger who might be near death. The man shivered and moaned, his tough exterior at odds with the soft sounds of pain and urgency. "No one. No police."

"We won't alert anyone until I find out more," she said. For some reason, Abigail believed this was a good man, and he needed her to hide him and help him.

Did she crave adventure so much that she was willing to risk her life and expose her family to danger?

Her head said no. But her soft heart, which seemed to beat faster now, knew she couldn't abandon someone hurt and in need. Someone who held her hand like a lifeline.

* * *

He woke in a sweat, memories of dark water and a burning pain causing him to lift up. But the pain hit hard, knocking him back.

"*Neh*, stay there," a soft voice said. He blinked, remembered that voice. He'd thought an angel had come for him. But somewhere in the mist and pain, he knew he wasn't worthy of an angel. So he'd taken the pain.

He lay back down, his head spinning. The warmth of a heavy quilt soothed him even while shivers shook him. "Where am I?"

"The Shadow Lake Inn," she said. "I . . . I found you on the beach."

"What lake?" His mind felt like dust, floating, thick, burning, and blank.

"Lake Erie, actually. We're off the beaten path, near a waterfall cove. Between Lake City to the north and Elk Creek to the south."

Lake Erie? Pennsylvania or Ohio? Michigan or New York? Where was he? The mist took over, dragging him down. Sleep. He needed sleep and he needed to forget. *No, no*.

"Where?" he asked again, not recognizing the places she'd mentioned. Wincing, he huffed a breath and realized he'd been out again. "Which state?"

"Pennsylvania."

"How did I wind up in Pennsylvania?"

He opened his eyes and looked up at the woman sitting by the bed sketching, her charcoal pencil slicing across the sketchpad. Amish. The light in the room had shifted and she sat in the glow of early sunset, her hair a shimmering red-gold. Maybe she was an angel after all. How long had he slept?

He stared at her, silent and jittery, his thoughts going back.

"I remember the water," he said on a rusty whisper. "I remember you."

She sat up and gazed into his eyes, studying him with apprehension and curiosity, her wide lips parting.

"How long have I been here?"

"Three days now," she said, her tone quiet and serene. "You've slept most of that time. You had a fever, but I managed to get some healing tea in you, so it's gone down now."

He lay watching her, trying to form his thoughts, trying to gather his scattered memories. "I remember you and the lake . . . but I can't remember anything before that."

The woman went pale, her skin glistening like porcelain in the muted sunshine that streamed through the small windows on both sides of the room. Several freckles fell across her cheeks like fairy dust.

"Do you know your name?"

He closed his eyes, saw shapes and heard noises. Gunshots, screaming, anger. He couldn't go any further into the recesses of his mind and he couldn't hide the panic in his words. "I don't. I can't remember."

She rose from the straight-backed little chair, placed her pencil and sketchpad on the bedside table, then gently pushed him back against the pillows. "I'll call you Jonah, because the lake swallowed you up and spit you back out."

He almost laughed. She was beautiful in that Plain way. The fact that he recognized her as Amish told him he must have known something about this area. But why was he here?

"I need to know," he said, trying to stay calm. "How did I get to the lake?"

She gave him a straightforward stare. "I have no idea. I was hoping you could tell me."

His gut burned, not from pain now, but with an urgency he couldn't explain. "I have to leave," he said, trying to rise.

"*Neh*. You have been wounded, shot in your side, but I think the bullet went through." Giving him a curious glance, she said, "I cleaned it and put some salve on the wound. It's bandaged, so don't mess with it."

"Shot?" He could feel the burn now, the heat radiating in his midsection. Touching the wound, he found a tightly bandaged piece of gauze covering a wide area under his rib cage. "Who shot me?"

She pursed her lips and held her hands together. "I don't know. I found you on the shore and dragged you out of the water. You must have hit your head somehow, too. You were unconscious and, at first, drifting in and out. Then you became unresponsive."

"Unresponsive?"

She cast her gaze down. "I . . . I gave you CPR. I had to learn it because we run this inn, the Shadow Lake Inn. You're in one of what used to be the servants' quarters. You'll have privacy here."

He glanced around. "This is not your home?"

"I live around back in what used to be the property manager's house. My family and I live there, that is."

Family. Why did that word feel like a knife in his heart? Was she married, with children?

Why did that idea hit him in the heart, too, with a pang

that seemed to stretch beyond the void of his mind? Did he have a family somewhere?

"What's your name?"

She fidgeted and adjusted the quilts. "Abigail. Abigail King."

"And I guess, for now, I'm Jonah."

"If you don't mind me calling you that."

"It'll do for now. But I need to remember something, anything." He couldn't for the life of him remember his own name, and that realization brought a panic he had to contain. He should be worried, but the petite, calm woman who'd apparently saved him had also brought him back to earth. He'd figure this out. Something in his gut told him he was good at that, at least.

He began to settle, to assess the situation. "Someone shot me and dumped me into Lake Erie?"

She fidgeted and then nodded. "I think so. You must have hit your head, too. I found you near the mouth of a tributary that pours directly into the big lake. That's all I know."

He needed more. "How did you move me here?"

She stood and paced. "My sister Eliza and I put you into a wagon."

"You got a wagon down to the beach?"

"We have a good draft horse—Samson. My sister brought him and the wagon around on the cove road. It's where people bring boats to launch into the lake."

A boat. He had a flash of a big boat, but then it was gone, leaving a sharp, pounding pain in his confused brain.

"You brought the horse and wagon down to the beach?"

"Yes, and together we got you up and into the wagon."

"I don't see how."

She smiled. "It got messy. She told our staff she needed to pick up something, but they are still wondering what. You weren't happy. We got sand and mud all over our clothes, and we had to take the old dirt road to avoid coming across anyone."

"I'm sorry." No telling what kind of words he'd used. No telling how much effort it had taken them either.

She looked down at her hands. "It wasn't easy."

Those words halted him. She'd gone above and beyond to save him. A gesture that could cost her a lot.

"No, I must have fought you. Why did you save me?"

Her eyes widened in surprise before she glanced toward the window by the door. "I felt it my duty to help someone in need." Then she looked directly at him, a silent strength in her eyes. "And you asked me to help you. You also asked me not to call the police."

Police.

That word jarred him, shook him. His headache grew in intensity. Holding a hand to his temple, he said, "You didn't have to listen to me."

She stood, all business now. "I saved you and dragged you here to this room, without my parents' knowledge. Do not make me regret that, Jonah. Or I'll throw you back to the whale."

CHAPTER TWO

A few days later, Jonah watched her go to the small kitchen and come back with a cup of steaming liquid. "If that's coffee, I'll kiss you."

She looked shocked, her high cheeks blushing. "You aren't my type."

He chuckled despite the situation. He'd expected her to give him a lesson from the Good Book. "I guess I'm not, at that."

When she handed him the mug, he frowned. "Not coffee."

"It's broth. Bone broth. You need your strength."

The frown turned to a scowl, so she'd know he wasn't happy. "It looks disgusting."

"Drink this and I'll let you have *kaffe* and a Danish later."

"You're a great host but a mean nurse." He took a tentative sip of the warm broth. It tasted pretty good, spicy and peppery. Trying to remember how long he'd been there, Jonah figured it was over a week at least.

She put her hands on her hips. "I am not mean, just firm."

"Yes, ma'am." Then he felt remorse for chiding her. "Do you make your husband drink this stuff?"

She stopped and pivoted away from the tidying she seemed to want to do, her gaze cast down. "I . . . I'm not married."

He had to remember she was different from him. She lived her faith in a community secluded and insulated from the world's evil. "I shouldn't pry."

"I'm sure you have lots of questions."

That he did, starting with his own name and his past, his life, the bullet wound in his side. The nagging headache. How could he remember things about Amish people, but not his own life?

"Abigail?"

"*Ja?*"

"Thank you for pulling me out of the lake."

"You're welcome, I think."

Setting down the almost-empty mug, he turned serious. "I don't remember who I am. I don't want to burden you, but do you have access to a computer or a laptop?"

"Why?"

The distrust hit him square in the chest. "I might be able to do some research."

"On yourself? When you don't even know who you are?"

He realized how impossible that sounded. "You make a good point."

She nodded, her full lips pursed while she stared at him. Her eyes glistened like emeralds. "Right now, you need to rest and get your strength back. But I can sketch you."

"Excuse me?"

"I like to make pictures." Grabbing the sketchpad, she pointed to the page she'd been working on—a sketch of craggy bluffs covered in shrubs and the lake beyond, with azure water and a light blue sky. "I can sketch your face and compare it to anyone who might have gone missing on the lake this weekend."

Sketching. Sketch artist. His head boomed with a deep pain that pushed the memories back so far, he couldn't grasp them.

His pulse raced as his past receded. What had happened to him?

"Jonah?"

He looked up to find her sketching away. Without thinking, he grabbed her arm. "Don't."

The fear that colored her eyes floored him. He didn't want to hurt this innocent woman, but somehow, he knew he had the power to do that. She dropped the pad and sat back in her chair, demure again, that streak of passion and defiance he'd seen in her eyes gone now.

"I'm sorry," he said. "I can't explain it, but I don't think I want anyone to know I'm here. Not yet."

She gave him that direct stare again. "If you can't remember, why do you refuse to let me help you?"

"I want help," he admitted, frustration making his headache worse. "You saved my life, and I'm grateful, but until I find out more, I can't explain. Let me rest here for a while. I heal quickly."

"You've been shot before?" Looking shy again, she

said, "I noticed some scars when I examined your wound and bandaged it. You must either be adventurous or dangerous."

He halted at that, his hands gripping the quilt. "I've been in dangerous situations before." Then he held up his hands and dropped them. "But I don't know what or why."

She stood and gathered her sketchpad and colored pencils, and what looked like medical supplies, into a big basket. Then she headed to the door, but turned to study him. "Are *you* a dangerous man, Jonah?"

"I don't know," he admitted. "I think I could be. I don't want to bring anything dangerous to you, Abigail."

"Then stay here and get some rest. I know your face. I'll do some searching of my own."

"Be careful."

She nodded, her back straight, her apron clean and white, her dress dark blue wool, her hair, so prim and proper, a shimmering reddish blond. "I'm always cautious. I'll be back to check on you later."

He watched her go, then sank back against the soft, fresh-smelling pillows. How had he wound up here in this bucolic Amish setting? Why had he been on the lake in the first place?

And why couldn't he remember who he was?

A few days later, Abigail hurried to the kitchen to make sure lunch had been served. The large, rectangular dining room had several rows of paned windows offering a full view of the lake out beyond the bluffs. The furnishings, left behind by the original owners, were antique and priceless. Chippendale curios, Hepplewhite mahogany sideboards, and Thomas Sheraton cabinets graced the walls around the Queen Anne–style dining tables. Landscapes and pastoral paintings hung on the walls. The view of the lake out beyond the wide, rocking-chair-filled porch added to the charm of the old place. The porch had been expanded through the years to add more rocking chairs.

Abigail had a lot of helpers who did everything from taking care of the white tablecloths and arranging fresh flowers from the greenhouse as centerpieces to working in the kitchen and cooking and prepping. The head cook, Edith Bauer, ran the kitchen with firm, no-nonsense efficiency and didn't allow slackers. Abigail's staff knew to get the work done. Edith loved to cook good food the guests came back for over and over, but Abigail, her sisters, and Mamm also helped with the cooking.

All were dedicated workers, both Amish and *Englisch*, but some of them loved to gossip. She couldn't let the *blabbermauls* get wind of Jonah. Or whoever he was. Why had she felt the need to save this man when she easily could have called the authorities and let them handle this matter?

Maggie Yoder greeted her with a smile. "You're late for dinner." While the *Englisch* called the midday meal lunch, Maggie and most of the others still called it dinner. Supper would come later for the Amish. The guests were on their own there, unless they asked for a special private dinner in their suite.

"Sorry, I had some things to attend to," Abigail said, guilt over her secret eating at her. "How many guests?"

"We have nine," Maggie replied. Married and waiting to have her first child, Maggie handled the midday shifts in a professional, no-nonsense way, with Colette helping her as needed.

Maggie scooted away with a smile. "And two of them are waiting for their *kaffe* and pie."

Edith came bustling around the corner, her brown eyes taking in the action, her hands on her hips. "Fresh *kaffe* coming up. I have three more pies in the oven for today and tomorrow."

"That should do it," Abigail said to the petite, buxom woman. Everyone feared Edith, a widow whose family had been part of the small group of Amish who'd settled here after leaving a community in Ohio. She was a sweet bit of mush beneath that bossy exterior, but Abigail kept that knowledge to herself. She needed a formidable chef in her kitchen.

Edith gave her a curt nod and spun on her orthopedic shoes, heading back to her domain before she left for the day.

"There you are." Colette grabbed Abigail by the arm and dragged her into a corner. "Were you with the mystery man?"

Colette had caught Abigail and Eliza sneaking to the carriage house with the hauling wagon. In her covert way, she'd followed them and reluctantly helped them, then let out a gasp as she stood at the door while they tried to get Jonah's clothes off.

After explaining what had happened, while Colette simultaneously shook her head and then stopped to stare openly, Abigail had made her promise to keep Jonah a secret until they could figure out what to do.

"Other than a gunshot wound and a bad bump on his head, he's fit as a fiddle," Eliza had noted.

Hard not to notice the muscles and the scars and that interesting face that held a hint of danger. Even passed out, this man looked troubled and haggard. But then, he'd been through an ordeal that could have killed him.

"This is like one of our books," Colette had said, dreamy-eyed and shocked all at once. "He could be a pirate."

Colette loved her books, even if Daed frowned on her reading a lot of *Englisch* fiction along with her Bible.

"We don't have pirates on the lake," Eliza had pointed out. "But he could be dangerous."

They'd left it at that, and her sisters had promised they wouldn't say anything, but she knew they worried just as she did. So far, Colette had not blurted out anything about Abigail finding a man and nursing him back to health— amazing considering the girl could not keep a secret.

And as secrets went, this was a huge one. She had to admit she hated making Colette and Eliza accessories to her deceit.

It had been over a week now, and Abigail had managed to sneak out and check on Jonah almost every day. She'd also been smuggling food to him every day. Then she'd sit with him for a while, to make sure he had someone to talk with, and to make sure he'd improved.

Abigail had urged her sisters not to mention Jonah unless they were alone. Now, however, Colette had an inquisitive, dreamy expression on her face as she stood there in the kitchen for all the world to see. Edith would get a spoon after them if she thought they were dawdling.

"We should get started on the wash," Abigail said, trying to scoot by her sister with a warning glare.

Colette didn't seem to be in a hurry, but she followed

Abigail. "Well? What's your plan? He's been hidden in that dank old apartment for weeks now. Summer is coming, which means more people will be here. Not to mention Mamm and Daed will begin to wonder why you take off toward the old path every day after lunch."

"Shh." Abigail tugged her curious sister away from the big, sunny kitchen and into the pantry. "I intend to check on him and get some food in him, as I've done every day since he came to us. That's the plan so far."

"Is he awake and feeling better? Does he know what happened? Is he on the run? Did he say who he is? Is he famous? Or is he a hardened criminal?"

"*Absatz*," Abigail said, holding up a hand for her sister to stop. "He's . . . weak but better. He still doesn't remember anything."

She didn't divulge that he had horrible nightmares that left him sweating and shaking. Abigail had soothed him several times as she'd watched over him during a bad dream.

But still, he had no real memories.

"What do you mean?" Colette's eyes, a mixture of blue and green, glistened like the lake waters on a summer day.

Abigail hadn't told her busy sisters about Jonah's lack of memory. Wishing she hadn't blurted that out, she made sure no one was within listening distance.

"He has no memory. Only bits and pieces. He can't tell me anything."

"And you'll keep nursing him and feeding him until what?" Colette's gaze softened. "You always did take in the strays, but this one is different, Abby."

Abigail shook her head and whispered, "Very different. I'm not sure what to do with him, but somehow I think he needs this time of rest." Giving Colette a warning glance, she said, "He has dreams, and he mumbles in his sleep."

She should know. She spent as much of her spare time as possible watching him. Watching him while she sketched or worked on quilting squares. Watching him while she read Bible verses to him or talked to him about the routine of her life. Watching him while she tidied up the financial records so she could enter purchases and expenditures into the laptop files.

She'd studied his face until she knew every inch of it by heart. Studying Jonah truly had become her favorite pastime. His rugged, ragged face reminded her of the constantly changing shores of the lake, full of mystery.

Colette eyed her with a frowning suspicion. "Oh my. You're beginning to like him. You *do* want to keep him."

Abigail shook her head. "I can't have him here forever. He's *Englisch*. Sooner or later, he has to remember and . . . then he'll be on his way."

Or would he? That was the burning question Abigail didn't want to think about.

An hour later, all the guests had been served and the kitchen had gone quiet. Edith had left for the day. She came in around four each morning, and her arthritis kicked in after standing on her feet for hours. Cleanup would come, and then they'd go on to the other tasks— scrubbing rooms, washing linens, and baking for the next day.

Abigail would check the front desk and make sure the reservation clerk, an *Englisch* man named Henry Cooper who'd retired from a corporate job and loved working part-time, would be there until they closed at eight tonight. The same routine over and over.

While Abigail loved this creaky old place and her work, she couldn't hide the exhilaration she felt helping Jonah. A mysterious man who couldn't remember anything—dangerous, yes. But also intriguing. Somehow, she knew in her heart this man would not harm her. She wasn't sure what to do next. She'd have to explain to her parents soon enough. After being so careful that no one knew about Jonah, she prayed *Gott* would show her the way.

"Handsome and with no memory. He's dreamy," Colette said on a sigh as they swept and mopped the kitchen floor. In the dining room, a worker cleaned the aged wooden floors. "I can certainly see why you want him all to yourself, but you can't hide him here much longer. He might think you're holding him hostage and try to escape." Then she lifted the mop and grinned. "Of course, if he can't remember, you could just tell him he's yours already and you are to be married this fall. Prepare him."

Abigail came back to real time. "I wish you and Eliza would quit saying things like that. He's not a stray dog. He's a hurt, confused human being and I'm not going to lie to him."

"And yet you're keeping his presence here from Mamm and Daed."

Abigail's guilt swept over her like a rogue wave. "I'm well aware of that."

But Colette's idea did have merit. Jonah would make a fine husband, looks-wise at least. But she'd need to know more about what was inside his head. "He might already be married."

Colette gave her a snarky smile. "He's an intriguing, mysterious man who washed up at your feet. What are you missing here? He's *Englisch*, true. But you could convince him otherwise."

"Stop it," Abigail replied, not daring to go down that forbidden path. "I will tell Mamm and Daed. Soon."

She grabbed all the dish towels to put in the big industrial washing machine in the laundry room behind the kitchen. "I'm not planning on marrying the man. I only want to get him well and safe."

Colette snorted and pivoted back toward the pass-through window. Abigail followed and wrapped the leftovers from the freshly baked ham and the juicy meat loaf, then did the same with the mashed potatoes and string beans. They served two entrees and three sides each day, and the help either took leftovers home or created a variety of new dishes with them. Today they'd served pound cake with strawberry sauce along with apple pie for dessert.

Abigail sliced cake and covered it with the sauce, then turned to slice the pie and placed both in dessert dishes on the counter of the pass-through window. Some latecomers had come in and asked for dessert, so she obliged and sent out fresh *kaffe* with the treats.

Shadow Lake Inn had a reputation for taking great care of guests, and they came back time and again. Tourists loved the waterfall up the hillside, and the bluffs along the lake. The quaint village and marina were a few miles away in Shadow Lake Township, so the restaurant served both visitors and locals who stopped by for breakfast or lunch. She also sneaked a piece of pie for her private guest.

Lord, forgive me for my deceptions.

Henry waved to her, and Matthew Mueller, the busboy she'd known since he was a baby, smiled shyly at her. Nineteen now and looking for love, Mattie had a bad crush on Colette. But her younger sister had grand standards and rarely noticed Matthew's whimsical smiles.

"*Denke*," Abigail said to Matthew to show her appreciation for his hard work. He did more than bus tables. He followed Colette around like a puppy dog, begging for scraps of her attention. Like now when he volunteered to help Colette finish up with the dusting and mopping.

While Abigail busied herself with these familiar tasks and kept an eye on her sisters, she thought about the man lying in the carriage *haus* apartment.

A strong man, chiseled in stone, with eyes that turned from blue to the deepest gray and a face that showed a world-weary façade, a scarred, carved face. This man wasn't just hiding from someone. He was hiding a secret deep within his soul.

She wanted with all her heart to find out that secret.

But what if he was right? What if he had the power to hurt her?

Time seemed to slip away like the sun-dappled lake that moved and shifted but remained pooled in the crater where it had been created. Jonah accepted that he couldn't remember who he was or why he was here. He couldn't get out of bed much that first week, but now he grew restless. Summer would come soon, but he barely knew the date or month. Frustration ate at him and circled around in his dreams, making him grumpy and jittery.

Strange, horrible, violent dreams kept him exhausted. Why could he remember the dreams but not his real life?

Today, to get away from those dreams, he'd managed to bathe himself and put on the clean clothes Abigail had brought him. A blue cotton shirt and some black pants that had a hook to close the waist. Amish clothes. Now he stood at the small window that gave him a partial view of the lake, his whole system alert and wondering. Something about the big lake made him edgy. Had he been on a boat out there? Had he been fishing? Or running away?

Fishing. That word stuck to him like water pulling him under. He went to the other window, which looked out toward a quaint, two-story cottage sitting on a hill. The cottage where Abigail lived.

A soft knock caused him to turn. He'd been waiting for Abigail, as he'd waited for her every day for the past few weeks. She came each morning and again in the late afternoon. She'd change his bandages with her eyes averted from his face, then rub herbal salve over his wounds while he tried not to wince, and while he tried hard to ignore the softness of her hands. She'd also bring newspapers and books, hoping to jar his memory.

He'd read everything she brought and learned plenty about the Amish in the *Shadow Lake News*, but remembered nothing about himself so far. Nothing about his name or his past. But the memory of her touch stayed with him long after she'd left each afternoon.

"Come in," he said, his heart doing that funny jump that happened each time she entered the room. Stir-crazy, he needed to get out into the fresh air.

She opened the door, a tray in one hand. He hurried to help, but dizziness overcame him, and he stumbled and grabbed one of the two chairs in the room. Letting out an expletive, he righted himself and hoped she hadn't noticed his dizziness or his language.

She noticed and immediately set the covered tray on the tiny table before she rushed to help him onto a chair. "It's your head. I think you have a concussion."

He nodded, swallowed the bile in his throat. "I discovered a really sore spot when I showered."

She blushed. "You showered? That explains the pleasant scent in the air."

"Did I smell that bad?" he asked, only because he enjoyed flustering her.

Looking even more embarrassed, she straightened and got serious. "Not bad, but . . . a good bath soothes the soul."

She soothed his soul, but he wouldn't tell her that. He'd used her visits like a lifeline to keep him from going under again.

"The concussion would explain my lack of memories, too."

She took the cover from the tray. "*Ja*, and the bad dreams."

Jonah looked up at her. "How do you know about my dreams?"

She fidgeted with the ham and mashed potatoes and a huge slice of apple pie. "I've sat here with you for days now, trying to figure out what to do about you."

"I can leave," he said, not wanting to go. "After I eat this pie, that is."

Her crestfallen gaze gave him hope. Would she miss him? "You don't have to go so soon. You're not well yet."

"I need to go outside and get some fresh air," he admitted.

"I could help around the inn." Anything to fight the angst that kept bubbling up inside him.

"You don't work here. People will notice." Her gaze slipped around and came to a stop on his face. "Although we do employ several *Englisch*. But with that long hair you could pass for Amish. You'd need to shave, unless you're married, and we can't know that."

"I don't know what I am," he said, the edge in his words causing her to lift her chin. "I can be single—no beard. Wearing a hat would help hide me—I mean, hide my face."

"Why would you need to hide your face?"

He shook his head. "I don't know. I don't think I like people too much."

"You have strange ways, Jonah."

"Apparently I'm a loner."

And he'd need to stay that way until he found out what had happened to him. Because how could he trust anyone around here, or out there, beyond this safe haven?

Getting back to his idea, he said, "I need something to occupy my mind, to take my mind off . . . not being able to remember."

She looked thoughtful, but he could see the concern in her eyes. "It would be a *gut* way to ease you into things. We can always use a helping hand and I do most of the hiring now. I could find you a spot." Glancing toward the back window that faced the gardens and the cottage, she said, "We did lose a yard man a few weeks ago. My *daed* and Mattie try to keep up, but we need more hands to keep the landscape looking pristine. We could start you there."

"That's convenient. Give me a job, then."

She finally took the chair opposite him. "Eat your food. I'll consider this, but first you need to heal. You were shot and your head needs to get better. You can't get your memory back if you go too fast."

He pulled over the plate and took the fork she offered. "I'm fine."

"You think so?"

He nodded toward the window. "You said that you need a maintenance man or groundskeeper?"

"We did lose some of our help in that area," she said. "My *daed* has been tending the herb and vegetable gardens, but with summer coming, he'll need to stay out of the heat."

Jonah wondered if he'd be here through summer. That could very well be a possibility. "I can work in the garden and the stable until . . . things change," he said, unsure what that would mean.

"You're still having dizzy spells," she replied. "We can't have you falling into Samson's feed or, worse, his stall."

"I need to meet this Samson. He must be a mighty strong horse if he pulled me out of the lake."

"The best," she said. "My sister Eliza has a way with horses. She's trained him and turned him into a big baby. She looks after the stable and takes our summer guests on rides around the property." Her pretty smile lit up. "Right now, she's training a pony for children to ride. We're planning on building a small arena with a carousel, so the pony can go round and round."

Jonah loved seeing her smile. "I could help build that. I've seen those at state fairs."

A memory jiggled through his nerve-endings. Popcorn, cotton candy, ponies.

"Jonah?"

The memory disappeared, leaving a slight headache behind.

"Tell me about your family," he said while he dived into the meal and fought to ignore those memories. "Thanks for bringing real food today."

"Soup is real food," she said on a soft chuckle that floated over him like wind chime notes.

"This is better. This is meat."

She ignored his exaggerated moans of delight. "My *mamm* and *daed* used to run the inn, but they're older now and both have had some health issues. Mamm is younger than Daed, but she had a tough life until she fell in love with him. Now she likes to putter around after him, making sure he takes care of himself. So, my two sisters and I have taken over most of the responsibilities. We have a *gut* staff, but I suppose I'm the boss."

Giving her a grin, he said, "I can see why."

She smiled at that. "Eliza and Colette would agree with you. They both have their ways, too."

"Has your family always worked at the inn?"

"My parents have since before they were married. They both worked here and, as I said, they fell in love. The Marshalls, the *Englisch* couple who owned it, had no children, so we were like their grandchildren growing up. They both died in a car crash while traveling to New York City."

Car crash. Car crash. Jonah's heart rushed and tumbled. He could hear those words over and over in his hurting brain. Before he could grasp why they were important, the wall went blank again. All he could see was a bright yellow balloon lifting through the air. The wall went dark. Did he want to look behind that wall?

"That's bad," he said to hide his discomfort. The mention of New York caused another charge of awareness to move through him. His head pounded away, forcing the memories back. He'd been there—to New York. That much he knew. "I'm sorry."

Hearing about her employers' death had also hit a mark inside Jonah. Did he have family thinking he was dead? Had his concussion happened because of a car crash? No. No. Why couldn't he remember?

"It was awful and so tragic. We did not know they'd planned to leave Shadow Lake Inn to us. The house that had been in their family since the Revolutionary War left to my family. They had no one else close."

Jonah stopped eating. "They must have loved all of you."

"They did," she said, her eyes misty. "As we loved them."

"So now you're in charge."

"I'm not in charge. I simply boss everyone around."

Jonah loved her wit and her sense of humor. "Including me."

"I'm not sure what to do with you."

"I told you, I can work. I'm used to working."

"Do you remember anything?"

"Sometimes, in the dreams, I remember a house with a tree swing."

She listened, her gaze caught in his. "What did the house look like?"

He hurt when he thought about that house. Hurt deep in his soul. "Small, two-story brick, with a big, white-columned front porch. A giant live oak out front. And that

swing—a solid rope with good, strong wood for the seat."
He squeezed his eyes shut and then opened them. "A huge
magnolia tree in the backyard. I can remember that smell,
lemony and wild."

"The magnolias were blooming?"

"Yes. Magnolia trees everywhere. I can see them in
bowls and vases, too."

"Someone liked magnolias."

"Someone," he said, wondering who and where.

"Do you mind if I sketch what you've described? That
might help you remember more."

His first instinct was to tell her he didn't want to remember the house in his dreams. The pain in his head
pushed at the pain of the memories. But he had to start
somewhere.

"You can sketch the scene, but not me."

"*Denke*." She gave him one of her quiet gazes, her expression as settled and serene as the starkness of this
room. "If I sketch your memories or some of what you
see in your dreams, we can piece things together, you
and me."

"Are you going to keep me here in this strange, wonderful prison until you shake up my entire life?"

"I'm not keeping you," she replied. "You are free to
go, but you're not well, Jonah. Take time to heal."

Then she placed her hand against his shirt, near the
bandaged wound. "Here." And moved it to his heart.
"And here."

A deep shock of awareness shot up his chest and into
his heart. He took her hand and gently moved it away, his
gaze on her. "You keep making pie like this and touching
me like that, and I think I'll heal nicely."

Seeing the bashful look on her face, as well as the flare

of fire in her eyes, he regretted what he'd said. "I'm sorry. I guess I'm a flirt in real life, too."

"This isn't the real world," she replied on a whispery note. "At least, it's not your world."

He'd need to be mindful of his careless attitude. This woman was different from those he'd probably known out there beyond these bluffs. "I don't even know my own world."

Abigail stood and turned to head for the door, her calm now shattered, her blush deeply beautiful. "I need to change your bandage, but I'll be back later to do that."

Jonah knew if she touched him again right now, he'd forget about being mindful. Restraint wasn't one of his traits. Why couldn't he remember what they were?

"I changed it after I showered," he said on a low growl. "Seems I know how to mend my own scars."

She stood, looking as if she wanted to leave. He stood, recklessly wanting her to stay. More than ever, he realized he shouldn't hang around here too much longer.

"*Ja*, or cover them with bandages," she said before she shot out the door like a scared fawn.

She'd hit on the deepest fears in his soul. What was he trying to cover up?

Jonah stared down at his food, his appetite gone now. This wasn't right. Confused and lonely and aggravated about not being able to remember anything or do anything, he was struck by loneliness. No need to think about things such as kissing an Amish woman he barely knew. A woman he'd bonded with because she'd dragged him out of the lake.

And yet he missed her each time she left. They'd spent a lot of quiet hours together in just a few short days. He knew he shouldn't miss her. He didn't know much about her, but he knew *her*. Her serene, quiet nature seemed a soothing contrast to the jagged anxiety of his dreams. He would not hurt the woman who'd taken him in and now protected him.

"I need to get out of here," he said into the still-sizzling air of the tiny room. "Before one of us gets hurt."

He couldn't remember much, but he knew in his soul *he* did not want to be hurt again. Could that hurt be what held back his memories?

CHAPTER THREE

"Abigail, are you all right? You seem quiet lately and you look pale. Are you eating enough?"

Abigail glanced up from the baked ham she'd brought home to find her *mamm* staring at her. Sarah King might be getting older, but she could sense when one of her daughters was off-kilter.

"I'm *gut*, Mamm. We've had a busy week. With spring here, we're getting more and more bookings."

"I remember those days," Mamm said, smiling. "If this arthritis in my spine wasn't so bad, I'd help."

Abigail patted her mother's hand. "*Neh*, you are to do what you want. Enjoy your garden, read your Bible and the books I've brought. I know you love a *gut* story."

"My one indulgence," Mamm admitted. "Your *daed* humors me on that and I humor him on pie and ice cream."

"Where is Daed? It's almost suppertime."

Mamm walked to the big bay window that framed a perfect view of the distant lake. "Oh, he said he wanted to find something out in the carriage *haus*. A hammer he's fond of, to fix some of the boards around our picket fence."

Abigail dropped the serving spoon, splashing mashed potatoes all over the kitchen counter. "He shouldn't be doing that all alone and this late. I'll go check on him."

She hurried out of the rectangular, two-story cottage that sat on a high bluff behind the big inn, then whipped through the white fence and ran breathlessly toward the carriage *haus*. Her *daed* might find Jonah.

When she got there, she breathed a sigh of relief. Colette had Daed by the arm, regaling him with stories of how one of the waiters had spilled a bowl of soup on the table of a favorite couple. The man and woman had driven across Pennsylvania to come back to the inn for their thirty-fifth anniversary. Instead of getting angry, they'd laughed and told the waiter that on their first date, the candle on the table had set the napkin covering the bread on fire.

Daed smiled and nodded, his precious hammer in his hand. Colette looked up and saw Abigail, a warning smile on her lips. "Look who I found wandering around in the old toolshed."

Abigail stopped to catch her breath. "I can see who. Daed, I could have gotten that for you."

Her father looked up, surprised. "Abby, I am perfectly capable of taking a stroll to find a hammer. Stop spluttering about. But you should know, I heard something in the carriage *haus* apartment. You need to call the pest man again."

Colette's hazel eyes went wide with mirth, her expression shouting, *I told you so*. Thankfully, she guided their sweet father away, looking over her shoulder at Abigail. "Could be rats, *ja*?"

"Musta been a big one," Daed said as they headed back to the cottage.

Abigail stared after them, then whirled to go to the apartment. She'd tried to keep her visits short since the day she'd touched Jonah's wound and her whole world had changed. The way he'd looked at her then had her blushing alone in her room at night.

She'd always heard of people being instantly attracted to each other, but she'd never dreamed it could happen to her.

And with the wrong man at that.

But he was her responsibility until she could come up with a better plan. When she knocked, Jonah didn't call out. She opened the unlocked door, ready to tell him to be careful.

Just as she entered the room, he walked out of the bathroom. Without his shirt. She couldn't avoid seeing him, seeing the scarred beauty of his lean, muscular arms and his hair-dusted chest.

Their eyes met, held for a moment. A rush of heat poured through her, causing her skin to grow warm. Swallowing, she gathered her breath. So much for trying to keep her distance.

"Oh, I'm sorry," she said, turning away, her head down. "I . . . my *daed* came to the toolshed. I was afraid—"

Jonah grabbed his shirt. "I heard him. I tried to stay quiet, but I accidentally spilled juice on my shirt and the glass rolled across the table and hit the floor."

She looked around, her eyes down. "I'll clean it."

"I've done that." He came over. "I'm dressed now, so you can open your eyes and lift your head."

Abigail felt the heat of her blush all the way to her toes. "I thought you'd fallen, or worse."

"My dizziness is better," he said. "I'm just clumsy."

Abigail nodded. "We have to decide what to do, Jonah. I've searched the local papers online and read the ones we keep here for the guests. No one matching your description has been reported missing. No boating accidents, nothing but traffic accidents and some break-ins farther up the lake."

He stood silent, his towering stance filling the little apartment and making Abigail aware of his nearness. Too aware.

He looked straight into her eyes. "I can find somewhere else. I should leave."

Abigail didn't blink. Instead, she gazed at him and saw the doubt in his frown. She should agree and tell him she wished him the best. She should make him go. Instead, she said, "*Neh*, I'll try harder to find out more."

Jonah moved closer. "What if we never find out?"

Abigail didn't know how to answer that. "If you'd feel better leaving, then go. But I'd worry about you."

He shrugged. "Honestly, I'm not sure where I'd go. I have no identification, no money, and no life."

Her heart broke for Jonah. "You are safe here. Whatever brought you here, you are safe for a while."

That simple statement seemed to bring him comfort. He relaxed, a sigh going through him. "A couple more days and then I'll go to the locals and tell them I have amnesia. I'll give them all the information we have."

Her pulse pounded against her temples. "You said no police."

"I got confused."

"Maybe they're after you."

Anger colored his face. Hitting a hand against the wall, he said, "I wish I knew. Wish I could see past waking up and looking into your eyes."

She put her hand on the doorknob in flight mode. His anger and the heat of his gaze only reminded her she did not really know this man. "I have to go finish supper. They'll be wondering."

The rage simmered into regret. "I hope I didn't get you in trouble. I don't want that."

"I stay in trouble. We all do. Three girls, *ja*?"

"Yes. I can see how a father would want to protect all of you."

Abigail's breath caught at the anguish in his words. "You must have family somewhere, worried about you. I hope you can find your family, Jonah."

"Me too," he said. "I wonder if I have anyone."

Abigail didn't want to leave him here alone, but she had no choice. "I'll check on you tomorrow," she said. "And I'll bring fresh gauze for your wound."

He nodded, his gaze like a dark sky as his eyes swept over her. "Good night, Abigail."

Abigail walked out the door and shut it behind her. Then she leaned against the wall to gather her nerves. When she came around the corner, Eliza ran toward her. "You'd better hurry. Mamm and Daed are wondering."

"But they don't know?"

"Not yet. But Colette is not exactly *gut* at keeping secrets."

The sisters walked arm-in-arm back to the cottage. "I

have to tell them the truth. That might be the only way we'll ever find out who Jonah really is."

"I think so," Eliza said, her eyes full of understanding. "But I'm not sure I want to be around when you explain."

"You will be around," Abigail said. "I need you there, okay?"

"Are you growing too close to your Jonah?" Eliza asked, her voice low but concerned. "He's handsome and he's like a project you want to work on, or one of your strays—remember our kitten, Peanuts, and that dog that ran away—you called him Noah because he survived a flood."

Abigail's eyes blurred with tears. "We never found him and he never came back. It broke my heart."

"This man can break your heart, too."

"I'm not falling for him," Abigail insisted. "I'm worried that . . . that he needs someone, that he needs a strong faith to guide him."

"But you might not be able to give him that," Eliza said, patting Abigail's arm. "We don't know this man or why he got shot and dumped in the lake."

"We don't know that he *was* dumped," Abigail said, sounding defensive. Jonah needed a protector.

"He got there somehow, and someone left him for dead," Eliza said, her tone low but neutral.

"I think that's why I'm hiding him." Abigail nodded and wiped at her eyes. "I should have handled this better. I should have called for help, but Eliza, he asked me to help him. *Me.*"

Her sister gave her an indulgent look. "That does not mean you are the one who can save him."

* * *

The weekend came, bringing heavy winds and a late April cold snap. Spring tried valiantly to blossom, but winter wasn't ready to give up the fight yet. Jonah watched it all from his little window by the bed. Watched and waited and walked to strengthen his body. He'd been shot, had received a head wound, and he'd had a bad cold that made his throat and chest hurt.

But Abigail had brought him herbal tea and salves to put on his chest. He felt more human now, and he smelled like an herb garden.

Abigail's days were filled with cooking and serving guests, keeping the eight bedrooms clean and ready, checking on her parents, and seeing Jonah every day. She talked about her work each time she came. He asked her questions, hoping to learn all he could. This place was old and steeped in history, off the beaten path, secluded and peaceful.

But he was restless and feeling reckless.

He made every effort to get up and move around more. "I'd like to go down to the beach," he told her when she came with his evening meal. "I want to see where you found me."

"I don't know if that's a *gut* idea," she said. "It would be hard to do." Then she stared out the window that had saved him from going mad. "There's an old path that's rarely used." Pointing to the right, away from the inn, she turned back to him. "I haven't been down that one in a while. It got messed up in a storm and it's a bit hard to maneuver the washed-out places, but together we could make it down."

"You'd go with me?"

She turned to nod. "*Ja*. I can't let you wind up in the lake again, ain't so?"

He gave her one of his serious looks, still trying to figure her out. "Did I have a phone when you found me?"

Shaking her head, she said, "*Neh*. Just your clothes."

"No phone, no ID." He silently let that information settle. "Nothing on me but wet clothes." Someone had wanted him dead. That he knew.

"Your clothes are clean and mended now. You might want to put on your black sweater if we walk to the beach. It's chilly out there."

She'd worn a shawl and a sturdy black bonnet. This world was so strange to him. Almost like another time. The inn was fairly modern, but Abigail's tone and attitude spoke of an innocence he'd long given up.

"Can you find the path?"

"I know every inch of this place," she replied. "But we'd better hurry. I have things to do before I head up the hill for supper."

He bundled up, the fresh scent on his old sweater making him feel warm and safe. She wrapped her scarf around her neck and then searched for a scarf for him in the old armoire.

"Here! I remembered bringing some things over when you first arrived."

The scarf looked moth-eaten in places, but clean—a deep navy blue. He sniffed it and wrapped it around his neck, the scent of lavender encasing him.

"Let me go first," she said over her shoulder, "to make sure no one is about. We only have a few guests, and they should be cozy inside. Most of our day workers have gone home."

After she gave him the all clear, Jonah followed her around the corner, past the toolshed and what used to be the carriage drive. "Is that the stable?" he asked as they slipped onto the hillside and passed a massive red barn.

"*Ja.*" She glanced that way. "Eliza is probably in there with Samson and the other horses. We recently got a new pony for *kinder* rides—Peaches. Eliza is training her, but she's a docile little pony."

Jonah studied the big building, but he wasn't worried about ponies. Instinct told him the stable could be a dangerous place. A hiding place. Why would that bother him?

He tried to follow the path, to memorize it. Abigail moved ahead, the wind pushing at a few strands of strawberry-blond hair that had escaped her bonnet. He lay awake at night, wondering about her hair. It had to be long and soft. Did it smell floral and sweet the way she always did?

"Here's the hard part," she said, bringing him out of his dreams as they approached an incline. "A few of the stone steps are missing."

Jonah saw what she meant as they moved through the still-bare saplings and trees. "Here, let me go first." He went around her and then carefully moved one foot down onto the next step. He turned to stare up at her, his hand out. "C'mon."

"I can manage," she said, shy again. But she glanced around, struggling to find something to hold on to so she could make the leap.

"Abigail, let me help."

Her eyes flared with awareness as she gazed at him. With a lift of her chin, she nodded and reached out to put her hands on his shoulders. Jonah grabbed her around her waist, thinking she felt small and fragile. Then he lifted her up and over the rocky washout and tugged her down onto the rock where he stood.

"There," he said, his gaze holding hers while he ignored the pain from his wound and instead breathed in her essence. "There."

The wind lifted her bonnet. She grabbed to catch it and stumbled right into his arms. Jonah caught her to keep both of them steady. She placed her hands against his chest.

The world seemed to still. Jonah saw only her, standing there in front of him, close to him. A deep yearning burst through his heart. He'd held another woman in this way. A special woman.

He blinked, swallowed. "We'd better get going."

Abigail dropped her gaze. "We should have planned this better. A storm is coming."

Jonah thought the storm was already here and it was brewing inside his soul. He shouldn't want to kiss this woman. She wasn't like him. He didn't belong in her world. And yet holding her felt right.

Too right.

By the time they made it through the rocky foothills to the beach, he'd convinced himself he had to get away from Abigail and this secluded, peaceful place.

Because he knew he'd not led a peaceful life before. He had a scarred, bruised body and a mind that refused to remember.

Something had gone wrong in his life.

He wouldn't sully Abigail's Plain, quiet ways just to satisfy his longing.

Out of breath, they reached the beach. Driftwood and

aged leaves left over from winter lay like a tattered quilt over the brown sand. She stood away from him, watching him, her arms held tightly against her shawl. Did she hope he'd remember so she could be done with saving him and protecting him?

"I found you there," she said, pointing to a curve in the shore. "Not far from the cove."

Jonah studied the lake, heard the lapping of the big water, felt flashes of anger battering like the wind through his mind. A boat, a huge, moving yacht. Others. Others had been with him.

He grabbed Abigail's arm. "A boat. I think—a big boat."

"What kind of boat?"

"A white yacht. Or a big fishing boat."

Fishing. Why did that activity, that task, seem to jump out at him? Had he been fishing for pleasure or fishing for something else?

Abigail moved ahead of him, silent and cautious, her long shawl and skirt lifting in the wind, her sweet, spicy scent surrounding him.

Like a dream. He'd seen her in his dreams. Must have happened when he'd drifted in and out of consciousness. She'd been there, close to him. Her lips on his.

Had he dreamed that? Or had that been when she'd given him CPR?

But before those sweet dreams of her, he'd lived a nightmare. His mind reached toward that dark place and recoiled. He did not want to go back there yet.

Of that he was sure.

"Did this boat have a name? Was someone with you?"

"I don't know a name," he said, his tone as biting as the wind. "I wish I could know." Then he nodded, held a hand to his pounding temple. "But yes, I think I was with someone. I think I had a good reason for being there."

Then the flash of memory disappeared, and he stood alone on the beach with a woman who touched his soul and gave him hope. A woman forbidden to him. And that could be more dangerous for them than anything else.

Chapter Four

They made it back to the apartment just as the wind died down and the sun settled over the trees and water around the curve.

Jonah stared out at the water, his expression tense and wary. "I wonder what happened out there. It looks so peaceful right now, with the sun glowing over the lake. I can see why you love it here. The world feels safe here."

"You're tired," Abigail said, seeing the fatigue rimming his eyes. He wanted to remember. Or . . . he wanted to forget. "That was too strenuous."

She guided him into the little apartment, which seemed to grow smaller the more she was around him. When they'd been out there again, in the spot where he'd washed up, Abigail had thought about how he'd looked, floating half dead in the water.

Different from how he looked now. He had his color back and his eyes, which mirrored the moods of the lake, held a glint that told her he'd already moved ahead, wishing for what he couldn't remember. A man like Jonah would always want to know. He'd want details and reason, the truth. He'd always want the truth.

Jonah sank down on the bed. "How can I get anything done if I'm as weak as a baby?"

"A *bobbeli* grows strong with time, patience, and practice," she said, trying to keep calm. Trying to forget being held in his arms. "Lie down and I'll make tea."

She didn't wait for him to do her bidding but went about making what he called her infernal herbal tea.

"I'm not a baby, Abigail. And I don't have the luxuries of time and patience, or practice, for that matter."

"How do you know that?" She poured hot water into the tea mug, the scent of mint and orange wafting in the air. Grabbing one of the oatmeal cookies she'd baked earlier, she said, "You might have all the time in the world."

"No, I don't. Someone on that boat wanted me dead."

"You remember that?" she asked, steadying herself against the chair beside the bed.

"No, but I'm putting things together. I was on a boat, and then shot and possibly hit over the head. Thrown overboard."

"You should have drowned. I don't know how you managed to stay alive."

"Well, if they tried to dump me close to shore, in a deserted spot, that may have helped me stay alive."

"You mean a spot such as the bend in the lake, near the cove?"

"Yes. Or I could have survived the gunshot and woken from the head wound, then jumped overboard to get away."

"Either scenario could have happened."

Or a far worse scenario. *Dear* Gott, *why did you bring him to me?* There had to be a reason.

She took up her sketchpad and started drawing what

she thought a big boat would look like. So far, she had the brick house with the wide, white porch, a tree swing, a magnolia blossom, and now a boat.

And she'd sketched Jonah's face, from memory, and while he slept. No one would see those sketches.

At night she cut out quilt remnants to make squares and patterns. She'd begun stitching the scenes he'd remembered into panels. She wanted to make him a sturdy quilt. Why, she didn't know. She might keep it for herself once he was gone. It didn't matter. She needed busy work to keep this time with Jonah registered and recorded. Every quilt told a story, as Mamm always said. Well, this one would be a doozy. It would be a primitive pattern of squares, more folk art than pure Amish, but she was becoming better at creating folk art quilts that showcased the Amish at work and at home. She'd sold a few at mud sales and festivals. The *Englisch* latched onto anything artsy and handmade. This one would be special. Her secret, his memories.

She'd never sell this particular one, however. It would be hers alone and it would go into her hope chest.

"Abigail?"

She looked up from her sketching, her thoughts all mixed up. "*Ja?*"

"You look pretty when you're doing that."

Those sweet, soft words coming from such a hard, harsh man brought tears to her eyes.

"*Denke.*" That was all she could muster after seeing the slow burn in his blue-gray eyes.

"Do your parents approve of your artwork?"

"They don't mind as long as the inn keeps running.

They worry we'll mess things up, but I find time to frolic and create."

He smiled at that. "How does an Amish woman frolic?"

"Not in the same way as an *Englisch*, I can assure you." She kept sketching. "We hold quilting sessions and baking sessions, we feed the men during a barn building. We gather for singings and we can and freeze vegetables and make jams and jellies. We like to have *schpass*, same as you. Fun; it means fun. Are you excited?"

He laughed, but it sounded rusty and odd; there was a huskiness to his deep voice. "You're right. That is not how the women I know spend their time."

"Do you know a lot of women?"

He stopped and stared at her. "I guess I do. Why can't I remember any of them?"

She saw that distant look in his eyes. "What is it, Jonah?"

"I had a feeling. I can't explain it. The feeling of a woman."

Abigail tried not to show any emotion or interest. "I'm sure you have someone waiting for you somewhere."

They didn't speak for a few moments. The wind hissed and chased shadows outside their warm little cocoon.

Jonah shifted on his pillows. "Have you considered letting me help out to repay you for your kindness?"

"I've thought on it, *ja*. If we get you out more and give you honest work, your memories could return."

"Maybe so."

She looked away, and so did he. What if he stayed here, memories or no memories? What would she do about that?

* * *

Abigail made it home in time for supper. Eliza and Colette had heated up some chicken and dumplings and put out a broccoli salad. She hurried to wash up and get their drinks.

"You were noticeably absent," Eliza whispered. "Mamm suspects something, so she kept Daed occupied by reading to him from *The Budget*."

Abigail glanced toward the sitting room. "I'm sure he loved hearing all the latest Amish news."

"As always. Missing hogs and a cow loose, mud sales and planting charts. Such excitement."

They grinned at that.

Abigail turned to place the tea glasses on the table, only to find her *mamm* giving her a thorough appraisal. "Why is your hair unkempt, Abby?"

Abigail put down the tea pitcher and touched the *kapp* she'd rushed to put on after getting home. "I went down to the beach to get a breath of fresh air, but the wind turned swift."

"*Ja*, I can see that from the shifting trees," her mother replied. "I also saw you coming from the carriage *haus* again just now. Seems you've been tidying up that old place for days."

Eliza gave her a warning smile. "I explained to Mamm how we're getting ready for the high season. April is almost gone, but May will bring sunshine and more guests." Giving Abigail a sharp stare, she added, "So that is why you took extra time in the carriage *haus* apartment."

"For sure," Colette said as she made her way to the

table. "Then we'll never know anyone else has stayed in that apartment."

Mamm's sharp gaze moved from Colette to Abigail. "What does she mean by that? No one has been staying there."

Abigail shot Colette a glare. "I'm sure I don't know."

Eliza looked down at the table.

"Abe, supper is ready," Mamm called. "But before we eat, I think our girls have something to tell us."

Daed strolled over to the big table, his dark, mirthful gaze moving over their guilty faces. "What is this?"

Abigail held her hands on the back of her chair, her knuckles whitening. She couldn't lie to her parents—not to their faces.

Eliza stood still, refusing to look up at anyone.

Colette had a shocked expression on her freckled face after blurting out her comment about the apartment. "I'm sorry," she said to no one in particular.

Mamm's dark eyes zoomed in on Colette. "You will tell me what is going on. What are you three trying so hard to hide from your *daed* and me?"

Colette's eyes widened, and then she blurted out, "Abigail found a man in the lake and she's been keeping him in the carriage *haus*."

"I cannot believe what I'm hearing," Mamm said a half hour later. She stared at the now-cold food on her plate. "My daughters conspiring to keep a strange, injured *Englisch* hidden right before my very eyes! I'm not sure I have words to express what my mind is thinking right now."

"It's my fault," Abigail said, bone-tired and almost

relieved that the truth was out. "I made Eliza and Colette promise they wouldn't tell. I had planned to talk to both of you. Soon."

Daed gave her a confused stare. "Not soon enough, ain't so? You've had this man here for several weeks now?"

"I haven't kept track of the days," Abigail admitted. "He was ill, barely conscious. He had a fever for days and still is not completely well."

"That explains why some of my herb pots are missing," Mamm said. "You know, Abby, I am only a midwife, but you should have alerted me when you first found him. I could have helped."

"You should have alerted us *immediately*," Daed said, slamming a hand on the table and causing the plates to rumble. "This will not set well with the bishop. It does not set well with me. I am going to this man, and I will ask him to leave."

Abigail stood with her hand up. "*Neh*, you can't do that."

Her sisters watched, bright-eyed and trembling. They never disputed Daed's word. Mamm looked pale, her eyes shouting what her mouth couldn't say. "You've upset your *daed*," she managed on a low whisper, her eyes accusing.

Daed didn't move. He only looked up at his oldest daughter as if she'd turned to stone. Which she very well might before this interrogation ended.

"I'm sorry," she said, dropping back down into her chair. "Jonah is not ready to go back out into the world. He needs more time, and he's willing to work here while he figures things out."

"Work here?" Her mother's shocked words bounced all around like a yo-yo.

"He can't remember who he is," Colette offered up. "Abigail calls him Jonah."

"You named him?" Mamm and Daed turned to each other and then back to Abigail. "What have you done, Daughter?" Mamm asked, shaking her head. "You've been nursing a stranger back to life and you don't even know his name. We have no idea who this man really is."

"He doesn't want anyone to know," Eliza said, shrugging when Abigail shot her a quelling glare. "He wants no police and he only wants to stay here for a while."

"He could be a pirate, or possibly a secret service man," Colette said, dreamy again. "He is not a bad-looking man and he and Abigail—"

"We have an understanding," Abigail cut in, afraid to hear what her misguided sister might blurt out. "He must leave soon, but he needs some money to travel, and he has to alert someone that he is still alive. He can't remember much."

Daed stood. "Enough of this. Abigail, take me to this man. Or better, bring him up here so no one sees you going to his room in the dark."

Abigail's pulse pounded like a mallet against her skull. "I don't think—"

"Neh, you did not think at all, and now we must figure out what to do with your Jonah," Daed said. "Go and get the man. Take one of your sisters with you."

Abigail stood and nodded. Eliza volunteered to go with her.

That left Colette staring miserably at her plate. She'd probably confess everything while they were gone. Abigail couldn't blame her. None of them wanted to lie to their parents.

As they walked toward the carriage *haus*, Eliza asked in a hushed whisper, "What should we do now, Abby?"

"Pray," Abigail said. "We need to pray that Daed doesn't call the police on Jonah. That's what I'm going to do until we can convince Daed not to send him away."

Eliza stopped her before they reached the apartment. "You still want to keep him?"

"*Ja*," Abigail admitted. "I'm not ready to let him go just yet."

But did she have the strength to defy her parents over this?

Surprised to hear a knock so late at night, Jonah got up and went to the door, waiting in tense silence. When he didn't speak, he heard a muffled, "Jonah, it's Abigail. We need to talk."

He opened the door, hoping she'd come to visit, but when he saw Eliza with her looking so glum, he backed up. "What's wrong?"

Abigail rushed into the room, her fists twisting against her shawl. "They know, Jonah. Mamm and Daed—they found out you're here and they want to talk to you up at the cottage."

Jonah didn't panic, but he should have. He should have run out the door and kept running until he found himself again. But for some strange reason, he wasn't so sure he wanted to know how and why he'd wound up here. Not yet anyway.

"Okay, let's go," he said, feeling that he wanted to get this all out in the open. He'd be forced to leave, which was what he needed to do. Before he got too close to

Abigail and hurt her, or caused her to be shunned or kicked out of her community.

Wasn't that a thing with the Amish? They had rules, a big book of rules. And he had probably broken all of them.

Abigail looked shocked. "You don't mind?"

"I can't deny them an explanation, Abigail," he said, grabbing his black sweater. "I appreciate all you've done for me, but maybe I should pack up and get on, after I talk to them."

Abigail's surprise turned to confusion and hurt. Her vivid eyes never hid much, but they remained a mystery to Jonah.

"We'd best get you to the house," Eliza said. "Before Daed comes with the shotgun."

Gun. Jonah stopped and held his head. A bang and a flash almost blinded him before the pain hit.

"Jonah?" Abigail was there, holding his arm. "Are you all right?"

He blinked, and the pain subsided. "Yes. Let's get this over with."

His memory kept returning, piece by piece, like one of Abigail's quilts. And with each flash of memory, he almost broke through to somewhere he didn't want to be. Whatever he'd been through, it had obviously left him damaged and doubtful. That darkness tried to pull him back, to lure him to the truth.

He wasn't sure he wanted to know the truth.

Abigail gave him another worried glance, then turned to head out the door. "You're right. The sooner we get this over with, the better. Then we can all get back to our real lives."

CHAPTER FIVE

She shouldn't have snapped at Jonah. Abigail knew he was anxious to get back out there to whatever world he'd left behind, along with his memories. But after today and the way he'd held her, Abigail didn't want to think about him leaving and going out there, all alone and confused. What would become of him?

What would happen now that her parents knew? Would they shun her, or make her go before the bishop?

The closer they got to the cottage, the more Abigail felt cold sweat pooling between her shoulders. She waffled between feeling contrite for her sins to feeling resentful of the strict demands of her life. She would take her punishment, but she didn't want Jonah to suffer any more.

Eliza took her arm, as she always did when Abigail went into a panic. "This is *entsetzlich*, isn't it?"

"*Ja*, the most awful anything could be," Abigail said, glancing back at Jonah. "Colette didn't mean to let it slip, and Mamm was already suspicious, so I guess it had to happen. I should have gone to them right away."

"Why didn't you?" her sister asked. "I'm usually the impulsive, secretive one, ain't so?"

Abigail had to smile at that. "Usually. But I believe I've taken that crown now." As they neared the house, she whispered, "Something told me to protect him. I panicked. I didn't know what to do except to help him, and keep him alive. He's holding a lot of secrets in that memory vault he can't open."

"And those could be dangerous secrets," Eliza whispered back, her eyes shifting toward the man trailing behind them.

Jonah caught up with them. "I'm sorry, Abigail. I've been a burden on you. If your father won't allow me to work off that burden, I'll go away. But I'm well now and able to help as needed."

"We could use some extra *hilfe*," Eliza said, patting Abigail's arm. "I'm on your side," she added. Then she bent her head to peer around Abigail and pin Jonah with her daring gaze. "And I pray you bring no harm to Abby."

Jonah looked confused and then glanced at Abigail. "I never meant to do that to her or your family. Your sister saved my life and honored my request that she not alert anyone. I won't forget that."

He looked into Abigail's eyes, his gaze heated with a commitment she hadn't seen before. She had to believe he was telling the truth, as much as possible for a man who couldn't remember his own name. He'd been sharp about wanting to get this over, but he must also be fearful of what he might find beyond this cove.

When they got to the cottage porch, she warned Jonah, "My parents are upset and angry at me. Please respect them and don't try to shield me. I didn't tell them about you and that was my choice. I will accept whatever they decide."

Jonah's eyes went dark with a whirl of emotions. "Abigail—"

"Let's go," Eliza said, giving him a curious glance. Then she nudged Abigail. "He doesn't want to leave you," she whispered in Deitsch.

Abigail couldn't respond, so she hurried inside the house, feeling as if she was about to face the bishop himself.

Mamm and Daed sat waiting in their hickory rocking chairs. Colette had been standing by the window, watching. Now she pivoted to meet them when they came in.

"I'm sorry," she said to Abigail.

Abigail took her sister's hand. "It's all right."

Then she turned to face her parents. "Mamm and Daed, this is Jonah."

Abe and Sarah King sat staring up at the man she'd named Jonah. He looked out of place in the old Amish clothes he wore and inside this Plain house. Not just an outsider, but a man who couldn't tell them much about himself, a man who didn't want to be here right now, as the tightening of his jaw muscles indicated.

Mamm stood and came to study him. "Jonah, I'm sorry our daughter hid you away and I hope your wounds are healed." Then she stood back and put her hands on her hips. "However, hiding you in the carriage *haus* apartment does not set well with her *daed* and me."

Jonah cleared his throat and lowered his head. His dark hair had grown long around his ears and forehead, making him look like the pirate Colette always called him.

"First, let me say that I'm sorry I've caused any

problems. Abigail found me on the beach, and she saved me. I asked her not to tell anyone about me. I can't remember anything beyond seeing her face that morning. I don't know who I am and I don't know what I am. But I'm grateful for her help. Please don't blame her or punish her because of me."

He stopped and stood with his hands folded over each other, his eyes downcast. Abigail knew he was a man of few words, suspected that quiet, eloquent speech had worn him out.

Daed sat silently appraising Jonah. "Why do you call this man that name, Abby?"

Abigail blushed, heat spreading all over her body. "Because he fell in the lake and the lake let him go, spit him out, like Jonah and the whale."

"The real Jonah had a purpose after that happened," Mamm said, her steady gaze looking from Abigail back to Jonah.

Jonah finally looked up. "Yes, he obeyed God's commands and turned his life around."

"Close enough," Eliza said underneath her breath.

Mamm frowned at Eliza, but she remained quiet while she studied the man standing before them. After giving Abigail a considering stare, she asked, "Abe, what should we do?"

Her father remained seated. When he started tugging on his long beard, Abigail worried they were about to see the last of Jonah.

But her always unpredictable *daed* stood and took her *mamm*'s hand. "We do need a gardener, as I'm sure Abigail has told you. You look strong and sturdy. What do you know of horses?"

Jonah stood silent for a moment. "Nothing, but I can learn. I'll clean the stalls and learn how to feed them. Whatever I can do, and I'll work without pay to replenish whatever I've been given."

"It will be hard, physical work," Daed replied in a stern tone. "And the job comes with stipulations."

"What?" Abigail asked before Jonah could say anything more.

Daed lifted his hand, demanding silence. "While I don't condone what my oldest daughter has done, we will deal with that later. She felt an obligation to help someone in need, but she kept secrets from us. She and her sisters."

His gaze flickered over Colette and Eliza, chastising them with a single look of disapproval.

"So, this is what will happen. You will work here for the next two weeks, the same amount of time you've been hiding here. Those two weeks are for free, as your payment. After that, if things go well, you will work in the gardens and the stable, away from the guests, but only long enough to earn some funds for when you go back out in the world. And . . . you are only to speak to my daughters when necessary for your work and your duties."

Abigail's head shot up. But her father's stern glance squelched whatever protest she had.

Jonah nodded and then glanced at her. "I could use the money—once I've paid you back. I'll need cash if . . . if I'm ever to leave."

"You can stay where you are in the carriage *haus*," Daed said. "We'll have Matthew check on you as needed and show you around. You can eat in the kitchen dining area, where most of the staff take their meals."

"It's like *Downton Abbey*," Colette blurted out. Then

she lowered her head and studied her hands. Their parents frowned on the girls watching the big television in the inn's massive lobby.

"When your two weeks are finished, if you have not abided by my rules, you will need to leave our property," Daed finished. "Abigail, do you understand?"

"*Ja*, Daed, I do," Abigail said.

But she didn't understand. She knew she was being punished in the worst way. Her father didn't approve of her being alone with an *Englischer*, or any man, for that matter. No wonder she bordered on becoming an *alte maidal*. She'd forever be the old-maid innkeeper.

Daed gave her a softened look, his sweet eyes beseeching. He never liked to dole out discipline, but if the bishop heard of this, he'd demand even more. So Daed had taken a stand and they'd all have to live with it.

But how could she possibly get through her days without speaking to Jonah except to issue work orders and make sure he performed them?

Where would that take them?

To a place that would keep her from doing something forbidden, such as falling for a man she could never have.

May had arrived, and with it a warmth that carried the soft wind across a thousand blossoms. Jonah lay in the little apartment, his pillows lined up with his window on the world. He'd opened both windows to get some fresh air. Now he stared out at the muted light the full moon cast over the sloping yard and the bluffs. The only other window opened on the other side of the room, toward Abigail's home.

He tried to avoid that one. The pretty old cottage made him long for something he couldn't explain.

After he'd agreed to Abe King's terms, Sarah had checked his wounds, explaining that she was a midwife and people around there considered her an expert on any medical problem. She couldn't write prescriptions, but she could give him advice and suggestions. When she deemed him on the mend, the family had wrapped up a plate of food for him and sent him back here.

Now, he had begun reporting to the kitchen, through the back door into the inn, at six o'clock every morning. After a quick breakfast, he headed to the garden, and then Eliza and one of the stable boys would keep him busy in the barn.

Gardening and barn work. Jonah knew without a doubt that he'd never done either of those tasks, yet now he relished each new day. He'd paid up his two weeks and would begin making a salary this week. But he wanted to earn some cash before he went on his way.

His way to where? That was the question.

He'd glanced at Abigail after he'd been dismissed that night two weeks before. Her bright eyes held a blue mist that filled his soul with longing. He'd wanted to take her in his arms and tell her this wasn't her fault. He'd hoped she wouldn't get a lecture, but he had to admit her parents had been firm but fair.

"You are hurt and you don't remember who you are," Sarah had said again before he left. "Our Abigail has always been keen on nurturing hurting people and animals. Fitting that she was the one who found you. It is not fitting for her to continue being the only one who feeds you and tends your wounds."

That was another warning to him to be mindful of staying away from Abigail.

Two weeks of working off his debt to the King family. Two weeks of trying to do the work, but also avoiding the woman who'd been by his side for most of the weeks that had passed. He'd found it hard to avoid talking to Abigail, making her smile or frown, asking her questions that might help him. Work had helped him heal physically, but seeing Abigail every day those first weeks had held his mind steady.

He missed her with a raw ache—missed seeing her with a tray of food and clean clothes. Missed her sitting and explaining Amish ways and Amish words to him. Missed her cookies and her smile, her sharp wit, and the way her brow twisted when she sketched her drawings.

If he stayed, he'd long for her even more. It wasn't meant to be. He'd only latched on to her because she'd been the one to bring him back from the brink of death.

I could get dressed and slip away, he thought. Go back out there and find work somewhere. Or go to the local authorities so they could run a facial recognition on his mug, take his prints, and find a match.

How did he know they could do that?

Jonah's head hurt with a flash of pain, the sound of a gunshot, and then darkness.

He blinked and rubbed his throbbing temples. Was this why he'd told Abigail no police? Had the police been chasing him?

He couldn't sleep. He needed Abigail here. She always soothed him with her calm, sweet voice and her pretty sketches.

He got up and walked to the window so he could see

the lake better. Then another memory moved through his mind, this one softer and less painful physically. A woman's laughter.

He could hear the sound so clearly, he opened the door to stare out at the path. Were there people out there?

But all he saw was the moon's lopsided grin and the dark water lapping against the shore. Jonah stood in the cooling wind, his eyes closed, the sound of sweet laughter filling him with an intensely deep pain.

He shut the door and stood staring at his little world. Then he grabbed the pad and pen Abigail had left for this very purpose. *If you remember anything, write it down.*

Jonah scribbled the two flashes of memory that had moved through his mind, the sound of laughter still echoing inside his head.

Tomorrow, I'll work hard. But soon, I'm going to find out who I am and what happened to me.

He now had a lot of reasons to find out his real identity. He needed to know if someone wanted him dead and he needed to find a way to stay alive. To get back to his life.

Then he thought of Abigail. He wanted to be sure for her sake, too. She'd saved him for a reason. She'd tell him it was God's will.

Jonah didn't feel as if he'd been a religious man before, but being here in this quiet cove had given him a lot of time to think about God. He'd also thought about why he'd washed up on this beach. Abigail had read to him while he dozed, her voice soothing as she repeated the 23rd Psalm. Jonah had heard her voice, felt her nearby, even in his dreams.

She'd talked to him and sat with him in silence at times, bringing him back from the edge, saving him.

They'd kept a distance from each other, only speaking when necessary over these last two weeks, but would he be able to avoid her if she became his boss on a more permanent basis?

Jonah lay back down and smiled. "I'll have lots of questions to ask you, Boss Lady."

What better excuse than to spend more time around her? He'd work hard and watch out for any clues to his past. He'd be careful around Abigail, but he wouldn't stop talking to her. She was still his lifeline. That much he knew.

CHAPTER SIX

"Chickens?"

"*Ja*, chickens," Abigail told him a week later in the busy employee break room. "You've become a capable worker and you've stayed away from me, so you're being promoted. Daed and I talked, and he agreed."

She gave him a glance that showed she'd missed him, too. They'd managed to avoid any time alone or any kind of private conversation. It had been hard, but Jonah had honored the stipulations.

"What kind of promotion am I getting?" he asked, feeling a great weight lift from his shoulders. Now he could really get to work and, hopefully, see Abigail more. As much as Jonah wanted to regain his memories, he did like the peace and quiet of this place.

Abigail gave him one of her soft, sweet smiles. "You are now in charge of the grounds and outside maintenance, and that means cleaning the horse stalls and the chicken coops. Everyone else has tried and failed."

"I can certainly understand why," he mumbled, wondering how he'd won such exciting tasks. But a job was a job, and he'd promised to do this one. For Abigail. "I accept, although this sounds more like punishment than a promotion."

Abigail leaned in and whispered, "Take it, Jonah, before Daed changes his mind."

She'd brought him a new set of clothes and left them in the employee room yesterday, guessing what he needed. The dark broadcloth pants and white cotton shirt fit him well enough. The brogans were new, and he had on warm wool socks. The black wool hat seemed strange, but he had to wear it. She'd told him he could switch to a straw hat as the weather warmed. The big jacket crackled, old and worn. He didn't need it now that the weather had changed, but it spoke of a long-term commitment. Would he still be here when winter returned?

"It's been good to be out in the open again," he admitted. "I must have been an outside person before."

Abigail gave him a once-over. "You look Amish."

"Well, that's the plan, right?"

She laughed at that. "But you still seem *Englisch*."

"Can I get to work?" he asked, impatient now that he didn't have to hide. Impatient, because he wanted to linger here with her and flirt with her, even touch her.

Abigail looked amused until she lifted her gaze to stare into his eyes. Then she blushed and turned to business. "I'll show you how to gather the eggs and clean the coop. It's not the most fun job in the world, but we like to use fresh eggs when we cook. We use pasteurized ones from the grocery store for frying and scrambling, but fresh for baking. We also sell them locally." Shrugging, she added, "That means we have to gather eggs every day."

"I think your father is trying to make a point with

me," Jonah replied before biting into a big, freshly made cinnamon roll.

"He's showing you hard work pays off," Abigail retorted. "And we both got off rather easy this time. But he's impressed with you enough to pay you to stay . . . until it's time for you to go."

Silence floated between them, but only for a moment.

Jonah shook his head. "We haven't done anything wrong other than your hiding me away, and I forced that issue."

"I wasn't honest," she said, guilt showing in her expression. "I don't know what made me think I could keep you a secret."

"Did you want to keep me a secret?"

"I wanted to protect you until you could figure out what to do. I don't normally deal with wounded men floating on the beach. A new concept, and one I didn't handle very well."

He studied her face, saw the shame there in the blush on her creamy, smooth skin. But he also saw the strength of her determination in her eyes.

"I'm glad to be out of that tiny apartment," he said. "No more hiding. But I still need to find out what brought me here."

"That might come with time. At least you can use the laptop in the office to do some searching."

"That I will do, after I've finished my work."

Jonah sipped his coffee and stared out at the lake, thinking there wouldn't be a next time with her father. Jonah had to make this right. He might not remember much of his past, but he had a gut instinct that made him think he had been on the right side of the law. He also wanted to work, so he must have some sort of work ethic.

Meantime, he didn't mind hard work at a place like this. This land sat quiet and rambling and held a stark beauty.

"Let's go," Abigail said. "The day won't wait for us."

She was so right about that. Jonah stood and looked into her eyes while the world awoke outside the windows.

The sun lifted over the trees to the east, its first rays causing the lake to glisten like a million diamonds. The sloping yard had progressed each day from winter toward spring, green sprouts popping through the gray of bare trees. Now, with June on the horizon, this natural world had come alive with lush, blooming trees and rich, green vistas. He hoped his memories would sprout like that and blossom into something tangible. Or they could turn dark and dreary, like a rainy day on the water.

He wished he could remember how he got on the lake. He wished he'd met Abigail in another life.

"Are you going to quit before we get started?" she asked, bringing his thoughts back to the chickens. "Standing there won't get anything done."

"Show me the eggs," he said, grinning. "I told you, it feels good to be up and able to go outside."

Abigail turned from where they stood in the office just off the kitchen to find her sisters and most of the other employees staring at them. They all scattered when she frowned and gave them her bossy glare.

Jonah's gaze followed hers, his pulse racing when he saw so many people milling around. Waves of panic took over, blocking out the sun and the freedom of moving on.

"I don't think I'm ready for this," he said, turning toward the back hallway between the kitchen and the office.

Abigail let him go, then called out to the employees, "Get to work. I have to show the new gardener where everything is."

Halfway to the stable, he heard her calling his name. "Jonah, stop."

He whirled and lifted his hands. "I'm not Jonah. I'm John Doe."

"What?"

She looked so innocent and confused, he had to stop and take a breath. "John Doe. It's what we call someone who can't be identified."

"You remembered that?" she asked as she hurried to where he stood. "But that's not your name either."

He shook his head and heaved a deep breath. "I like Jonah better."

He'd used the term "John Doe" as if he'd said it a hundred times. What was wrong with his head?

"Are you still willing to work here?" she asked, a note of fear in the question.

"Yes. I had a bad reaction to seeing everyone huddled there, staring at me as if I'm a bug under a microscope."

Her smile returned. "You are a bit like a bug at times."

Jonah had to admit he loved her wry sense of humor. That smile had held him up during some dark days. He liked to tease her just to get her riled up.

"You'd like to squelch me, right?"

"I thought you were leaving," she said, the soft smile gone. He saw a longing in her eyes that reflected the longing in his heart.

No more teasing.

"I'm here, Abigail. And I need work to keep me busy so maybe I can relax and figure things out." Pushing at his hat, he said, "I'll work during the day and research the past in my spare time. I won't be in anyone's way."

She nodded at that, her light shawl lifting in the wind to touch against his work shirt.

"Well, the chicken coop is a *gut* place to start. The hens will chatter and the rooster will mark his territory and try to prove his superiority. You can't show any fear."

Jonah nodded as they approached the coop and its fenced-in yard. "Actually, I'm more terrified of you than of any rooster."

Abigail stopped and gave him a curious stare. "Why would I scare you?"

He glanced around. "I'm not even supposed to be speaking to you right now. I don't want to get you in trouble. Those people back there will talk."

"I have nothing to hide," she said, her indignation impressive. Her green eyes were changeable, like a dark forest. "Well, except you, of course."

"That's the problem. You hid me and got in trouble. I won't let that happen again. I won't make more trouble for you."

"I told you, now that my parents know the truth, and now that you are an official employee here, I have nothing more to hide."

"But I might," he retorted. "I want to work, to help, but I don't want to make things hard on you or your family."

"Then let me show you what duties we expect of you, and you can work all day."

She took off again toward the yard, where the chickens

had gathered to cluck. They wanted to be fed. Jonah caught up with her and almost reached for her arm. But he stopped himself, holding back. He felt exposed and raw out here in the wind and the sun, with people coming and going back at the inn.

"Abigail," he said, almost out of breath. "Do you understand?"

"I do," she said, her tone all business. "Nothing personal anymore. No quiet conversations where I try to help you remember. We are working together, and this old place requires a lot of attention."

"I have a lot of time."

"Then it will all be as it should."

"No, it won't. Not when I see you every day. This morning I already miss having you all to myself."

She stopped and turned. "You can't say such things. We are wrong to think of each other in that way."

"But you have thought it, haven't you?"

She lowered her head, her bashful ways taking over. "*Neh.*"

"Then you're in denial," he replied, pushing past her. "Show me how to feed the chickens. Then I can get some pointers from Old Red here."

She looked from him to the strutting rooster. "*Ja,* because you two seem to be a lot alike."

Jonah laughed despite the sizzle that buzzed around them. He'd have to ignore these strange feelings he'd developed for Abigail. She was off-limits, and now his boss.

He didn't want to get fired on the first day.

"*Kumm,*" she said. "The chickens will eat while you gather eggs. The feed and equipment are in this small barn."

She pointed to a shed attached to the coop and yard. Jonah did a scan of the structure. The long coop was set at the back of the big, fenced-in yard, raised slightly from the ground. It had a walk-in front door. All the structures were painted a deep red, making the coop look like a miniature barn.

"Have you ever been around chickens?" she asked while he continued to take in the area.

"Only the human kind," he retorted without thinking, his focus on the woods surrounding this structure and the stable nearby. Vast acreage where anyone could hide and watch.

They both stopped and stared at each other.

"What does that mean?" she asked, her tone bordering on hopeful.

"I guess it means I've been around a lot of cowards," he replied. "I can't explain the things that pop into my head." Nor could he explain why he'd tried to memorize his surroundings and possible escape routes.

Abigail gazed at him, sympathy flashing in her eyes. "Then we work, and we try to find more pieces of the puzzle."

"Is that going on your quilt?" he asked. "The cowards?"

"No, but a picture of you feeding the rooster you've named Old Red might wind up on that quilt."

"I'll show him who's boss," he replied, feeling somewhat better. When they stopped near the chicken coop, he lifted his head and took in the air, enjoying the thought that she breathed the same air. That gave him hope.

"This is the run," she explained about the big yard enclosed with a tall wire fence and a wire ceiling. "It's built tight like this so it will be sturdy enough to keep predators away."

Predators. Again, Jonah got a funny feeling, as if he knew all kinds of predators. Human ones?

Abigail turned to open the shed door, but when she tugged it back, it stuck fast. She tried again, and this time the jammed door flew open, causing Abigail to fall back toward Jonah.

As he caught her against his chest, the floral scent of her essence surrounded him like a flower garden.

"Oh," she said, not moving for several heartbeats before she whirled to stare up at him. "I'm sorry."

Jonah held her there, savoring the feel of her in his arms. A forbidden feeling, but he couldn't deny it. This woman made his heart boom. He'd become attached to her the way a lost animal became attached to the first human who showed it any attention. But he would leave one day. They both knew that.

Right now, he didn't want to think about it.

You can't do this.

He let her go and turned to look at the shed door. "It's swollen. Probably from too much snow, and now it's drying out. I'll see if I can level it off."

"*Ja*, of course," she replied, her words breathless and rushed. Moving away, she pointed to the items inside the dark shed and then straightened her *kapp*. "We keep the chicken feed up top and in this heavy plastic bucket so varmints can't get to it. We also keep this door closed and latched at all times. The smaller bucket here is for gathering the eggs. We switch that out each day after we wash the eggs, and we bring a clean bucket back to the shed as needed. Because we serve food to the public, we follow strict FDA guidelines on cleaning and storing the eggs. We refrigerate them immediately after washing them. So getting them to the kitchen is important."

"Got it," he said, not able to look at her again. And he didn't dare go into that small shed with her. Too tempting.

Abigail, who'd seemed so willing and shy before, now looked formidable. "We have ten hens," she said, her voice firm again. Pointing to the coop, she walked over and opened the door wide so he could look inside. "The hens roost on that row of slats."

Jonah studied the henhouse. It squatted up on stilts about a foot off the ground and had a wide, slanted walk with grooves so the chickens could climb up to the enclosure.

"Don't they get tired or cold?"

"No." She pointed to the ceiling. "We have a heat lamp. They sleep, and they stay warm in the winter by snuggling."

That word hung in the air as she gave him one of her shy glances. "In the summer, they still roost, but they have more air coming in." Pointing to the mesh vents located at the top corner of each wall, she said, "We open the vents for circulation, even in winter."

Jonah tried to get back on task and studied the round roosting platforms and the big, square nesting boxes. "Okay. I guess they get used to the cold and the heat."

"This coop is used all year long. In the winter, we put up plastic walls around the chicken yard to absorb heat. This coop is built from stone to do the same. We insulate with pine shavings—never cedar. Cedar isn't good for the chickens. We used to clean the floors every spring and several times during the hot days, but now we keep the pine shavings heavy on the floor, and nature and the air vents in the top of the shed take care of the rest." Lifting her hand, she shooed away some of the clucking chickens. "We still clean the shavings and the floor several times a year."

Jonah tugged at his hat. "I never knew taking care of chickens required so much work."

"They like being pampered," she said with a laugh. "And like all women, they want their houses neat and clean. We get many eggs, so we try to keep the hens happy."

Jonah loved her laugh, so bright and full of life. He missed laughter. That he knew in his gut. But why?

Keep your mind on the chickens.

He listened as she continued to explain what to do. This would be an easy but somewhat dirty task. They were coming out of the shed when he asked, "What other kind of punishment has your father planned for me?"

"Let me be the one to explain that," a deep voice said from behind them.

Abigail pivoted and almost collided with Jonah.

Jonah reached to steady her and met the wrath in her father's eyes. Abe had come to check on them.

CHAPTER SEVEN

"I'll take over now," Abe said, his dark eyes holding a quiet anger, his stance a firm reminder that he had the last word here.

Abigail gave Jonah a quick glance, her eyes full of apology and the shame of getting caught with him so soon after her father had forbidden any intimacy between them.

"I'll get back to the kitchen then," she said. "He'll need to know—"

"—I know what needs to be done," Abe said, his gaze centered on Jonah. "He'll soon know enough, too."

Abigail hurried away, her head down. Jonah hated seeing her in that submissive posture, but he knew how things were. She glanced over her shoulder, subdued and embarrassed. That made Jonah angry. She hadn't done anything so awful after all.

He wouldn't be that submissive. "I can handle this," he said to Abe, hoping her father would quit glaring at him.

"I have no doubt," the older man said in a firm tone. "We will work together to make sure you know what you're doing. Chickens are fickle creatures, but the rooster rules the roost."

"That goes without saying," Jonah replied while they tried to stare each other down.

Again, Abe made his point. He might not run this place anymore, but he still held authority here. Jonah knew the Amish had traditions and deeply embedded rules. He sensed that he followed the rules, too, but did he follow official rules? Or his own? That could be what had nearly gotten him killed.

Abe moved into the shed and gathered the feed, his face like a solemn wall of stone. Then he handed Jonah the egg bucket. "I'll feed and water. You'll gather the eggs from the nesting boxes. Then we'll tidy the place up."

Abe moved from the shed to the chicken coop. Inside, Jonah realized that as clean as this place looked, the smell wasn't so pleasant.

As they worked side by side, Jonah decided to set things straight. "You don't like me, do you?" he asked Abe while he reached over to gather the eggs from the square, open boxes.

"I don't know you," Abe replied, his earlier anger now simmering. "I might have liked you if you'd come here in a different way. I would gladly have helped you without hiding you. That put a big burden on a daughter who already carries a heavy load around here."

Abe made a good point. Jonah couldn't deny that.

"I understand," he said. "I asked Abigail not to report me. I thought my memory would return." Then he stopped and stared at the distant lake. "Your daughter saved me in more ways than just by pulling me out of the water."

Abe put away the feed buckets and watched as Jonah

carefully placed the eggs in the gathering basket. He'd been careful not to drop any. Once he finished, Abe handed him a packet of sanitizing wipes.

"You don't want to get salmonella while you're still weak."

"I appreciate your letting me work off my debt to you," Jonah said before tossing the wipe in a big trash can outside the coop. "And I'm glad I'm official now. I like working around the place. I can't sit in that apartment all day."

"But you don't know why you came to us with your wounds and your empty head," Abe pointed out as he checked the nesting boxes and dropped more pine shavings onto the roosting floor.

"No, I don't. I hope I'm a good person. I want to repay Abigail for her kindness."

"You did work to repay us," Abe said. "You did a *gut* job and proved you know how to work hard. But one day, Jonah, you will want to go back out there and find what you left behind. I won't have my *dochder* getting silly dreams about a man who is not our kind."

Jonah could never imagine Abigail dreaming *silly* dreams. The woman was sensible and full of backbone. She didn't deal in folly or pretension. Anything she dreamed about would be practical, and something she longed for and could make happen.

Except falling for Jonah. Her father didn't want her to fall for an *Englisch* man who didn't even know anything about himself. Jonah would abide by her father's wishes, no matter how Abigail made him feel. They were from different worlds, and he would only be in her world for a brief time. He hoped. Yet he'd miss her every day, even when his memories took over.

He could understand Abe's need to protect his daughter, though. He would do the same if he had a daughter. He would do the same for his child.

That gut-piercing feeling hit him again, leaving a vast hole in the dark wall hiding his memories.

He finished helping Abe clean and freshen the floor and the nests. "I am not going to hurt Abigail. I know I don't belong here. But right now, I don't belong anywhere. I only need some time to search for the truth." Then he stared out at the land. "Besides, I like it here. It's peaceful and beautiful, and who wouldn't find this a haven in hard times? Being here has helped me more than I care to admit."

Abe came to stand next to him, a shovel in one hand. "You might not have any ill intentions, but my daughter is a gentle soul. She takes to things—animals, projects, people."

"I guess I could be all of those things," Jonah admitted. "I'm human, but I'm sure I've acted like an animal at times. I might be a project to her, but I won't push her into something she'll regret. I respect your daughter too much to do anything that would upset or confuse her."

Abe's direct stare never wavered. He kept his eyes on Jonah, as if trying to find his memories and pull them to the surface so Jonah had to face them. Jonah held that stare, never blinking, refusing to feel any guiltier than he already did.

Finally, Abe nodded. "You truly don't remember much, ain't so?"

"Did you think I faked my amnesia?"

"I did not know," Abe said, "but I had to be sure. My daughters are all smart, but they are also still innocent when it comes to *Englisch* ways." Abe took off his hat and slapped it against his pants, then repositioned it. "They work hard because we all love this place. It's our livelihood and demands a lot of upkeep. They meet *Englisch* every day and know many of our return customers. But they also know not to mingle too closely, you understand?"

"I do," Jonah replied. Glancing toward the house, he said, "I think Abigail worried about me on my first earning day. That's why she wanted to show me everything this morning. Once I get the routine down, I can work by myself."

Abe slanted out his bearded chin. "I don't know if you are an honorable man, but I will hold you to that. Abigail doesn't have to guide you through every task."

"You don't believe I'm honorable or innocent?" Jonah asked, his stomach burning with the sure knowledge that he couldn't be dishonorable.

"I won't judge you," Abe replied as they put away their tools and buckets. "But I will watch you and correct you and . . . I can send you away if you step over the line."

"I wouldn't expect anything less," Jonah said. "Now, what's next on my list of chores once I deliver the eggs to the right place?"

"The stable," Abe replied. Then he locked up the chicken yard and motioned to Jonah. "Give me the eggs. I'll leave them in the back of the kitchen. I'll meet you in the alley inside the stable and explain how to muck out stalls."

"No pine shavings in there?"

"Straw," Abe said, the basket steady in his hands, even if his gait wasn't. "Messy, dirty straw."

"You're enjoying this, aren't you?" Jonah asked, figuring directness would win him points.

"That I am," Abe replied without looking back. "That I am."

"Daed is bringing the eggs," Eliza announced as she rushed into the office behind the kitchen. "What if he knocked Jonah out with the shovel?"

"Our father is not violent," Abigail retorted, but her nerves were stretched to the limit. She'd worried about Jonah all morning, which irritated her because she knew she shouldn't worry about a grown man. He'd done his two weeks, working on the outskirts of the property, away from her. Ignoring her, really. She'd tried to avoid him, too. But now he worked for her. "Daed is probably making sure I don't interact with Jonah too much."

"Define interact," her sister teased, her eyes wide with wonder.

"We talk," Abigail replied, shaking her head at how her sister picked up *Englisch* phrases. She was close to her sisters, but she couldn't tell them she dreamed of kissing Jonah. That would be her secret. "He's used to having me around, and now he's out there struggling."

"I don't see Jonah as struggling," Eliza replied. "He seems able to take on any task we shove at him, or anybody who messes with this family, for that matter."

Though she was good at observing people, Eliza clung to her books and her animals. What would she know of human nature?

Probably more than Abigail realized.

The back door opened and Daed stepped in. "Eggs," he called to anyone who wanted to come to get them.

Matthew rushed up, his shaggy, dark blond hair lifting. "I'll take that bucket, Abe."

Abe nodded. "*Denke*, young Matthew."

Matthew must wonder why Abe had been in the hen-house, but he was wise enough not to ask. Instead, he glanced at Eliza with a questioning lift of his eyebrows.

Eliza shook her head, forcing Matthew to move on.

Daed turned to Abigail and Eliza. "Eliza, I'm going to the stable to show Jonah what needs to be done. You might be needed to explain the horses. I doubt he's been around any farm animals."

"I can do that, Daed," Eliza said, trying to hide her mirth. "We don't want him to get kicked in the head again."

Abigail wanted to jump up and ask how everything had gone, but instead she studied the computer screen as if her life depended on it. Her father could see right into her soul sometimes.

"He did a *gut* job," Daed offered. "For an *Englisch*."

Then he turned and walked out the door.

Eliza shot Abigail a wry smile. "My turn to get to know your Jonah," she said as she rushed around the desk and scooted away before Abigail could protest.

Abigail moaned in frustration. Her sister would flirt and ask too many questions. What if she said things to Jonah that would give him the wrong impression of all of them? Did Daed plan to pass him from daughter to daughter to keep him confused? Was this a test of Jonah's merit? Abigail began a silent prayer to steady her wayward soul.

At least Daed had reluctantly given Jonah a compliment, and that one comment had offered her some reassurance. She'd been afraid he'd admonish her for showing Jonah the chicken coop. But what could they have done other than talk with chickens clucking and other employees walking by?

When she heard a crash in the kitchen, Abigail jumped up and ran out of the office. Someone had dropped a goblet, and she helped clean up the orange juice all over the floor. The rest of her morning involved putting out breakfast food on the buffet, cleaning up after the guests were done, and helping Edith cook for the heavy lunch crowd.

Once the restaurant had settled down, she looked out the wide row of side windows to find Jonah walking across the backyard tugging at Samson's reins, alone and solemn, while the docile horse followed his lead.

Her heart held that image close. It would go on the quilt.

Jonah stood in the stable, rubbing Samson's broad, gray-haired nose. The big, gray-and-black-speckled Percheron had taken a shine to Jonah.

Once Abe had shown Jonah what to do, he'd left him alone. That gave Jonah some time to walk the long alley and take in the other horses. Samson was the leader, but there were two mares, both smaller draft horses, and a beautiful roan named Pickles. Little Peaches had her own private area and a small corral for training. Eliza told him he could watch and learn how to train Peaches, too. She planned to give pony rides once Peaches learned to behave and follow Eliza's commands.

Eliza had finished her work, but she'd come back to the stable with a ham biscuit and some lemonade. "Abigail sent this out," she explained. "She's fretting about you something awful."

Surprised, Jonah asked, "Is she okay?"

"She's fine," Eliza teased. "I just wanted to get you frazzled."

"Your family has a cruel way of making someone pay penance," he'd told Abigail's pretty little sister.

Eliza was different from Abigail. Abigail was all golden and fresh-faced. Eliza tended to be more serious, even though she had a humorous side, but her hazel eyes changed from brown to dark green at times. Her hair was darker, with a few golden streaks. She could easily be a forest waif. Abigail made him think of wind and water. Eliza was more earthy.

He liked her immediately, because she didn't make his heart rush ahead or his soul want to rebel. He didn't dream of holding Eliza close the way he thought of Abigail.

"Daed wanted me to show you around," she'd explained, her expression full of mirth.

"I heard you're good with the horses."

"I love them. They're my babies. Samson is my favorite, and then we have the two mares—Rosebud and Sunshine. Peaches is coming along on the carousel, and we will continue training her. Pickles, the roan, is the outsider."

"Like me," Jonah had said, smiling.

"So, have you found some of your memory yet?"

Direct, that Eliza.

"I have flashes," he replied, not giving her much to chew on. She didn't ask any more questions, thankfully.

She'd been direct with him as she explained in precise detail what each horse required and expected. Not too much food, and none after they'd been worked hard. Lots of water, but not too much before they worked. Too much food could cause colic, which could be painful and life-threatening.

Jonah didn't know if he'd been around horses before, but the big, beautiful animals soothed his bruised soul. They each took to him after he'd learn to mix the bulk food such as oats with chaff or bran. He and Eliza had given them a morning feeding and he'd helped her with the midday feeding, too. The evening feedings would be his last task of the day. Jonah learned he'd need to fill the hay bend full at night, so the horses wouldn't start eating the hay on the floor, or worse, biting the stalls.

Jonah still needed to learn all the various feeds—maize, wheat, bran, and several more. He only knew horses liked carrots and apples and, apparently, they also liked turnips, peas, and beans on a limited basis. They seemed as fickle and fragile as newborns.

Newborn.

He stopped now, Samson behind him as they took a walk to get used to each other. He remembered a baby. A crying, laughing baby. A warm, soft baby he'd held in his hands.

Jonah's heart was pierced, as if a thousand arrows had struck it. He turned Samson around and headed back to the stable, his throat tightening.

Samson snorted and pawed. Did the horse sense Jonah's

anxiety? Trying to calm himself and the big animal, he held the reins with one hand and tried to open Samson's stall with the other. But the horse grew more agitated.

Jonah glanced around. No one but him. He'd have to handle Samson and get him back safely in his stall. He reached for Samson's long nose and tried to talk to him. Samson's eyes rolled back and his hoofs came up.

Jonah held the reins tightly and patted the horse's flank. Samson snorted and turned. Would he kick?

But a shout and feet running brought both him and the horse dancing around. "Stop!"

Abigail.

"Samson, stop it," she said, taking the reins from Jonah. Grabbing a carrot out of her apron pocket, she motioned to Jonah. "Open the stall."

He did, his hands sweaty and shaking, the image of a baby crying making his head swim. He watched, helpless, as Abigail got Samson back into his stall by offering him the carrot. Her voice stayed low and soothing, steady.

She brought the horse and the man back to calmness.

After she had the Percheron safely stabled, she turned to Jonah. "Are you all right? What happened?"

CHAPTER EIGHT

He sank down on the dirt floor and put his head in his hands. Abigail kneeled in front of him. "Jonah?"

She'd never seen him like this: shaken, sad, tears forming in his always stormy eyes. He looked broken. "Did Samson harm you?"

He shook his head, wiped at his eyes. "A baby. I remembered a baby. A child crying in my arms."

He looked up at her, saw the shock on her face, then grabbed her hand. "Abigail, I think I might have a child somewhere."

A child.

Abigail let that revelation sink in, her heart battling to control her emotions. Jonah might be a father, a man with a child. If that were true, he had to have a family somewhere.

He belonged with that family.

"Did you have another memory?" she asked, holding his hand tight, wanting him to remember even as she wished he hadn't come here without his memories. But he had, and now they must deal with their return, one memory at a time.

He nodded, his breathing calming down now. "I heard a baby crying. In my head, I heard a baby. Then I could see him in my arms."

"Him?"

Jonah's expression changed, clarified as he accepted yet another fragment of the truth. "A boy. I know it was a boy."

Abigail didn't dare let go of Jonah's hand. She could feel him shaking. His fingers were clammy with sweat. His pulse fluttered against her skin like a plea. He'd had some sort of emotional breakthrough, but she feared the results would not be good. How could she help him? How could she ease the deep, raging torment she'd seen in his eyes?

"Did you remember anything else?"

He ran his free hand down his face and then pushed back his hair. He'd lost his hat in the scuffle with Samson. "No. But I panicked and . . . Samson felt it. I didn't want him to run away."

"Samson is fine," she said, her eyes misty. "He's a big oaf at times, but he always knows where home is. He's safe. Are you sure you're okay?"

Jonah's gaze lifted to her. His eyes held hers for a long moment. "What if he's looking for me? The boy—what if he needs me?"

"If he's a wee thing, he won't be looking, but I'm sure he'd be missing you," she said, her mind whirling with the many reasons she had to put her constant thoughts of Jonah out of her mind. She could have nothing to do with this man beyond helping him to find the truth. And even that pushed her toward forbidden territory.

"He might be older now," Jonah said, letting go of her

hand before he stood and then reaching to help her up. "He might need me."

Jonah was the kind of man who'd want to be needed. She knew in her heart he was a *gut* man. But how to make him see that himself?

Abigail stood so close she could reach out and push the deep brown locks of hair away from his forehead. But she resisted the gesture. If Jonah had a son, he must have a wife. Or he'd had a wife at one time. He'd been with a woman. Intimately.

He searched her face, his eyes dancing over her. The torment of not remembering had darkened them to black. "I have to know, Abigail. I need to know."

"Of course you do."

"Abigail," he said, taking her hand again. "What's wrong with me?"

They heard footsteps coming up the long aisle. Samson snorted and gave them an eye roll.

"Abigail, I've been looking for you." Eliza hurried to them. "Daed is on the watch." Nodding her head to Abigail, she said, "Go out the back and head to the house. Mamm will need you."

Abigail gave Jonah one last glance. "Are you going to be all right?"

He nodded, his skin pale, his eyes holding a warning. "I overdid it, I think."

He didn't want anyone else to see him like this.

"I'll try to check on you later," she said as she hurried away.

She'd have to sneak out to do that, but she wouldn't sleep a wink without knowing.

* * *

"What was that all about?" Eliza asked, her head swiveling from Abigail's departing figure to Jonah, who was holding on to the stall.

"Nothing."

"Did you do something to upset my sister?"

"No."

"You aren't going to tell me."

Jonah finally looked at Eliza. For some strange reason, he trusted her. Not like he trusted Abigail, with his soul. But enough to be honest. "I had a panic attack."

"Oh-oh," she said, rushing toward Samson. "Did Samson try to knock you over with his hooves? He's notorious for that, but really he's only playing."

Jonah held up a hand, his hands steady now. "Samson got frightened because I lost control and . . . I don't know, I got all shaky and my anxiety spiked."

"He can sense that," she said, her hand reaching for the big horse's nose. "Hey, boy, I told you to be kind to our Jonah."

Jonah wanted to shout that he wasn't really a Jonah and he could never be *their* Jonah. He was a man from nowhere who had nowhere to go. But he might have a son.

"I had a memory, but it got lost, and I panicked."

"I'm sorry," Eliza said. "But right now, we need to finish the evening feedings and I have to get back for supper. One of us will bring your meal."

"I'm not very hungry," he admitted. His stomach roiled and coiled with his need to know about his son. If he had a son. Could he have been holding someone else's baby? Did he have siblings or cousins who'd become parents?

"You'll be hungry later," Eliza said in her calm, no-nonsense way. "I think we're having chicken potpie and trust me, Mamm's potpies are the best."

Before Jonah could argue, she said, "But before we refill the feed, you and Samson need to get past this little incident."

She pointed to the big draft horse. "Samson, you are not to upset our new helper."

Samson snorted and tossed his silvery mane.

"Jonah, show Samson you are still his friend."

Jonah took a deep breath and stepped toward the big horse. Placing his hand on Samson's nose, he said, "I'm sorry, Samson. I had a moment, but it's over now. I really do like you."

Samson lowered his nose and looked at Jonah. The big horse didn't waiver. Jonah stared back, thinking everyone, from the chickens to the entire King family, had tried to test his mettle. He'd almost lost it today. He rubbed Samson's black nose and made a peace offering with the apple slices Eliza had told him to keep on hand.

Samson ate the gifts and tossed his mane, his dark eyes like deep, black pools. Jonah wished he could look down into his own dark pit of despair.

But he now knew he couldn't hide here any longer. He had to report himself to the police and let them search for his identity.

If he had a family waiting out there, he wanted to find that family, and he wanted to hold that child in his arms again.

* * *

That night, Eliza, Colette, and Abigail all sat in Abigail's room, assessing the situation as they'd analyzed other problems through the years.

"I thought he did okay for his day of doing all the outside chores," Eliza said. "He's *gut* with the horses and chickens. Tomorrow, he'll come head-to-head with the goats and cows."

"Butting heads?" Colette asked with a grin. "I didn't get to help teach our interloper today. I can show him the ropes with the goats." Her grin proved she'd made that rhyme on purpose.

"I'd buy a ticket to that," Eliza said, grinning back. Then she searched Abigail's face, as if looking for open wounds. "Did Daed catch you with Jonah this morning?"

"*Ja,* but I managed to explain why I was there. He didn't admonish me too much." She'd run away before he could.

"Did you and Jonah talk?" Colette asked.

"About chickens, mostly," Abigail admitted. "I still can't believe he had a panic attack today."

"He wouldn't tell me what triggered it," Eliza said, giving Abigail a questioning glance. "Do you know?"

"I didn't press him," she said. She'd wanted to know more about Jonah thinking he'd remembered a baby. It could have been anyone's child.

"And you don't want us to press you," Eliza replied. "Secrets, always with the Jonah secrets."

"They are mine to keep," Abigail pointed out, glad they'd gotten through the evening meal without any questions. Supper had been quiet until Eliza told Mamm and Daed about Jonah and Samson's standoff.

"I had to force Jonah and Samson to apologize to

each other," her sister had reported. "I think they will be friends now."

"Always hard when a new helper takes over with an animal," Mamm said, her tone gentle while her eyes were sharp. "Did something happen with Samson?"

Abigail couldn't speak up. Still reeling from what Jonah had revealed to her, and his emotional response to possibly having a son, she didn't want to hear Eliza's version.

"He got anxious," Eliza said. After Abigail shot her a warning glance, she went on. "I was a bit late getting out to the stable today. It's his first day alone with all the horses."

"Is he afraid of the animals?" Mamm asked, her shrewd eyes moving from daughter to daughter to find any weak spots.

"*Neh*, he is *gut* with the animals," Eliza said. "But we did throw him out there without much supervision."

"He is a grown man who wants to work," Daed said. "Why are we discussing this at the supper table?"

Colette, who usually remained quiet, spoke up. "He's come to us, Daed. From the lake. What purpose does *Gott* have in mind with this stranger washing ashore?"

Daed studied his daughters, then turned his gaze on Mamm. "I do not know, but I hope we can come up with an answer before the bishop pays us a visit. You do remember we have church here the third week of the month."

"Jonah might be gone by then," Abigail blurted out before she could stop herself. "He is remembering a few things."

"I plan to have him gone soon," Daed replied, giving

her a knowing, fatherly appraisal. "But for now, he is a hard worker and we needed someone like that to handle the outdoor tasks and the animals. If he continues as he did today, doing his chores and working hard, I will continue to pay him a small salary—to send him on his way with some spending money. That is our purpose with Jonah. To get him well enough to leave. Once we've done our duty, he can get back to whatever life he left behind."

Abigail glanced at Eliza. Eliza glanced toward Colette. Mamm studied all of them, her gaze serene and hard to read.

Daed finished his meal and got up to stare out the big bay window that gave a view of the inn and the lake, and a glimpse of the carriage *haus*. Even in the moonlight.

"Well, what's the plan?" Colette said now, bringing Abigail's mind back to the present.

They sat on the big bed, crossed-legged on the starburst quilt that Abigail and Mamm had made for Abigail's sixteenth birthday. Ten years ago. By Amish standards, she was an *alte maidal*.

"He needs food," Eliza said, bringing her mind back to Jonah. "I told him about the potpie."

"But Mamm didn't offer to fix him a plate," Abigail said. "She thinks he ate in the inn kitchen, but he didn't."

"I could go down and take him something now," Eliza said. "If they notice, I'll explain that he worked too late to get any leftovers. Which is true."

"How will you get it to him?" Colette asked. "They won't let any of us go alone."

"We'll go together," Abigail decided. "We have nothing to hide, and the man needs to eat."

They marched downstairs and began fixing a plate.

Daed was, thankfully, up in the bedroom, probably reading his Bible by the propane lamp. While the inn had modern conveniences, in their home, they still adhered to the old ways.

Mamm sat finishing up some knitting. "What are you three up to now?" she asked in the same tone she'd always used when they were younger.

"We realized Jonah never had dinner," Colette offered. "We thought we'd all walk it over to him."

"How thoughtful," Mamm said, her smile sweet. "Too bad your *daed* already took Jonah a plate."

"What?"

Had they all three said that together?

Abigail fidgeted underneath her mother's stern stare. "That was kind of Daed."

"Your father is a kind man." She spoke with an emphasis that meant *but don't push him*. After gathering her yarn and tucking her work into the basket by her chair, she stood and stretched. "I think we all need to go to bed now, ain't so?"

The girls glanced at one another. Finally, Abigail said, "*Ja*, I'm tired. We had so many people for breakfast and lunch today."

"More coming for the weekend," Eliza said, her yawn a poor effort to disguise her wide-awake interest.

"I have some reading to do," Colette said, her tone pure innocence.

Off they all trotted while Mamm brought up the rear to keep anyone from straying as they marched in unison up the stairs. Though they were all grown now, their mother still had the ultimate authority.

Abigail and her sisters each went to their rooms.

But once she heard Mamm settle into bed, Abigail grabbed her shawl and her quietest slippers and lightly, slowly, made her way down the back steps and out onto the back porch. Then she hurried to the edge of the woods and followed the path around the stable and on toward the carriage *haus*. Glancing behind her, she made sure no one had noticed her. She had to see Jonah.

CHAPTER NINE

Jonah lay awake, staring at the white ceiling. Moonlight danced through the trees, leaving a pattern over his head that kept twisting and moving, like his memories.

The baby. He couldn't get that sound out of his head. He knew how it felt to hold a baby close, to smell the freshness of newborn skin and baby powder. He knew the deep, gut-wrenching agony of loving someone so much you'd do anything to protect them.

Where was the baby now? Did Jonah have a wife and child? Or just a child? Where was the mother?

A gentle knock at the door brought him up. Grabbing his clothes, he hurried into his shirt and pants. "Who is it?"

But he knew, of course. Only one person would come to his room this late at night. He opened the door before she said, "Abigail."

Abigail.

Why did it seem as if he'd been waiting for her a long, long time?

"What are you doing here?" he asked.

"I wanted to see if you'd eaten and ask how your day

went. It's your first day of taking on new tasks and finally drawing a salary."

"I ate the potpie your father dropped off, and you already know how my day went. I did great until I had that memory flash."

"What brought on the memory?" she asked, leaning against the wall as if she wanted to be invisible.

He lowered his head, then lifted his gaze up to her. "I was thinking about how horses have to be pampered and cared for—like a newborn."

"Newborn? That brought your memory?"

He bobbed his head, unable to speak for a moment. Swallowing, he lifted his chin. "I heard the baby crying, saw the baby in my arms, my hands so big around his tiny head."

Abigail inhaled a breath, the look in her eyes telling him she could picture that scene, too. "A *bobbeli*," she whispered. "You might have a son out there somewhere."

Jonah touched a hand to her cheek. Her skin was so soft, and she always smelled like spices and flowers. He wanted to tug her hair out of that white cap and see how it would look flowing over her shoulders. It had to be long because Amish women didn't cut their hair. Long and lush, like a waterfall flowing into a spring valley.

But, for her sake, he couldn't touch her like that. He watched her eyelashes flutter at his touch, saw her chest lift, and then he dropped his hand away.

Her eyes opened wide, as if she'd come out of a dream.

Jonah stepped back, giving himself some time and space.

"I have to go to the police, Abigail. I've been here

long enough. I need to go into town and see what I can find out. I want you to go with me, to tell the police how you found me."

She backed away. "Me? I can't. Daed won't allow that."

"If you don't go with me, they'll only come here to question you and get more information. I don't want to bring that on you and your family, or your business. I still need this job for a few weeks. While I'm working here, they can search for my identity."

Abigail glanced all around. "I have to go. I'll find you tomorrow and let you know if I can do that."

Giving him one last fleeting glance, she ran out of the apartment and turned right to go to the far side of the building. To stay out of sight.

Jonah watched her until she disappeared around the side of the carriage house, his heart fluttering with each step she took to distance herself from him.

Torn and disoriented, he fell back into bed and went to sleep. He dreamed of a little boy playing on a tree swing underneath a big oak tree. A little boy who laughed as he lifted into the air.

Back and forth, the swing moved, and the boy giggled and called out, "Daddy, I go high."

The giggles made Jonah think of bubbles drifting away.

The swing went up, up into the air, but when it came back down, it was empty, the ropes still shifting in the wind.

Abigail came up with a plan.

"You want to do what?" Eliza asked the next day as they sorted the linens in the laundry and folded them.

Colette shook out a pillowcase. The big washroom,

adjacent to the kitchen on the back end of the house, turned warm with steam from the industrial-size washing machine and dryer.

"She wants us to stand watch while she sneaks off to be with her *Englisch* fellow."

Abigail rolled her eyes and shook her head. "He is not my fellow. He is Jonah, the man who came from the lake. He needs my help."

"He's always needing your help," Colette retorted. "And Daed is always watching."

"Daed knows I go into town on Wednesdays to get the best prices on meat and staples at the market. I'll take the same taxi van I always take because it holds a lot of supplies."

"I'm with you on that," Eliza said, her hair curling against her neck as she ironed the bed linens to make them smooth and crisp. "What I'm not understanding is, if you're with Jonah instead of at the market, what will you bring home?"

"Colette will go with me," Abigail explained. "Colette will do the marketing while I go with Jonah to the Township precinct."

"Colette is standing right here," her sister said. "And Colette has not agreed to this plan yet."

"I know you use your business phones to talk to boys," Abigail replied, staring at her sisters. "You both do."

"Oh, you're good," Eliza said. "We might talk to boys, but we're not hiding one, or trying to figure out how to sneak off with one. Seems you're becoming the expert on those things."

Abigail didn't want to sound desperate, but she needed

to do this for Jonah. "If I don't go there to talk to the authorities, they will come here, and then everyone will figure out what's been going on. The *blabbermauls* will enjoy my discomfort and it will hurt Mamm and Daed."

"She really is good," Colette said, her eyes full of amusement and concern. "Using our dear parents to make us feel guilty."

"Did it work?" Abigail asked, her voice low. Staff members also loved to gossip.

"I'm in," Eliza said. "You haven't given me an assignment, so I'm guessing I have to distract our dear parents from finding out that you and Jonah have both left at the same time."

"Exactly," Abigail replied. "You're good at that."

After her sisters agreed to help, they planned the timing and the distractions. Abigail and Colette would leave early for the market, getting in the cab together.

Jonah would get up an hour early to feed and care for the chickens and other animals; Eliza would help him as she sometimes did.

Then he'd walk along the fringes of the property to the main road and wait for the cab to come by. The driver sometimes picked up others at the cabbie station. So that would work.

Abigail and Colette would exit the cab first, then Jonah. They'd go their separate ways and meet back up at the cabbie station near the town market.

"A *gut* plan," Abigail told Jonah the next day while they ate a quick lunch in the kitchen. "Eliza is going to take Mamm visiting, and Daed already has a meeting with the other church elders to discuss having church at the inn next Sunday."

Jonah stared over at her, his eyes full of appreciation. "You're risking a lot for me, Abigail."

"I promised to help you and to see you through this, Jonah."

"I hope this works. I don't want your parents to be angry at me or to punish you."

"I'm a grown woman," she replied. "I might be admonished, but my parents know they can trust me."

"Not if you keep secrets from them."

"Who's keeping secrets?"

Abigail and Jonah looked up to find Mamm standing at the door to the kitchen, her eyes square on them, her expression tense.

"Besides you two, of course."

"No one," Eliza said as she rushed into the kitchen. "Abigail and Jonah were talking about before, when she was hiding him. But now we all know about him, and Jonah likes that we can trust one another, or rather how our family trusts one another. It's hard to trust with secrets between people. But he's learning our ways and he agrees with some of the tenets of our faith, ain't so?"

"*Ja*," Abigail said. "Jonah has learned a lot being here."

"I can see that with my own eyes," Mamm said, giving them a long perusal. "Jonah would be wise to remember our ways, I think."

Jonah nodded and gave Mamm a soft smile. "I'm

gaining new memories every day. And a new appreciation for the Amish."

Mamm didn't miss a beat. She plastered her gaze on Abigail. "*Ja*, I can see that with my own eyes, too."

"What brings you to the kitchen, Mamm?" Eliza asked, offering their mother a cup of peppermint tea. "We have freshly baked oatmeal cookies."

"I came to bake an apple pie," Mamm explained. "You know I like to bake in that big oven. I waited for Edith to leave, so she wouldn't hover over me. And I wanted to see how things were going, too."

Abigail decided trust worked both ways. Her mother had come to check up on her and here she sat with Jonah, making secret plans. She'd have to say extra prayers every night for the rest of her life.

"I'll help you cut up the apples," she offered as she stood to go toward the pantry, where they kept the store-bought fruit. "The afternoon crowd will appreciate a fresh pie."

Mamm looked around her to Jonah. "Are you all right?"

Abigail pivoted to Jonah. He'd gone pale, his eyes wide with the look she was beginning to recognize. He'd remembered something. "Jonah?"

"An apple orchard," he said. "I remember an apple orchard. I went there to pick apples. For pie."

Abigail made a mental note for her quilting squares.

"Was anyone with you?" she asked, holding her breath. This was the first time Jonah had shared his memories with anyone besides her. That meant he trusted her family, too. But would he tell her if a woman and child had been with him?

"No. I just remember the orchard. Trees everywhere, bees humming. A pretty day."

Mamm's whole countenance changed as she went to sit down next to Jonah. "It must be a horrible thing, not having all your memories," she said, her tone low and full of understanding and compassion. "I can see now how this would make you afraid to go back out into the world. You want to be sure."

Jonah's eyes filled with a mist that hovered like a fast-moving fog over the lake. "I need to be sure. I need to find out who I am and why I landed here. What's out there waiting for me."

Mamm put her hand over his. "Of course you do. I understand how this must be weighing on you. I hope you continue to bring up your memories, Jonah. You can only heal if you are whole again."

Jonah nodded, his gaze moving from Mamm to Abigail, as if he wasn't sure what to do. "*Denke*," he said, smiling.

"You spoke Deitsch," Abigail said.

He looked surprised. "I did?"

"Stick around," Eliza said. "You'll be speaking it a lot before you know it."

Jonah stood, his gaze hitting on Abigail. "I need to get back to work or I won't be around at all."

After he left, Mamm looked at Abigail. "Now, Daughter, might you trust me enough to tell me what plans you have next for our Jonah?"

CHAPTER TEN

Abigail couldn't lie to her *mamm* this time. Not when she'd asked outright for Abigail to be honest.

Swallowing back her anxiety, she said, "Jonah wants to go into town to talk to the local authorities, so they can do a search to see if he's been reported missing."

Mamm sat silent, her eyes revealing nothing. "And why would that involve keeping secrets?"

"He asked me to go with him—because I'm the one who found him."

Mamm lifted her chin. "Were you going to do this without telling your *daed* and me?"

Abigail nodded. "I thought Daed would forbid it."

"You knew he would," her mother said. "So, you've planned this and enlisted your sisters to help?"

Mamm had always been good at outwitting her children. She always knew things, was able to get the truth out of each of them.

"Abigail?"

"*Ja*, but I have to go with him, Mamm."

"I understand he needs you there to speak on his behalf," Mamm said. "So, you may go with Jonah."

"Really?" Abigail couldn't believe she'd gotten off without punishment.

"Really," her mother replied, her hands folded on the table. "And I will accompany you."

"What?" Abigail stood and started pacing. "But why?"

"Because your *daed* will not allow this, not without one of us there with you. You knew that already, and that is why you were going to sneak out like a schoolgirl up to no *gut*."

"I'm not a schoolgirl," Abigail retorted. "I'm practically an *alte maidal*."

"Well, a mature woman would understand not to sneak around with an *Englisch*."

"He needs me," Abigail blurted out, her anger causing her to be bold.

"Or is it the other way around?" Mamm asked, her tone quiet. "That you need him?"

"*Neh*," Abigail replied. "I only need to help him."

"You say that, Daughter, but your eyes and your actions seem to indicate you care for this man."

"I do care for him. He's been through a horrible trauma and he needs someone to help him. He has no memory, no money, no way of going back out into the world. Someone shot him, Mamm."

"*Ja*, and you found him. They could shoot you, too, because you saved him and helped hide him. He might be a wanted man for all we know."

"All the more reason to get him to the police."

"You can go and be a witness or vouch for him, Abigail. But only if I'm there with you. I will have to explain to your *daed*, but if you go, I go. That is the only way."

Abigail saw no way around this, so she nodded her head. "I'll tell Eliza and Colette you'll be there with me, but Colette still needs to pick up supplies at the market."

"She is capable of doing that, so she can come with us."

Mamm stood, clearly proud of how she'd handled the situation. "Do you understand me, Abigail?"

"*Ja*, I do," Abigail replied, remembering other conversations like this one. "It seems I have no other choice."

"*Neh*, unless you think concealing and lying are good choices."

"I don't want to do either of those things," she admitted. "I only wish you and *daed* could trust me more."

"We can only trust where trust is deserved," her mother stated. "If you continue to keep secrets and sneak around to help Jonah, or see Jonah, *even after we've gone to bed*, you will not have our trust." Lowering her head, Mamm went on. "We can't trust Jonah if he expects you to continue this sneaking around and withholding things from us."

Abigail held her comments. It would do no good to go against Mamm. Instead, she nodded. "Are you ready to make that pie?"

"I am," her mother said. "Would you like to help?"

Abigail bobbed her head, afraid of all the emotions bubbling inside her like sugary apple juice trying to break through a piecrust. "I would," she said, her voice low and raw.

Mamm smiled and held out her arms. Abigail ran straight into the soft warmth of her mother's shoulder. Amish weren't the touchy-feely type, but Mamm gave the best hugs.

She held Abigail there tightly for a moment and then

she lifted her away. "Guard your heart, Abigail. This man is not right for you. This can't be."

Abigail bobbed her head again and blinked back tears. "I only want—"

"—to help," Mamm finished for her. "Make sure that's really all you want."

Abigail peeled apples while Mamm made her special piecrust with pure butter and a dash of nutmeg. They all knew how to make this pie, but none of the three King daughters could get it just right the way Mamm did.

That was the kind of tie Abigail held on to, twisted in her mind and twirled into a pretty bow. But sometimes she wanted to untie all of it and release her hair and her heart, so she could run along the shore barefoot and free.

And that tie had now bound her to Jonah.

No matter what happened from here on out, she would always have a connection with him. A connection she stitched each night into a quilt, patterns threaded with his interesting smile and his brooding frown, sewn and patched with his memories, and the memories she'd help him create.

How did she choose between the strings that now seemed to be unraveling before her very eyes? How did she mend her life without tying in all the threads that made no sense?

Turning to her mother, she stopped peeling and sighed.

"Make the pie," Mamm whispered. "Just make the pie."

Abigail did as Mamm said, because Mamm was so good at these things.

* * *

The next morning the taxi arrived, and Colette, Mamm, and Abigail climbed in the back while Jonah got up front. She'd had to get word to him that the plans had changed.

He did not say a word, but got in and shut the door. He wore a set of clean clothes she'd provided. Amish clothes and a hat, so he didn't stand out.

Not to anyone else, at least. But Abigail knew him well enough to see the pulse ticking along his jawline and the tense way he sat straight up and stared out the window.

Once they were in the Shadow Lake Township proper, the cabbie stopped at the market. Jonah glanced back.

"We get out at the taxi station," Abigail explained. "Then we all go our separate ways."

Jonah got out and opened the door to let Abigail and the others pile out. "Are you going with me?" he asked, his eyes on Abigail.

"We both are," Mamm said, her smile hiding the definite dare in her tone. "I thought you could use some extra support."

Jonah didn't argue or dispute. He understood Mamm, which would work well for him over time.

Abigail guided him into the small police station; her mother went in right behind them. Jonah looked around, that faraway light in his eyes. Then he took over.

"I'm here to speak to an officer—about me. These nice Amish women found me half drowned in the lake. I'd been shot, but I managed to make it to shore. I also had a head wound, I think from falling off a boat. Other than those details, I can't remember who I am or why I got shot and left for dead."

The officer, a young, blond-haired man with a badge

and a name tag identifying him as Sergeant Palmer, stared at Jonah, and then glanced at Abigail and Mamm. "You're not Amish?"

"I'm not," Jonah replied. "I don't know who I am or what I am. I need help."

Jonah watched as the young officer at the desk stared at him in shock. "What kind of help?"

"I thought you'd be able to help me identify myself," he said, his heart beginning to beat louder. A roaring in his ears told him he was about to have a panic attack. "I don't know how. Fingerprints, photos, asking around."

"Let me get the chief," Sergeant Palmer said. The man didn't look convinced, and he acted like he didn't really care.

After he walked away, Jonah asked Abigail, "Is this how they treat all Amish people?"

"They don't go out of their way for us," she said in a quiet voice. "They think because we don't follow *Englisch* ways, we shouldn't bother them when we're in trouble. We don't bother them on most things, but when we are forced to, they do their jobs and help, but that's about it."

Sarah King glanced down the hallway. "But Jonah is *Englisch*. Of course, he does not look *Englisch* right now."

"Let's go," Jonah said, his gut burning with dread and fear.

"What?" Abigail's shock made Jonah's anxiety shoot up. "You want to leave?"

"Yes. I said no police originally, and there must have been a good reason for that."

Abigail's mother followed them to the door and out onto the sidewalk. "It could be a bad reason," she said. "Are you hiding from your crimes?"

"I didn't do anything," Jonah said. "Nothing like that."

"How can you be so sure?" Sarah asked, her expression grim. "I thought you wanted to get this over and done. Did you change your mind because I insisted on coming? Or because you remembered something else?"

"No," he said, his head spinning. "It's just that . . . I see things in my head. When we're in this building, I can see myself at another station, arguing with someone."

"The people who wanted to arrest you?" Sarah asked, her tone firm, her dark eyes reminding him of Abigail.

"No. Different." He looked back, seeing again what his mind had envisioned. "I was the one wearing the badge."

Abigail gasped. "Are you saying you might be in law enforcement?"

Jonah's heart did a fast run while dread poured over him, making him break out in a cold sweat. "I don't know. But if I told you no police, and I did work in law enforcement, then as I said, there has to be a good reason why I resisted telling them everything."

"But that officer knows now," Abigail said. "What if he recognized you?"

"Let's go before he returns," Sarah replied. "Jonah, I don't know you very well, but I pray you are right. I wish I could believe you're on the right side of the law."

He hurried them around the corner until they were out of sight.

"Until I find out more, I can't tell you that," he said. "But I can tell you that come what may, I will do whatever it takes to find the truth—on my own. And I will protect your family while I'm at it."

"My family is not accustomed to violence, Jonah. You know that."

"I do," he replied. "And I won't let any harm come to your family."

They made it to the cab station and sat down. Jonah took a long breath, using the technique Abigail had shown him to help calm down.

He glanced over at her. "Why am I so afraid of my memories?"

She looked at her mother and then back to him. "You have painful memories, Jonah. I've read up on concussions and memory loss, and I've learned that sometimes we suppress memories as a way to protect ourselves from whatever trauma we went through."

Sarah sat staring ahead. Then she stood. "I'll go find your sister. You two need to talk about how this should be handled. Your *daed* will want answers."

Jonah watched as Sarah walked toward the market. "Your mother is a good woman. She wants to protect her children. I can understand that."

"Because you think you might have a son?"

He nodded. "Why can't I remember? Why would I want to forget having a family?"

"As I said, possibly because something happened to you that you're not ready to face," Abigail replied.

Jonah studied her, saw the concern and caring in her eyes. "I don't want to hurt you," he said.

"You won't. I'm a grown woman and I care about you."

"I'm going to find the truth. Can you accept that?"

"I can, because *Gott* is in control, not me."

"Then why won't he tell me what's going on?" Jonah asked.

"He will, one day," she said as she stood. "He will, and I hope on that day you'll finally be at peace."

Jonah stood and reached toward her, but she pulled away and cut her gaze to the left. Her mother and Colette were coming back with several grocery bags. Jonah rushed to help them, the scents of flowers and spices following him like the touch of a white ribbon.

CHAPTER ELEVEN

Jonah waited in the kitchen the next morning. He'd taken to eating with the rest of the staff because he couldn't sleep past dawn anyway. He helped with the heavy lifting and assisted in cleanup.

But he waited today to talk to Abe and Sarah. They'd sent a message through Eliza that they would meet him here.

The staff had cleared out, as if they knew a meeting was about to take place at the big table in the back of the kitchen. He had coffee ready, and Abigail had put out some muffins.

They arrived and walked in, solemn as ever. Abe, a tall man, Sarah more petite. Abigail had some of her father's height, but she didn't tower or look as intimidating as Abe, no matter how she tried.

Abigail, however, was not here. Just Jonah.

After he'd refused to finish things up at the police station yesterday, the ride home had been quiet. He'd gone to work the minute they'd gotten all the groceries inside and put away.

Jonah knew Abigail had questions, and so did he. Lots

of questions always. But after yesterday, he'd accepted that he wasn't ready to go back out there all alone.

His gut told him he liked to be prepared. And he couldn't do that—prepare for whatever lay ahead—if he didn't take some time to find out the truth.

Yesterday, he'd also needed time to think about why he'd become so apprehensive in the police building. The reaction had come from the smell of stale coffee and the musky offices connected to a three-cell jail, the sound of inmates arguing and talking trash with one another. He'd recognized the boredom in the young sergeant's eyes and the way those same eyes had widened with surprise and interest when he'd told the man he didn't know his own identity.

All kind of red flags had gone up, and Jonah knew in his heart he had to get out of there. Now he needed to explain to his hosts why he wanted to stay with them longer than he'd planned. Jonah felt he needed to be here, despite the attraction he felt for Abigail. Or because of it—he couldn't leave right now.

"Jonah," Abe said. "We are here. Why do you want to talk to us?"

Sarah nodded and automatically poured coffee and passed around muffins. The sounds of chattering voices, and pots and pans being shoved and stored, came through the swinging doors into the long kitchen. The room was filled with sunshine because it had several windows. Abigail had told him the staff dining room used to be a sunroom.

He needed that warmth this morning.

"I want to thank you for letting me work off my earlier stay with you. I'm also glad you've given me more duties, and that you're willing to pay me. I know I'm supposed to leave soon, but I want to stay here and work indefinitely while I try to figure out my life."

Abe glanced at his wife and back to Jonah. "Is this why you didn't tell the authorities everything yesterday?"

"Partly," Jonah said, his hands curved around his coffee mug. "I panicked, but I'm learning that each panic attack brings a new memory, and yesterday I saw myself behind an old desk, in some sort of police department building."

"Ours?" Abe asked when Sarah handed him his coffee.

Obviously, Sarah hadn't shared everything he'd told her and Abigail. "No, different, but . . . the sounds, the scents, the feelings were all the same. I've been in a police department before, and I saw myself arguing with someone. I felt the anger, the frustration of that argument, but not what we were discussing. That's why I had to get out of there. What happened to me in that other police station, I don't know. But I'm beginning to think I must have worked as an officer somewhere."

"Now you want to continue to live here until you get all the answers?" Abe asked, his shrewd eyes holding Jonah's. "You've already been here for over a month, but you'd like to stay even longer?"

"Yes, I would. I know that wasn't part of our original agreement, but you did decide to offer me more work." Jonah leaned forward. "I don't mind the work. It helps me to relax and remember things. I need the pay, and I appreciate that you're willing to give me a chance. I can't say how long I'll need, but until I have a better under-standing of things, I'd like to stay here, where I'm safe. And . . . I can keep watch so none of you are in danger."

"I haven't agreed to a long-term arrangement," Abe pointed out with gentle admonishment. "And I do not condone the idea of violence coming our way."

Sarah had remained quiet, but now she spoke up. "Jonah, I told you yesterday how I feel about this. As long as you do no harm to anyone here, you can stay. If you bring harm to our home and this inn, you must leave. If you remember who you are and discover you are a dangerous man, I hope that you will leave and take your problems with you."

"I promise," he said, his heart shifting at the thought of leaving Abigail. "You've been too kind to me. No matter what, I won't allow anything bad to happen to you."

"How can you keep that promise?" Abe asked. "If you're on the run from danger, it will surely show up here one day."

The swinging door burst open. Abigail came through it as if she'd been standing on the other side. "I should be in on this meeting, ain't so?"

"Says who?" her mother asked. "Why do you feel the need to be here?"

Jonah gave her a nod that wanted to be a smile. "Abigail has helped me in so many ways. She has a right to know I've asked to stay here a while longer."

"You have?" She hurried to the table and took a seat by her mother, her hopeful gaze on Jonah. "You're not leaving?"

"Not if your parents will let me stay and continue to work for longer than they had expected." He shrugged. "I have nowhere to go and frankly, I'd rather stay here until I can figure everything out."

"He means to find out if he's *gut* or evil," Sarah said, a half-smile on her lips.

But Abe didn't smile. "I have not agreed to this new request yet."

"But Daed," Abigail said. "Jonah is *gut* at everything. The chickens and the horses, even the milk cows, and that old bull. They all like Jonah." Grabbing a muffin, she added, "And we need a maintenance man and gardener. Eliza says he's done wonders in the stable, too."

Abe tugged at his beard. "You are a hard worker, Jonah, but that's all we know beyond what little you've remembered."

Abigail stared at her mother. "You seem pleased that he might stay, Mamm."

"I'm not pleased," Sarah replied, her eyes on Jonah. "I'm trying to be kind to someone in need."

Abigail shot Jonah a hopeful glance. "He is in need, but we also need him—to help out around here. Our last maintenance man didn't really care all that much about what was fixed or broken. He did as little as possible, and that's why I had to fire him."

Sarah lifted her eyes to her husband. "What do you think, Abe?"

Abigail glanced at Jonah, and he gave her a warning look in return. If she was too insistent, Abe would be suspicious.

"I'll do my work and keep my nose to the grindstone," Jonah said. "I will buy my own electronic tablet as soon as I can, so I can do online searches that might give me some clues as to who I am."

Abe tugged at his pointed beard, the crow's feet at his eyes shifting each time he frowned.

"You are a hard worker, Jonah from the lake, but you must respect our ways if you stay here. I can't turn away a man in need, but you are not one of us. If you stay, you need to respect our ways. Not saying you have to go by our tenets, but you will respect our beliefs and our guests. Do you understand what I'm saying?"

Jonah understood all too well. "You have three daughters, and you want me to be respectful of them. I only want to be a friend and a worker here. I will do whatever needs to be done for your family and the people who come here. Nothing more."

"Nothing more can be," Abe said, standing. "You're hired for the rest of the summer. We'll be so busy, no one will have time for any trouble."

He sent Abigail a sharp stare and then did the same to Jonah. "If that should change, you will have to go, and next time I won't listen to any excuses."

Jonah stood, too. "I appreciate that. Should we shake on it?"

Abe looked reluctant, and then reached out his hand. Jonah felt the strength in his grip and saw the warning in Abe's dark eyes.

"Thank you," he said. "Now I'll get to work."

As he turned to leave, he heard Abigail speak. "*Denke*, Daed. You have been kind and understanding."

"I won't be so kind if you stray, Daughter," Abe said.

One last warning to both of them.

Jonah left the kitchen and stood outside. Taking a long breath, he took in the spring air wafting through the trees. The grass sprouted green and fresh, and the early blossoms had popped out all around him. Abigail and Eliza had shown him where the hostas and the lilies were beginning to peek out. Soon all the gardens would fill with colors and blooms. The sprawling acreage stretched all the way back to the woods and the cove, twisting around a curve in the land and road, where a waterfall connected the tiny cove to the big lake. He'd mow the yard in the next few weeks and help weed out the underbrush along the walking trails through the woods.

Instinct told him to mark all the ways in and out, too. He had no idea where that instinct came from—unless he truly had been involved in the law somehow. The memories nagged at him, there in the dark recesses of his tired mind. Maybe, like these tender blossoms that had popped up through earth and snow, his memories would continue to return.

As restless and edgy as he felt, Jonah was thankful to be in such a beautiful place. Whoever had tried to kill him had messed up big-time and sent him to paradise. This place was like living in another time.

A sense of peace settled over him and held him for a few minutes, but his muscles tightened again in wariness. Then he thought of Abigail, laughing and walking toward him, happy and free. He remembered her voice when he'd come awake on the lake's shore. The voice of an angel. He could almost welcome death after seeing that angel.

He'd hold that memory dear since he couldn't hold the woman herself.

Except in his dreams.

A few nights later, Colette checked the hallway and then gently closed the door to Abigail's bedroom behind her.

Abigail and Eliza were waiting in Abigail's upstairs

room for one of their nightly sister talks. Abigail had been anxious all day, but busywork had kept her from talking to Jonah.

He was her only guilty pleasure, but try as she might, she couldn't put the man out of her mind.

"Did you get to talk to Jonah any more today?" Colette asked as she offered both of them one of the three brownies she'd swiped from the kitchen.

Abigail gladly took one. "I haven't had time to eat much, and I wasn't hungry at supper."

They all sat in a circle as usual. This was a ritual that had begun almost as soon as they could walk and talk. Her younger sisters would sneak into her room, because they loved their big sister and because she slept the farthest down the long hallway from their parents' room.

If Mamm and Daed knew about these before-bed meetings, they never mentioned them. Abigail was thankful for that now that they were all older and discussed more serious things than cloth dolls and mean boys. Sometimes a girl needed her sisters.

"*Neh*," Abigail said between bites of brownie, in answer to Colette's whispered question. "I have to be careful that Daed doesn't see too much, but it's hard not to stop and visit with Jonah like I did those first two weeks. Nice to have our talks to look forward to each day."

"I suppose so," Colette replied, her brownie torn in half. "To have a handsome man all to yourself. What woman doesn't dream of that?"

"But we are not to dream of *Englisch*, Sister," Eliza said.

She got up and went to the big hickory cabinet in the corner, then reached in underneath some blankets. "I want to see how the quilt is coming."

"How do you know where I'm hiding the quilt?" Abigail asked, her hand full of brownie. "You should stay out of my things."

"You hide everything in the same spot," Eliza replied with a shrug and a tug that brought the unfinished quilt out into the open.

"I want to see." Colette grabbed a corner and helped Eliza spread out the beginnings of the quilt on the bed.

While Abigail fumed, her sisters clucked and fussed over the colorful patterns. The quilt had become too private and meaningful to share it with everyone, but these two didn't seem to realize that.

"Tell us about it," Eliza said, her dark eyes bright with curiosity. "You've been working on it ever since Jonah washed up."

"I've had to do it at times without a quilting table," Abigail said. "I did the first patterns while I sat with Jonah after he began to remember. I started with sketches and then decided I'd make a quilt, I think because I want him to remember us and the inn when he leaves. But I keep adding panels, so I've used the quilting room at the inn when I can sneak it over there."

"Soon you won't be able to do that," Eliza reminded her. "Quilting classes are popular with our guests."

"I know." Abigail would have to find a way to finish the quilt in private. She would do it, for Jonah and for her own reasons. Her need to record his existence could go hand in hand with his need to find out where he belonged. This quilt might bring back his memories.

"It's growing," Eliza said. "Soon you won't be able to carry the thing or hide it. You need to find a *gut* spot to finish it."

They each examined the square patterns, which looked like primitive picture frames lined up across the top of the quilt. She'd used bright colors to lighten Jonah's dark thoughts. Reds and greens with natural colors of rust, yellow, and brown, all stitched with big, creamy stitches and a soft, navy fabric on the back. She planned to add in some blues when she did the beach scenes.

Colette pointed. "Explain each square, Abby."

"A tree swing and a house," Abigail said, her fingers touching the first picture. "He remembered the house and tree first, and the swing. He also has memories of magnolia trees. I'm working on a blossom for that panel."

"And this?" Eliza's eyes lit up at the next one. "That's a new one. Is that Samson?"

"*Ja*, with Jonah," Abigail said.

She studied her efforts, trying to see the quilt as her sisters might. While her style leaned toward the primitive and folksy, she'd captured the big, gray-and-black draft horse, and she'd tried to capture Jonah. At least, he looked like an Amish man. Yet he remained difficult to frame inside a square pattern.

"Right after that, he had a memory of a baby crying." She stopped, slowed her breath. "A baby he held in his arms."

Her sisters looked at her, shock and understanding merging in their eyes. She had not mentioned this to anyone. "Jonah is a *daed*?" Eliza asked.

"He does not know," Abigail said. "He thinks he might have a son."

Colette shook her head. "A little one out there somewhere, waiting for his *daed* to come home. How can he stand it?"

"He's struggling," Abigail said as she brushed a hand over the fabric, her fingers touching the image of Jonah and Samson. "But since he asked to stay longer, he seems more resolved, a bit calmer. I think he's accepting that for now, he's well and safe and has work to occupy him here."

"Most men come to that realization sooner or later," Eliza said, her tone pragmatic. "That's what settles them. Along with marriage."

"But this man is different," Colette reminded them. "He is restless, and he wants to find the truth. I think he should."

Abigail and Eliza glanced at Colette. "Well, if the man has a family, we can't keep him here." Reaching for Abigail's hand, she leaned down and lifted her gaze to meet Abigail's. "You cannot have a man who is not Amish and who might also have another family waiting for him. A married man, Abby. *Denk* on that."

"That is all I do think about," Abigail replied. Standing, she grabbed the quilt. Her quilt. She'd find a new hiding place for it. "I can't help my feelings, but I know they are wrong. I have to fight them. I've never had such a thing come over me before."

"You've walked out with other boys," Colette said.

"Boys," Abigail said. "All immature boys."

"Jonah is no boy," Colette replied. "And that makes him dangerous to you, Sister."

Abigail tugged the quilt to her chest, the memories she'd stitched there holding her with a fragile thread. "I won't act on these feelings," she said, her tone hushed and desperate. "I can't."

Eliza stood and touched a hand to Abigail's arm. "*Neh,*

or you'd risk losing everything—the inn, your family, maybe Jonah, too."

Abigail felt the metallic taste of blood as she bit her lip while trying to hold back the wave of need and dread that seemed to wash over her this time of night. Her lonely time. Once she lay in her bed, she could think only of Jonah.

Forbidden thoughts of a man she could never have.

"Jonah is not mine to lose," she replied, her eyes burning, her heart rending while she questioned *Gott*'s plan for her life.

"Then when are you going to put the *bobbeli* Jonah saw in his memories on that quilt?" Colette asked.

CHAPTER TWELVE

"This is the vegetable garden," Abe explained to Jonah a couple of weeks later. "Now that June is here and it's warmer, the weeds will try to take over. We'll need to hoe the rows and thin the plants. Do you know anything about growing vegetables, Jonah?"

Jonah couldn't remember doing that. "I think I probably ate a lot of easy meals, fast food and grocery store stuff."

"No wonder you gobble up food like a hungry dog," Abe said, his smile as sharp as his gray eyes. "You've never had *gut* cooking."

Jonah stopped, the pounding starting up in his head. He couldn't have a spell here with Abe. Not after they'd gotten along so well over the last few days.

"I do like the food around this place," he said, taking a deep breath. He stopped as they reached the greenhouse and the budding rows of vegetables hidden behind it and leaned his hand against the frosted glass. "I remember a vase with flowers. And tomatoes. Fresh tomatoes."

Abe's eyebrows shot up. "Jonah, are you seeing something?"

Jonah nodded, a hot sweat breaking out on his forehead and along his backbone. "I think so."

"Do you need to sit?"

He shook his head. "No. No. Thanks to Abigail, I'm learning to let the memories come and then pass."

Abe's eyes held that disapproval Jonah had seen more than once. "Look, Abe, she helped me a lot when I was so ill. I'd have horrible dreams and she soothed me, telling me to breathe deeply so I wouldn't panic. Your daughter saved my life. I'm here for now and . . . she's my friend, the one I tell things I don't like to talk about."

"You mean, such as your memories?" Abe asked, his tone unyielding, but his eyes less judgmental.

"Yes. I don't want you to think I'm going to make a move on Abigail."

Abe scratched his head. "Make a move?"

"Court her," Jonah replied, forgetting the Amish didn't understand slang.

"You are not allowed, *neh*."

"Can I be her friend? Can't we establish that and let it go, so I don't get a lecture every time her name comes up?"

Abe glanced at the garden, his gaze on the sprouting corn and the rows of string beans. Jonah didn't know what half of these vegetables were, but anyone could recognize corn and tomato plants. Had he once planted those in a garden somewhere?

The vase of flowers came back in view in his brain. He'd have to tell Abigail about that. She had a way of sketching his memories. She'd mentioned something about a quilt, too. He missed her.

Abe finally spoke. "Can you keep it to friendship alone, Jonah?"

"I will," he said, thinking that would have to be it. Abigail was his friend. That had to be the reason these erratic emotions kept bubbling over in his head, why he lay in bed and thought about her at the same time he wondered about his past. The two had somehow merged in his dreams. "I won't cross any lines, Abe. I just need a friend."

Abe finally smiled. "I'm not pretty enough for you?"

Jonah checked to make sure that was a joke. "You're a great friend," he admitted. "I mean, I hope one day you'll call me friend."

Abe walked toward the greenhouse. "I'm concerned that a friendship with Abigail could turn into something more. She cares for you enough already. Enough to hide you away and sit with you in secret."

The greenhouse air was lush and warm, the whole place full of flowers and budding plants. Eliza had told him they grew things in here during the winter and protected some of their more delicate plants.

"No more secrets," Jonah said. "At least not about my being here. I'm going to find out the rest one day."

"That is what concerns me," Abe said as they moved through the rows of tender plants. "The day you remember all and decide to leave."

"*You'd* be glad, though," Jonah replied, still thinking about Abigail.

"I might, but my daughter may consider you more than a friend by then. She won't be so glad."

Jonah understood, and he'd hate to hurt Abigail. "So, what do you suggest? It's hard for us to avoid each other."

Abe turned and touched a budding fern. "How about this, Jonah from the lake? This Sunday is church, here on the grounds. You'll attend and sit with the men, and then you'll eat with the men."

Jonah wasn't so sure about that suggestion. It sounded like a command until Abe said, "And later, you can visit with Abigail after dinner is finished. The men usually put away the tables and chairs and the women clean up. There is plenty of time to say hello and catch up."

"In front of the whole congregation?" Jonah didn't feel comfortable with that.

"The *Leit* will be aware and watching," Abe said, using a word Jonah had learned meant the congregation, or the brethren. "This way, they'll accept you as one of us for now, and it also will show me how you handle being around the whole community."

"And how I deal with talking to Abigail in passing?"

"That's what friends do, ain't so?"

Jonah knew he'd been whipped. "I'll come to church, Abe, and I'll be careful to follow the rules. I probably need a good soul cleansing anyway." Then he gave the other man a level stare. "I will also make sure I get to visit with my friend, Abigail, a little bit. With a lot of chaperones."

"*Gut*, then that's settled," Abe replied, clearly proud of himself. "Now, let's talk about hoes and pitchforks."

Jonah nodded, wondering if Abe would ever use one of those implements on him. Probably, if he didn't behave on Sunday.

* * *

Abigail couldn't believe Jonah wanted to come to church. She'd spoken to him only briefly all week. Eliza was keeping him busy in the stable and barn, and Daed had him gardening from dawn till dusk.

Were they deliberately making sure she wasn't ever alone with him again? Well, he'd be here today, and she could at least find a few minutes to say hello to him.

While the men worked at setting up the church benches out in the backyard of the inn's property, the women took food into the cottage to keep until it was time to serve a light dinner and dessert.

Rows of sandwiches and side dishes were lined up on the counters and long table, while *kaffe* and tea would be prepared directly after the worship service. The ministers and the bishop could go on a long time, but Abigail would use that time to get her head on straight and catch a glimpse of Jonah sitting with the men across the aisle.

How would he handle being confined to a hard, wooden bench for over two hours? The Shadow Lake Township Amish community was smaller than the bigger communities in Spartansburg and Lancaster. But although they only had fifty or so members, the community held strong.

When she came out of the back of the cottage, she spotted him laughing with Matthew by a row of long, backless benches underneath the spreading live oaks that would shade the small gathering. People would talk, but she'd find a way to speak to him later. Daed had told her Jonah remembered possibly having a vegetable garden. Had it been behind the house with the white porch?

He looked up and caught her staring at him. Thinking

he'd try to approach her, Abigail didn't move. What would she say?

But Jonah didn't walk toward her. Instead, he smiled and lifted a hand in greeting. Matthew did the same, but his gaze wandered past Abigail.

"Are you flirting already?" Colette asked from behind her, looking fresh in a green dress that complemented her blue-green eyes. No wonder Matthew's gaze shifted. "Daed is testing Jonah. Don't make him fail."

"And how do you know that?" Abigail asked, wishing her family would stop controlling her life. Then she changed her thought. *Gott* was in control, not any of them.

Colette waved back at Matthew with a distracted lift of her hand. "I heard him telling Mamm before supper last night. She was concerned about Jonah showing up in church, but Daed said he'd told Jonah he shouldn't speak to you, except in passing during lunch and cleanup."

"Ah, so that explains why Jonah is being so distant." Abigail wanted to stomp her foot, but she reminded herself again—Jonah was forbidden to her. They could never be more than friends.

Did Daed mind if they were friendly? He had said they could visit in passing. That wasn't exactly an order to stay apart.

"Why didn't Daed discuss this with me?"

Colette made a face. "He shouldn't have to remind you of how things are. But he did have to remind Jonah. And he got him to come to church."

"That's almost mean, forcing us together and yet forbidding us to be together."

"Jonah has to keep his distance, or have you forgotten?"

"I can't ignore the man," Abigail said on a pouting note.

"You can if you stay busy," her sister suggested. "*Kumm* and help me set out the fried chicken legs Aenti Miriam cooked this morning."

"Aenti Miriam is here?" Abigail had hoped her mother's older sister would stay home today, as she sometimes did if her arthritis acted up. Abigail would need to pray on that attitude, too, even if Aenti tended to be keen on everyone's life and business. "She notices everything."

"She's here and she's noticed Jonah," Colette whispered. "She is badgering Mamm for an explanation."

"I'm sure she is," Abigail replied. Now she understood why Daed had set this up. She and Jonah were both being tested today.

She'd pass the test and make the most of cleanup, and she felt sure Jonah would, too.

What other choice did they have?

"Hurry," Eliza said, checking the area behind a copse of young oak saplings and some shrubs that had a great view of the lake. "I saved you and Jonah a spot."

Abigail grabbed her plate and followed Eliza. "But we aren't supposed to meet like this."

"I'll be nearby, and it should be okay if you didn't plan it, ain't so?"

"Only you *are* planning it," Abigail replied, not ready to turn down this opportunity, but also not ready to upset her *daed*.

"We always eat in this spot when church is held here in *gut* weather," Eliza reminded her. "Adding one more shouldn't be a problem. Now go and find the quilt I laid out and I'll be back in plenty of time to chaperone properly."

"You?" Abigail obliged her sister with a smile. "*Denke*, Eliza. We'll be quick." Her sister moved from discouraging to engaging, depending on her mood. Eliza's heart warred in much the same way Abigail's seemed to be doing.

She found the old quilt spread out by the huge oak tree the three of them had always loved. A perfect spot for privacy, and a favorite of the sisters through the years. They could see the lake and the lane leading to the inn, but no one could spot them behind the holly shrubs and other vegetation growing in a wide oval around the tree. A big rock jutted out near the secret path she'd shown Jonah a few weeks ago. She used to sit on that rock and stare out at the water, her dreams drifting on the wind.

Now, she sat down on the soft, warm, floral material and took in the sunshine and the buzz of bees. Late spring blossomed all around the lake in the formal beds and out in the woods. They'd celebrated a chilly Easter the week before Jonah had shown up. April had gone by in a whirl, and May had passed with a few storms and the promise of summer. June would bring more guests at the inn, and probably more mayflies to the lake. Abigail closed her eyes and held tight to this world. She loved her life at times, but at other times, she wanted to sail away on that lake and find new adventures.

Her eyes still closed, she thought about the day she'd taken Jonah down the secret steps to the lake. How he'd caught her there and they'd come so close to a kiss.

She'd never been properly kissed, but if she ever were to be—she wanted Jonah to be the one.

She opened her eyes and found him standing a few feet away, watching her, his chiseled face etched with longing, his expression so intense it made her take in a breath. His eyes flamed, blue-tipped with a heat she could almost feel on her skin.

"Jonah."

"What were you dreaming about, Abigail?"

She couldn't hide her blush. "I wasn't dreaming. I'm enjoying this beautiful day." And wishing he could kiss her, but she would never reveal that.

He nodded and came to sit down beside her, his scent like the lake's fresh air mixed with a touch of sweat. "I heard you were down here eating alone."

"I . . . I haven't taken a bite yet. I can share."

He lifted a fried chicken leg from her plate. "I've been eying these."

She smiled and got her equilibrium under control. "My *aenti* cooked these. She's famous for her fried chicken."

"Eliza sent me," he said between bites. "We're finished with loading all the benches and tables. I can't believe the men set up and remove the benches every two weeks."

"They are used to it," she explained. "How did you fare during the sermon?"

"I had a good view of you," he admitted with a sheepish smile. "Most of it was in High German, so I couldn't figure it out, but I had something pretty to focus on."

She blushed all over again. "Did you not hear anything the ministers preached?"

"I got enough to know that Amish people are serious about worship and about the Lord."

Abigail beamed at hearing that. She had never asked Jonah about his own beliefs, but she wanted him to see that *Gott* loved him.

"I hope the sermon brought you some peace," she said after nibbling on a chicken salad sandwich. "Daed meant well, asking you to *kumm*."

"Oh, he meant more than well," Jonah replied, taking some of the potato salad she offered. "He said we could visit in passing, so the whole congregation could see us." Glancing back down at the inn, he leaned close. "We're not where they can see us now, however."

Abigail wondered if he'd noticed how the men usually ate first and then the women fed the children and themselves before cleaning up. Part of their customs, but she also knew that courting couples often found ways to be together after church.

Of course, she and Jonah weren't courting. Far from it.

"We did visit in passing," she replied. "Now we are sharing our meal." Over the last few weeks, they'd waved to each other and talked when in groups with others. Today, when they'd finally found an opportunity to talk alone, her Aenti Miriam had frowned and rushed in like an angry hen, scattering anyone who wasn't busy with the break down and cleanup. "I think we have been well-behaved so far."

"I wonder if I was ever well-behaved," Jonah replied, his eyes full of a daring shine. "I promised your daddy I would mind my manners and yet here I am, flirting with his oldest daughter."

Abigail shook her head and tried not to imagine the implications of that statement. She glanced at the water glistening on the lake to stop her mind from wondering about stolen kisses. The caws of seagulls made her heart happy, but right now she had a handsome man staring at her.

"He wants the community to accept you, Jonah. That means he accepts you."

"Within reason," Jonah replied. "He warned me six ways to heaven."

She giggled at that. "I have never heard that term before."

"You'll see it in use if I don't follow your father's strongly worded suggestions." He gazed over at her, reminding her of how he'd been watching her earlier when she'd sat there with her eyes closed, dreaming about kissing him. "Is he this protective with all the men you've . . . dated?"

Her whole body grew warm, and then she lowered her head. This time from shame. "I don't have many suitors."

Jonah put down his plate. "That's hard to believe."

"I went through a boring Rumspringa," she explained. "I walked out with a few boys, but no one I ever wanted to be with the rest of my life." Shrugging, she said, "The inn takes up all my time."

"You must have high standards."

She laughed at that. "*Neh*, some of them didn't seem to want to be with me, and the ones who showed interest were more excited about taking over the inn than marrying me. They made it clear how they would change things, and how I should accept that."

"Idiots," Jonah said. When she lifted her head at that admonishment, he gave her a soft smile. "I won't apologize. I don't understand how any man could resist you."

Abigail let out a dainty snort. "I've barely been kissed."

Then she clamped a hand over her mouth. "Why did I say that?"

Jonah's eyes lit up again. "Maybe because you *want* to be kissed?"

They gazed at each other in the quiet of the afternoon. Abigail couldn't take her eyes away. Her gaze slid down his face to his wide, full lips, then back to his eyes. Eyes that burned with the same need she felt deep inside her heart.

"Let me know if you need to practice," he finally said, his words husky and low.

She glanced around, the warmth of the sun, his words, his eyes, his lips, heating her skin. "You shouldn't say such things."

"You mean calling those men idiots, or saying that you are so hard to resist? Or . . . offering to kiss you?"

She lowered her gaze. "*Ja*, those things."

He lifted her head with a callused finger beneath her chin. "I won't apologize."

They sat, their gazes on each other again. The trumpeter swans and gulls were fussing and squawking down on the lake, the spring breeze moving over them while the trees swayed and danced all around.

Jonah reached toward her.

"Abigail!"

Abigail came out of her stupor and hopped up. "Aenti?"

"I've been looking for you everywhere," Aenti Miriam shouted, her hands on her ample hips, her eyes burning with condemnation. "*Kumm* quick. Your father is not well."

CHAPTER THIRTEEN

"I am fine."

Abigail stood over her *daed's* bed and touched a cool rag to his head. "You passed out," she said again. "You need to be checked. I'll call the doctor."

"*Neh*, I got overheated, nothing more."

He looked so frail, his skin pasty and flushed, his hands shaky as he tried to wave her away.

"Mamm says you have a slight temperature. Don't be stubborn. Let me call the town doctor. He makes house calls."

Daed grimaced, his face etched in pain. "I won't call a doctor on Sunday."

Abigail gave up and went back into the living room. "He refuses to let me call Dr. Murphy."

"I don't know that the doctor could do much without giving him a thorough checkup," Mamm said, her hands wringing despite her calm countenance. "I will keep watch on him for the rest of the day, and tomorrow, hopefully he'll consider going to see the doctor." She gave Abigail a warning glance. "I'm afraid he'll have another spell, though. What if he's having another heart attack?"

"I'll stay the night and help," Aenti Miriam said in a tone that shouted *because I know better than you do*.

"That's not necessary," Mamm replied, her gaze lifting to Abigail. "My girls are here."

Mamm loved her older sister, but Miriam liked to be in charge too much. She'd only make Mamm worry more, with all her suggestions and lectures on what might be wrong.

"I'm here and I will stay here tomorrow," Abigail said, the guilt of being with Jonah earlier grating on her. Yet she would not cave in to her *aenti*'s demands. "The inn can do without me for a day or so."

Aenti Miriam gave her a shrewd frown. "I do not understand why you were alone with that stranger, Abby. That did not look proper to me."

Abigail refused to get upset or to admit to anything. "Jonah works here, and it was his first time at church. Eliza planned to sit with us before Daed got ill."

"It does not matter," Miriam said while she scrubbed an already clean kitchen table. "People will assume."

"Assume that my daughter wanted her lunch, because she was busy the whole time everyone else was being served?" Mamm asked, clearly aggravated by Miriam's busybody ways.

"She was alone with that man who does not look or act Amish."

"Jonah is no threat," Eliza said, taking Abigail's side. "He is a *gut* worker and he sat with the men, properly, until it was time to head home. I told him he could take some of the leftovers and visit with Abigail and me. I was going to join them when you came running."

Mamm's head shot up at that. She had not believed anyone else had been involved, it seemed.

Colette entered the room, carrying clean silverware. She glanced around. "Is Daed all right?"

"He's resting," Mamm said. "I'll go and sit with him. Miriam, go on home. As you can see, I have plenty of help."

Aenti Miriam glared at each of them in turn. "I do not condone what is going on here."

Mamm touched her arm. "*We* know what's going on here. We hired a new man to help with the work and he is a friend. And a *gut* thing, I'm thinking, because at the moment my husband is not well. It's best you return to your own home, ain't so?"

Miriam huffed and puffed and then turned to gather her bonnet and dishes. "Eliza, where is my buggy and Rutabaga?"

Her ancient horse. Abigail wondered why Rutabaga, notorious for running away, always managed to be found. It showed something about a woman when even the family horse didn't like her.

"I'll bring Rutabaga and the buggy around," Eliza said. "Why don't you wait on the porch?"

Colette put down the basket she'd been holding while she'd listened in rapt attention to this whole exchange. "I'll sit with you, Aenti. We didn't get to visit much today."

Miriam's indignation calmed to a pout. "Very well. I don't stay where I'm not needed."

She turned and stalked out the door.

Mamm pivoted toward the bedroom, her frown aimed at Abigail. "We will discuss this later."

Abigail finished cleaning the kitchen and living room,

then sat down on a chair, her nerves jittery. Her mind held a blurred image of Jonah coming close to kiss her. She closed her eyes and asked *Gott* to take these feelings from her heart.

When the door opened a few minutes later, she stood and glanced at Eliza. "Where is he?"

"He's out in the stable. You can't go out there."

"I'm not going to," she said, wishing she could. But she'd done enough damage today. She'd failed her *daed* and now he'd become sick. "I only want to make sure he is all right."

"Jonah is a grown man, Abby. And Aenti is already too curious."

"Aenti is an unhappy widow who messes in everyone's business, but she is right. I appreciate your inviting Jonah to eat with us, but I should have declined."

"I tried to help, but I made things worse," Eliza whispered. "I'll take the blame."

Abigail pulled her sister into the kitchen, away from the short hallway leading to the bedroom upstairs. "Eliza, why are you helping me . . . with Jonah? I know it's wrong, and yet I like being with him. But you have no reason to push me toward him. You've warned me over and over to stay away from him."

Eliza's big hazel eyes filled with a mist of tears. "I don't know. You seem so happy when he's around. Today, he looked lost and lonely at times. I thought I'd do something for both of you."

"I see," Abigail said. "You feel sorry for your older sister who is still not married."

"It's not that," Eliza quickly amended. "You know, we are all romantics at heart. Mamm and Daed have encouraged us to read and learn and we've read a lot of fiction. We both know real life doesn't always have a happy ending."

"The Bible didn't always have happy endings either," Abigail said. "But *Gott* used all kinds of people for *gut* purposes."

"Do you think Jonah has a *gut* purpose?" her sister asked.

"I hope so." Abigail sat down at the table and watched as Eliza made two mugs of mint tea. "I can see the good in him, Sister. I can see that he needs someone to believe in him."

"But . . . you can't take it any further than that," Eliza replied, her hand over Abigail's. "And I should not encourage this. Especially after what happened today. I hope Daed didn't find out, and that my meddling didn't cause him any stress."

"*Neh*, I was the one to do that," Abigail said, wishing she'd stayed in the kitchen today instead of trying to meet up with Jonah. "But it won't happen again."

Eliza's eyes filled with understanding. "You need to be his friend and nothing more. I should remember that myself, next time I want to do something nice for you."

Abigail loved her sisters, and she wanted them to be happy. They wanted the same for her. "I am fighting my feelings," she admitted.

Eliza's eyes got a faraway look in them. "It is romantic to think of impossible love. Only you must not act on your feelings."

"You talk to a lot of young men," Abigail said. "What do you think? Are you interested much in any of them?"

"I talk, I flirt, I search," Eliza said. "I don't know if I'm ready for marriage yet."

"I thought I wasn't," Abigail said, glancing up toward the bedroom. "But now—"

The partially closed bedroom door burst open and Mamm came running out. "Call for help. Your father is having some sort of spell."

Jonah heard the sirens from where he sat near the secret path to the lake. He'd taken to coming up here after work to catch his breath and try to remember things.

He hopped off the outcropping of rocks he'd been sitting on and ran at full speed toward the cottage. Bursting through the door, he hurried to the bedroom.

"He won't wake up," Sarah shouted, grabbing Jonah's arm. "Can you help?"

"Mamm, the ambulance is almost here," Colette said, tears streaming down her face.

Jonah didn't speak. He inherently knew Abe was going into cardiac arrest. He hurriedly unbuttoned the top of Abe's shirt and checked his pulse. Weak. Then he took all the pillows away and lowered Abe's head and proceeded to give him mouth-to-mouth, pumping his chest while he counted in his head after each attempt to give Abe air.

He was still pumping Abe's chest, hand over hand, when the first responders arrived. One of the paramedics touched Jonah's arm. "We'll take over, sir."

Jonah stepped back, and a fog seemed to blow over him. Clutching his head, he stumbled. Abigail came to take him into the living room.

"Sit here," she said, her voice soothing.

He sat, the images in his head frightening him. Putting his elbows on the table, he placed his head in his hands.

Abigail looked toward the bedroom, her eyes filled with dread.

"Go," he said, pushing her away. "I'll be okay."

"But you're having a flashback."

"It's fuzzy. Let me sit here. Go check on your father."

Abigail's hand swept over his as she hurried away.

Jonah sat and focused on the images he'd seen. He'd done this before. He'd tried to save lives. He could hear his voice, shouting, "Don't leave me. Don't go."

The darkness surrounded him. He couldn't go any further.

A room with a vase of flowers, muted shadows. Him trying desperately to save someone's life.

But who had he been trying to save?

Abigail stood with her arm around her mother as the ambulance carried her father away.

Jonah stayed in the kitchen and witnessed the unbearable distress of the sisters and their mother. He hated seeing Abigail and her family so upset, so he finally went to her side. "Do you need to go?"

She shook her head. "We've called a cab."

"I can try to drive the buggy," he offered.

"*Neh*, the cab is on the way and it's quicker. Mamm and I will go, and Colette and Eliza will stay here. Will you look after them?"

"Yes, but—"

"Jonah, please, stay here."

She turned and hurried out of the house, a small tote bag in her hand.

Jonah watched, helpless, as she held her mother's arm and waited for the cab.

Eliza came up beside him. "I'm going to get the animals settled." When he didn't respond, she said, "I could use some help."

Jonah nodded absently. "I hope your father will be okay."

Eliza gave him a worried smile. "The paramedics said you probably saved his life."

Jonah barely remembered what he'd done. "I must have learned how to do that, somehow."

"Mamm is grateful," Eliza said as they walked to the door and went out toward the stable.

Jonah didn't want gratitude, but he'd take it. He wanted to remember why he'd been trying to save someone's life. If he truly had been a police officer, it could have happened while he was on duty. But . . . a memory on the fringes of his mind told him it was something important.

His mind swirled but refused to release the memories.

"You had a spell of your own, ain't so?" Eliza led the way to the tack room, where they kept the horse feed and other supplies.

He nodded. "I'll jot it down so I can talk to Abigail about it."

"She's still working on your memory quilt," Eliza said. Then she slapped a hand over her mouth. "I shouldn't have told you that."

"She's mentioned it," he said, wondering how Abigail

would depict the tidbits he'd given her. "But this one is hard. I was saving a life."

Eliza's eyes misted over. "*Ja*, my *daed's* life. Jonah, how can we ever repay you?"

Jonah lowered his head. "You've all given me more than I deserve. But you could help me with one more thing."

"What's that?" Eliza asked while she fed Samson.

"I need to get on the Internet again to see if any local police officers are missing. I'm convinced I worked somehow in that capacity."

Eliza nodded. "I'll take you up to the office as soon as we're done here, and I'll tell the night shift you're going to use the computer. You can lock the back door when you're done." Sighing, she said, "I'll wait at the cottage with Colette. I hope we hear something about Daed soon."

"Me too," Jonah said. "Me too."

Then Eliza surprised him. "I purposely sent you to see Abigail today, in our secret place. I shouldn't have done that, but my sister deserves a little happiness. She takes care of all of us. I thought she could use a friend."

Jonah's heart bumped against his chest. "I understand. Friends. We can only be friends."

"Or you could become Amish," Eliza said with a soft smile. "Something to think about."

Abigail paid the cab driver and helped her mother into the house. The sun began its descent for the night, the sky shot with orange and pink hues that looked like a blanket thrown over the trees and water.

Colette and Eliza met them at the door.

"How is Daed?" Colette asked, her voice shaky, her eyes glistening.

Mamm let go of Abigail's hand and reached for all her daughters. They gathered around her in a circle.

"Your *daed* had a mild heart attack," she explained. "He will be in the hospital for a few days, and when he returns, he'll have to be careful. But the doctor says if he follows instructions and takes his medication, he should be all right. If not, he might have to have surgery to replace a heart valve."

Eliza and Colette nodded, tears in their eyes.

"We'll need to make sure he eats healthy and doesn't get all worked up," Abigail said. "But we can do that. We know what needs to happen and most days, we get things done."

"Daed won't be able to do much for a while," Mamm explained.

Colette took Mamm's hand. "Let us get you some supper."

"I'm not hungry," Mamm said. "I think I'll go on to bed."

"I'll bring you some tea," Colette offered.

Mamm nodded and walked slowly up to the bedroom.

"She's tired," Abigail said. "But we are grateful Daed is alive."

Eliza hugged Abigail close. "Jonah saved him."

"I know," Abigail replied, weary to the bone. "The doctors said it could have been much worse."

Then Eliza leaned close. "He's up at the inn, in the office."

Abigail glanced toward the bedroom. Colette nodded as she carried in the hot tea. "I'll sit with Mamm."

"I shouldn't," Abigail said. "We talked about this, Eliza."

"Someone should," Eliza replied. "He saved our *daed* today. And . . . it brought back a memory. He needs a friend, Abby. He said he'd share what he remembered with you. I took that to mean only you."

"I'll hurry," Abigail said, thinking she was about to break her own rule again.

But her feet carried her at a swift pace to the back side of the inn and the employee entry. The weekend staff had a small lounge where they stayed during their shifts.

She only wanted to tell Jonah how thankful her family was for his help. Nothing more.

But when she opened the office door and saw him sitting there with his head in his hands, she lost all her resolve.

Abigail rushed to his side and fell to her knees. "*Denke*, Jonah, for keeping my *daed* alive."

He lifted his head and looked down at her, then touched a hand to her cheek. His eyes were dark with the torment that troubled him so. "Is he going to make it?"

She nodded, putting her hand over his. "He had a heart attack, but he is grateful. We all are. He is alive and the doctors have given us reason to believe he will heal, with the right food and medicine."

Jonah nodded. "I had a memory of doing the same— CPR on someone."

"Did you remember more?"

He glanced at the screen. "I feel something, something buried so deep I don't know if I'll ever remember it."

"I hope one day," she said. Then she stopped, her eyes on the computer screen. "Did you find anything there?"

"No missing police officers anywhere in this area. I'll search more tomorrow. I believe I was in law enforcement, but why can't I find out any information?"

"I don't know how to help," she said. "You should rest."

He moved his hand down her neck and then dropped it away, leaving a sweet warmth on her skin. "You need to rest, too."

Then he turned and shut down the laptop. "I'll walk you halfway."

She nodded. "I told myself I'd stay away from you, Jonah. When he gets home, my *daed* can't get upset about anything."

"You mean . . . about us?"

She nodded as they walked out and took the path toward the cottage. When they reached the fork where the path split toward the carriage *haus*, she turned to face Jonah.

"We must take care."

"Yes," he said, while his eyes seemed to tug her like the lake's waves. "Yes."

"Tell me exactly what you remembered so I can make a sketch."

"A vase of flowers," he said. "Beautiful, colorful flowers in a yellow vase. I saw it on the table. I could almost smell the scent of a garden."

"But you were . . . saving someone's life?"

He nodded. "I wish I knew who and how and when. I hope they lived."

Giving her one last heated glance, he turned toward

the little apartment, his broad shoulders slumped, his head down.

Abigail slowly made her way toward her family's cottage, her heart heavy with worry for her *daed* and for her Jonah.

Because no matter what he remembered or where he went from here, he would always be her Jonah.

CHAPTER FOURTEEN

Things changed after Abe's heart attack. It was almost July, and the inn was always full of people wanting to celebrate the Fourth, when fireworks would shimmer over the lake. Some went down to the beach and others put lawn chairs and blankets along the yard near the bluffs.

Jonah took over handling tasks Abe had done before. He settled into a quiet routine, taking care of everything from gathering eggs and cleaning the chicken run and coop to helping Eliza with her beloved horses and learning more about the other animals that belonged to the King family. Eliza knew the lineage of each horse, and they had become his favorites.

Samson ruled as the prince, the leader, with the pride of a Percheron whose French lineage included warhorses both in Europe and the United States. Pickles, the smaller roan, was a quarter horse and a hard worker. The two dainty mares, Rosebud and Sunshine, loved to pull the smaller, summer buggies, while Samson and Pickles handled the bigger, enclosed winter buggies, as well as plowing and planting. Peaches was a miniature version of Sunshine, but with her own personality. She'd be good with the youngies, as Eliza liked to call children.

Jonah might not remember much, but he felt fairly certain that in his former life, he'd never had to rely on a horse or buggy. Next, Eliza planned to teach him how to safely drive a buggy with cars flying past. He learned more about the Amish culture every day.

He thought he could go into organic gardening if he ever went back to the real world. He'd learned how to plow the garden behind Samson and plant tiny green buds that would turn into corn, tomatoes, or beans, squash and zucchini, or mustard and collard greens, even potatoes. Beyond the garden, the apple orchard rose up in four symmetrical rows that provided apples for tourists and locals alike. Already, the apple flowers had bloomed. The apples were beginning to form, growing larger in the warm July sun. Would he still be here when fall brought apple-picking time?

Jonah hadn't been to the apple orchard yet. Now, sitting here on his favorite rock, he glanced back at the trees in the distance. His head buzzed with a shard of pain. Another memory. This one as distant and far away as those budding trees. Brief but clear. An orchard, a woman laughing, a little boy giggling.

"Daddy!"

Jonah held his head, hoping that would capture the image, but the laughter drifted away; the little boy stopped calling out.

"Daddy," Jonah said. "Was he calling out for me?"

He sat waiting, holding his breath, but the flashes of memory in his head taunted him day and night, making him want to rejoin the world and find the truth. He could no longer stay here, safe and cocooned and protected by a woman fierce in her faith and reckless in her loyalty. He needed to find his own life and go back to it. Were they waiting for him—the woman and the boy?

When he didn't have chores to do, he went to the office and did as much digging as he could to see if anyone matching his description had gone missing. He'd searched every newspaper and online missing persons site in the state of Pennsylvania, then gone on to the states surrounding the lake—Ohio, New York, Michigan, and on to Niagara Falls, where the Niagara River flowed north from the lake and through the falls, and on into Canada. The lake was two hundred and forty-one miles long and fifty-seven miles wide. A lot of area to search, and a lot of lake for a boat to travel through. He'd tried over and over to remember that boat trip.

Jonah's impatience grew and made him angry, but he couldn't give up. Next, he'd do a nationwide search. Going to the police would be simple, but his gut told him not to do that. He could have a photo made and sent out to social media sites, but that might bring curious people out of the woodwork. Or bad people who might hurt Abigail and her family. Not knowing ate at him. If he'd been a law officer, that meant he'd lived a dangerous life. He wouldn't bring that danger here.

Why? He'd even taken to praying now and then, asking God that one-word question. Jonah figured God heard that question a lot, but he hoped the Lord would help him, for Abigail's sake at least. Somehow, he knew God mattered. Jonah learned that more every day, being here.

Glancing back at the apple orchard, he decided he'd find time to go there tomorrow. If he could walk among the trees, he might remember better.

The memory of that laughter and the boy calling out for his daddy—that would stay with him well into his dreams. Jonah thought about taking the walk to the orchard now. Or finding something else to occupy his thoughts.

He liked staying busy. If not, he'd probably go out of his mind wondering why he'd landed here in this bucolic place, with no memories. Seeing Abigail every day made him smile, even when he tried to keep his distance. It had become a sweet torment.

I can't have feelings for an Amish woman. That wouldn't be fair to her.

It wouldn't be right either. He'd never forgive himself if he caused Abigail to be shunned by her family.

And yet being around her seemed to be a balm to his weary soul. She never preached to him or admonished him. She only listened and gave sage advice, her eyes bright, her hair gleaming, and her smile like a jolt of pleasure that burned through his system in a cleansing heat.

The kind of pure heat that could burn and brand a man forever.

Until he became whole again, Jonah could only work hard so he'd be exhausted enough to sleep. Each night, he prayed he'd wake with his memories intact again.

But what if he'd been hiding from those memories?

"Jonah?"

He turned on the rock he'd begun to think of as his

own. He came out here a lot after work and tried to read or to jot down shards of memories.

Abigail. Had he sensed she'd show up as she sometimes did? That could be why he'd waited until the sun slipped away before heading down to his lonely little apartment.

"Hi," he said. "Did you need something?"

The look in her eyes told him everything he wanted to know. And also showed him everything forbidden to him. Her emotions flowed like the waterfall on the other side of the property, freely and softly and clearly. If he pushed, she'd allow whatever he wanted.

He would not push.

She stopped a few feet away from the rock and tugged at her hair, which was always trying to break free of its bun. "I wanted to alert you that my sisters and Mamm and I are having a frolic this week, in the employee dining hall at the inn."

Chuckling, he gave her a smile. "A frolic, huh? Sounds bold."

"It's not what you think," she replied, moving closer as the summer wind tugged at her light blue skirt. "A frolic means we get together to have fun, sometimes to sing, or do some sewing, some canning, and putting away vegetables or baking cookies. This one will be a quilt frolic."

"Are you going to work on *our* quilt?"

Her eyes widened at that question. Too late, he realized how it sounded. They both knew nothing could ever be theirs, together.

"I mean the quilt you're creating from my memories."

"I know what you mean," she said, a touch of sadness

in the acknowledgment. "I'm bringing it out for the first time. Only my sisters know what it represents."

Not sure he wanted that quilt to go public, he asked, "And if others have questions, will you tell them more about me?"

"*Neh*, I don't have to explain my sketches or my imagination. I will tell them that I'm learning how to make primitive designs, and this is my first attempt. Which is true."

"My being here has forced you to lie. It shouldn't be that way." He moved over and patted the rock. "Abigail, sit with me."

When she hesitated and glanced back toward the inn, he said, "I had another memory a few minutes ago. I thought I'd tell you about it."

She moved toward him like a frightened doe and sat down on the very edge of the big rock. "I have not lied about anything. I just choose which topics I want to discuss or talk about."

"You are pragmatic, I'll give you that."

"The Amish are known for being pragmatic. We *kumm* up with ways of making sense of things."

"Then I need to be more pragmatic," he replied. "I can't make heads or tails of anything."

She laughed at that, the sound dancing along his spine like musical notes. "I don't think I've ever heard that said before."

"It means I'm mixed up. And . . . I could say a lot of things you've never heard before."

"Would I be embarrassed?"

"Very."

"Tell me what you remembered just now."

He told her about the apple orchard. "A tree. I was near an apple tree. I heard them, Abigail. A woman and a little boy. He called out, 'Daddy! Daddy!'"

Abigail's expression showed sympathy, but Jonah also saw pain there. Pain and acceptance. "You might have a wife and a son, something you already suspected."

"I don't know," he said. "I'm going to walk through the orchard soon to see if I can remember more." Then he smiled a weary smile at her. "Would you come with me?"

She looked down at her apron. "Shouldn't you go alone? I don't want to intrude."

"You have never intruded. I need you. I need you to help me stay calm. I don't like having these panic attacks."

She glanced back at the path to the cottage. "I will see if I can meet you here and we'll go together one day soon. After the lunch crowd has died down or later, near sunset, so I won't be in a hurry."

"Next week's the Fourth. I know your family doesn't do anything special, but it would be nice to have you with me for part of the day. Let's plan to visit the orchard then."

"Did you remember something about the Fourth of July?"

Shaking his head, he said, "No, nothing yet. I know about the day, but I don't remember much of anything happening other than fireworks."

"I promise I'll find a way to walk with you through the orchard on the Fourth of July. That can be our celebration."

"I'll get my work done and be ready. *Denke*."

She laughed. "You are using Pennsylvania Deitsch more and more often."

Surprised, he said, "I guess I am."

They sat smiling at each other until the sun slowly sank over the water and trees across the way.

"Beautiful," Abigail said.

Jonah kept his eyes on her. "Yes, beautiful."

She turned toward him. "You shouldn't look at me that way."

"You shouldn't be so beautiful."

She ducked her head, the blush he'd come to enjoy making her look even more innocent. "I've never considered myself as such."

"Have you ever taken a good look at yourself? I hear the Amish think mirrors are vain, but surely you've been curious."

"We have one mirror in our house. We only use it to adjust our *kapps* and bonnets."

"And what do you think when you look into that mirror?"

She shrugged. "That I'm Plain, and soon I'll be an old maid who watches her nieces and nephews and bakes bread all the time."

"Then you need to look again, Abigail," he said, gripping his hands into fists to keep from touching her. "You need to see the beauty and grace and kindness I see when I look at you."

She stood in an abrupt denial. "I must go before one of my nosy sisters calls out and alerts Mamm that I'm missing."

He wished she could stay. "Yes, go."

Giving him that unsure, doubtful glance, she said, "I will see you tomorrow."

"Yes, tomorrow."

"Have fun at your quilt frolic."

She nodded, proper and serene.

But he watched as she walked away, then glanced back, and he saw that hungry longing in her eyes. The same longing he'd felt since he'd first seen her there on the beach, and later, in his dreams. That unsettling longing held them together like a stitch sewn in one of her quilts, in *their* quilt.

Shaking his head, Jonah stood and looked out at the choppy lake waters. At least now he had something to look forward to—a walk through the orchard with Abigail.

A date of sorts, but he didn't dare voice that opinion.

He had to find a way to leave. Because if he stayed, he didn't know if he could resist the sweet temptation of Abigail King.

CHAPTER FIFTEEN

Colette watched as Abigail folded the unfinished quilt squares to take over to the inn's big conference room. The room used to be part of the servants' quarters, but the former owners had taken out walls to make it a nice place for group retreats or business meetings.

Today, however, Abigail had reserved it so they could hold their frolic in the spacious room. The inn had a big quilting rack that they set up for quilting lessons. Visitors loved learning to make quilts. Then Abigail and her mother and sisters each had their own circular quilting frames that could be held on their laps, or on a small table, and were used to stitch individual patterns.

"You're going to share this new quilt idea today?" Colette asked, her eyes shining bright.

"I'm going to work on my patterns," Abigail said in what she hoped was a nonanswer.

"Oh, I see. Now we are playing word games to hide the fact that you have a huge crush on a man who does not belong here?"

Her younger sister could be so sweet at times. Other

times, Colette had the bluntness of a worn-out kitchen knife.

"I'm making a quilt for a person who has come into our lives, to help him regain his memories."

"That's a wonderful *gut* way to *frame* it," Colette said, her big, blue-green eyes reminding Abigail of the colors of the lake.

"I'll be framing a lot today," Abigail said, refusing to take the bait. "What are you working on?"

Colette smiled and gave up. "Just some starburst patterns."

"Always a *gut* choice."

"I wish I could come up with something such as you have," Colette quipped. "But I haven't seen any more men washed up on the lakeshore this summer."

Abigail gave her sister a scowl. "Stop it."

Eliza came in. "Everything is under control in the kitchen. Maggie will be here soon. Mattie is mopping up, and I'll bring in our refreshments later. What needs to be done?"

"We need to be aware that Abigail is working on her primitive patterns," Colette said, hoping to shock Eliza.

"*Ja*, well, the whole community saw Jonah during services last month. The quilt doesn't have his name on it, ain't so?"

"Colette is fretting about how I will explain all the patterns," Abigail said. "I want to work on it, and this is the best time." She glanced around to make sure the rest of the kitchen staff was still in the kitchen or dining room. "I'll be working on a vase of flowers today. That's normal."

"But what about the rest of your creation?" Colette said in her fretting voice.

"I have added a man and a horse," she admitted, not naming either. "And an apple orchard."

She wanted to add the picnic she and Jonah had almost had, until things went wrong and Daed got sick. Perhaps she'd show a picnic blanket and a basket to remember that day.

Eliza's gaze moved between her sisters. "Who will know unless we blab?"

Colette rolled her eyes. "All right. I will be cautious and pretend our sister is eager to learn primitive quilting."

Abigail gave them a curt nod. "I have always wanted to learn, and I have lots of ideas."

Colette snorted. "*Ja*, and one of them is brawny and has deep blue eyes." Giggling, she whispered, "I think she has lots of ideas for that one."

"Stop it," Eliza said. "Leave her be."

"Touchy?" Colette replied, sticking out her tongue.

"What's this?" Mamm stood at the double doors to the big, long room. "Colette, why is your tongue hanging out like a puppy dog's?"

Colette looked guilty. "I was only teasing my sisters," she said, lifting her gaze to Abigail. "But I'll go help gather the refreshments."

"I think that is wise." Mamm glanced at her. "Your *daed* is napping, but he should be up soon. The bishop will sit with him while we quilt."

"Is Nan coming, then?" Abigail asked in a squeak. The bishop's wife enjoyed gossip. She'd probably purposely decided to come today to get information regarding Jonah.

"She is," Mamm said. "Aenti Miriam will be here soon, too."

All three girls stopped what they were doing.

"Why?" Colette asked without thinking. Then she gave Abigail an apologetic shrug.

"Colette, that is no way to act," Mamm said. "I know my sister can be a pain, but she loves to quilt, and she's won awards for her work."

"Exactly," Colette said, her head down. "She'll criticize every stitch we make."

"But she'll notice the beauty in the work," Mamm said, her gaze suddenly locked on Abigail. "I'm anxious to see what you have there, Daughter."

Abigail glanced at her sisters and then back to her mother. "It's a primitive. I'm working on patterns and I've stitched part of the quilt. I need to add the other squares."

"And is this your quilt?" Mamm asked, her hands folded against her apron. "The one you've been so secretive about? What will you do with it?"

Abigail willed the blush heating up her neck to go away. "I don't know. I might . . . give it away. Or display it."

Mamm smiled and nodded. "I'm anxious to see the story it tells."

"No story," Colette said, too fast.

"Every quilt tells a story, Colette," Mamm replied. "And I sure want to hear this one."

Abigail saw big trouble ahead. Why had she believed this was a *gut* idea?

* * *

Jonah fed and watered the chickens, then had a heated discussion with Old Red regarding dating manners and how to handle hens and their delicate sensibilities. Everyone now called the territorial rooster Old Red ever since Jonah had given the ornery rooster that name, weeks ago.

Old Red truly ruled the roost around here, but he needed to tone things down at times. Jonah had learned that same lesson.

After gathering the eggs and cleaning the chickens' fancy castle, he'd moved on to the stable and cleaned out the stalls, where he fed and talked to Samson. Then, to be fair, he'd told Rosebud and Sunshine they were the best-looking mares in the stable. Now he moved on to Pickles.

"How did you get that name?" he asked the docile little horse while he brushed him down and hand-fed him some sort of mix supposed to keep him healthy.

The horse lifted his dark head, his black eyes widening before he tossed his mane. Jonah liked working with the animals. They were easy to be around.

Pickles didn't respond too much. He dipped his nose back into the feed pouch, his eyes showing a grateful gleam.

"I see. Don't want to talk about it." Jonah felt the same way. "I can't talk about a lot of things, Pickles. Because I have no memory."

He put a finger to his temple and tapped it. "Nothing much up here, except the memories I'm making now at the Shadow Lake Inn."

"I see you tell your troubles to the animals."

Jonah pivoted, thinking if he'd had a gun, he'd be

holding it on the person standing about ten feet away. Instead, he went tense, feet braced apart, hands curled into fists.

"Can I help you?" he asked, shadows dancing across the plains of his open mind. Memories hovering like low-hanging clouds.

The stranger was Amish from his dress, but Jonah didn't recall ever meeting him.

Stepping forward with a hand up, he smiled. "I'm John Zook, the bishop for this community."

Ah. Jonah had figured he'd have to answer to this man sooner or later. "I saw you at church a few weeks back."

"*Ja.*" Bishop Zook stepped forward. "I got called away before I could properly meet you."

Jonah grabbed a damp rag and wiped his hands. "I'm sure you have questions."

The bishop, an older man with a salt-and-pepper beard, nodded. "Such as, what is your purpose here?"

Jonah moved closer, his senses hyperaware of his surroundings. "Right now, I'd like to finish cleaning the barn."

John Zook laughed. "Could you use some help?"

"Isn't this below your pay grade?" Jonah asked.

"I'm not sure what you mean."

"Do bishops muck up stalls?"

"We do whatever task is at hand."

Jonah handed him a rake. "I was about to put down fresh straw."

Bishop Zook followed him into an empty stall and started working, the ease of his actions showing Jonah he knew hard work. But then, Amish people did work hard all the time.

He thought of Abigail and the burden of running the

inn. She never complained, but he could see her fatigue, and he'd also seen that faraway look in her beautiful eyes.

The bishop gave him a thoughtful perusal. "We don't get many people here with amnesia. I imagine that is a frightful feeling. Would make a man angry and aggravated."

"That it does," Jonah admitted. "But the King family has taken good care of me. Loaned me some clothes and fed me, gave me a job."

"They are a loving family. Kind and considerate. But there have been some concerns."

Jonah stopped spreading straw and turned to the bishop. "What do I need to do to make everyone around here feel okay with me?"

"If you could remember the truth, that would help," the bishop said. Then he held up a hand. "But I understand you have lost your memory, and that something *baremlich* happened to you."

"That about sums it up," Jonah said, interpreting the word to mean terrible. "I don't even know my real name, but I feel safe here. I've asked for more time before I go back out into the world."

The bishop put his rake to the side. "I believe you, Jonah. Perhaps there is a reason the lake spit you out, as I've heard Abigail explain. I am not here to condemn you. I've heard you are a hard worker and you've been a big help here."

Jonah wanted to be relieved. Yet he felt uneasy. "But?"

"But we are set in our ways and we follow our own tenets."

"I understand and I respect that. I'm learning more

each day, and the more I hear, the more I'm impressed with this way of life."

"*Gut*. I believe the King family needs a helper right now. If you follow our ways and respect our rules, all will go well." Then he unrolled his shirt sleeves and nodded. "I must get back to my friend Abe. He was snoozing when I left him. I worry about his recent health issues." After adjusting his clothes, he said, "Nice to have this discussion with you, Jonah from the lake." Then Bishop Zook said, "*Gott segen eich*."

God bless you.

Jonah smiled, a genuine feeling of relief washing over him. He didn't think he needed the bishop's approval, but he was glad to have it. For Abigail's sake.

He stood quietly watching as the bishop walked out into the morning sunshine. He'd never had such a calm, measured dressing down. Not that he remembered, he thought with grim humor.

But he'd been warned. One wrong move and he'd have to leave Shadow Lake Township. And Abigail.

"Abigail, you are concentrating so hard you'll have a permanent frown."

Abigail glanced up from her stitching to find her Aenti Miriam staring at her with a frown much worse than her own. "I want this to come out the way I saw it in my sketch, and in my head."

"*Ach, jah*," Miriam said with a clicking disapproval that reminded Abigail of the hens clucking at each other. "I've never heard such—a woman doodling on paper all day."

"I don't doodle, Aenti," Abigail replied between gritted teeth. "I draw the things I see around me."

Miriam leaned over the quilting rack, her brown eyes burning with criticism. "Well, you do have a way with quilting, and your *mamm* has shown me some of the pretty pictures you've created."

Abigail's surprise must have shown on her face. "Really?"

"Did you just give my sister a compliment?" Eliza asked with a grin.

"I give praise where praise is due," Miriam replied in a huff. "But I am anxious to see the finished product on that square she's been stitching over there in the corner."

"Why don't we stop for refreshments?" Mamm said, standing so Miriam would do the same. "I'm ready for some of that pound cake Maggie made."

Maggie Yoder beamed with pride. "I have to say it turned out better than I had expected. But it's a true pound cake—a pound of flour, sugar, butter, and eggs, with a touch of vanilla."

"Sounds wunderbar *gut*," the bishop's wife said. "I must cut a piece for John."

"Of course, Nan," Mamm replied. "I'm so grateful he's keeping Abe company. Abe frets that he can't get out and do more."

"He is wise to rest and follow the doctor's orders," Miriam said. "I warned both of you long ago that you needed to slow down."

"*Ja*, you sure did, Aenti," Eliza said with the sweetest smile.

But Abigail saw the glint in her sister's hazel eyes.

Nan stood and stretched. Her mother, Nan, and Miriam

had been working on a wedding quilt for Nan and John's oldest daughter, Beth. "You know John loves a *gut* discussion with Abe. I'm sure they had much to discuss today."

Her gaze drifted to Abigail. Abigail had put away her quilting ring and gone about her business, filling tea glasses and *kaffe* cups. "I've sliced some strawberries and we have blueberries, too, to serve with the cake."

Nan looked disappointed that she hadn't gotten a rise out of anyone. "It all looks so nice, Abigail."

"*Denke*," Abigail said with a soft smile. "We have lots of help around here."

"And how is the new yardman coming along?" Nan asked, finding the perfect in, which Abigail had inadvertently set right up for her.

Abigail finished handing out the food and turned to smile at Nan. "Jonah has been a blessing. He takes care of all the gardens and the crops. And the animals, too, since Daed had his heart attack."

"Why does he dress Amish?" Miriam asked between bites of cake, the crumbs settling against her apron top.

"He didn't have a lot of clothes when he arrived," Eliza offered, giving Abigail a sympathetic glance. "We loaned him some things we found in a closet."

Miriam let that sink in. "But he can go and buy his own clothes."

"He is fine wearing what we gave him," Abigail replied. "He works outside most of the time, so he needs work clothes."

Miriam continued, clearly glad they were addressing the elephant in the room. "I suppose so. Very odd how he almost drowned. Everyone's been so curious as to how he came to be here."

"But we are thankful he did not drown," Mamm said, a surprising resolve in her words. "He has become a big help to all of us."

Abigail sank onto a chair, her appetite gone. But she ate a couple of bits of cake so Maggie's feelings wouldn't be hurt. Maggie worked in the restaurant, but she had a hard time actually cooking the food. Her *mamm* had died young and her older sisters hadn't trained her up very well.

Miriam took a sip of her tea but didn't give up on her interrogation. "Abigail, will you show us your quilt? It must be so special for you to keep it a secret up until now."

"It's no secret, but I don't think it's ready," Abigail said, wishing she'd chosen something else to work on today. Was she asking for condemnation? But she didn't really have anything to hide. Her imagination had created this quilt. Or so she told herself.

More like she'd wanted to remember her time with Jonah. Now she had to share those private moments because of her own stupidity.

"I'd like to see it, too," Mamm said, her tone brooking no argument. Was she testing Abigail?

Everyone waited, some with gleeful anticipation and some with understanding and empathy.

Abigail couldn't say no. She'd opened up this can of worms with her need to work on the quilt during her afternoon off. Now she had to face all her doubters.

"I'll show it, but remember, I'm piecing together bits and pieces to make sense of things."

"What an odd way to make a quilt," Nan said, her tone kind. "I suppose we each have our own way of working."

Abigail had brought in the portion of the quilt with the panels she'd already stitched together, hoping later she could spread it out and work alone after everyone left. Now her sisters, ever loyal, helped her to spread it across a big bench on one side of the room.

Once they were finished, she stood back and held her breath while she took a glimpse of what she'd created so far. What would these women say? Would it be obvious why she'd created this quilt? What would Mamm think if she figured out that the quilt's story was all about Jonah?

CHAPTER SIXTEEN

Jonah could hear women talking and laughing. He wanted to turn and run away, but Matthew had told him one of the sinks in the men's bathroom down the hall from the restaurant had sprung a leak. He figured he could check it and alert Abigail to call a plumber if he couldn't figure things out.

He took the toolbox he'd found in the barn and headed into the small, two-stall bathroom. But he was working near the room where the women were, so he couldn't help but hear.

"It's beautiful, so beautiful. You're right, it does tell a story."

He didn't recognize the voice, but they must be admiring quilts.

"It's wunderbar *gut* for a first effort, Abigail."

Wonderful good. Abigail.

Was she showing a quilt, then? His heart stopped. *Their* quilt?

"I'm not finished." Abigail. Her voice sounded foreign and shaky.

Lowering his head, Jonah went to work, finding a

stripped washer valve on the sink faucet. He had it fixed in no time once he'd found a couple in the toolbox.

Wondering how he knew to do this kind of stuff, but he couldn't remember his name, he thought maybe he did have hysterical amnesia. He'd read up on it while he'd been online the other day. What could be so horrible that it could cause a man to forget everything personal about his life? Maybe that knock on his head had been worse than he'd thought. He still got headaches, but usually they came when he started having a memory. The nightmares also brought headaches and more torment. Murky, shifting shadows, laughter he couldn't find, faces that turned from him.

He twisted the wrench against the new washer and then tested the faucet. No drip.

"I love the little boy in the swing."

Jonah stopped, held his breath. *The little boy in the swing*.

Maggie. About to have her own child, she'd notice that kind of image right away.

Jonah sank down and leaned against the wall, his knees up, his head down, and listened, unable to leave. His breath came in huffs while his pulse hammered at his temples like a sharp, heavy nail. Abigail had told him she might work on the quilt today, but he'd never thought about others seeing it.

"And that vase of flowers you finished. It's like they're real."

That sounded like Eliza.

"That's a mighty big boat. Not the usual kind for anyone Amish."

The boat. The yacht he'd mentioned the day they went down to the lake.

"I saw a boat like this once, on the lake," Abigail said. Had she really? No. She was trying to cover, to hide the truth.

"The man and the horse—that horse looks a lot like Samson. But who is the man?"

Silence.

"Abigail, who is this?"

"Aenti, it's an image I have in my head."

"Well, your image looks like that man, Jonah. I still don't know why you are keeping him here. He's not Amish and yet he dresses as such. That's deceitful and . . . it's not right."

"I think Abigail is ready to clean up now, Miriam."

Sarah, protecting her daughter.

"Why is she showing us this anyway? I can't believe you continue to condone this, Sarah."

"Miriam, let's take these dishes to the kitchen."

He heard footsteps moving around, so Jonah stayed still for a moment longer, forcing himself to breathe deeply and push the dark images away. Things would be even worse for Abigail if they found him eavesdropping on their conversation.

Abigail was showing *their* quilt? The quilt she'd been working on since he arrived. Why put herself through that kind of scrutiny? Unless she wanted to be found out, wanted to expose him, so he'd leave and . . . save her from any more embarrassment? Or did she want someone to validate her talent? He could see her talent and her worth easily enough, but some couldn't.

"I do need to go and check on the kitchen," Abigail

said. "I have a lot more to do on this quilt. I want it to be perfect."

"There are no perfect quilts, Abigail."

Her aunt again. That woman sounded brutally blunt. She did not like Jonah. And could he blame her? He was an interloper, and too mysterious for the Amish and their simple ways.

"Miriam, we all know that, but Abigail wants it to be beautiful, ain't so?"

"*Denke*, Nan," Abigail said. "It's bits and pieces of things I see and hear . . . and sketch."

"Why don't you stop sketching and use traditional patterns?" Miriam again. Abigail's aunt sounded judgmental and bitter.

Jonah almost dropped his wrench to go into that room and protect Abigail. But he knew she could protect herself.

And she did.

"I won't stop now. My sketches help me to work on my quilts. One day, I might start making patterns for profit. I don't think anyone would object to that."

That's my girl.

But she really wasn't his girl. Abigail deserved someone who could take care of her and help her run this inn. A man who believed as she did, lived as she did. Abigail should be married to an Amish man. Not someone who couldn't even remember what he'd been before. If he'd come here with all his memories intact, Abigail still could never be his. Everyone from her sisters to her parents to the bishop had told him to back off.

Not his to have. Not his to think about, dream about, worry about.

Even though he was the man with the horse she'd stitched on that quilt.

"Abigail."

Abigail turned to find her *mamm* waiting for her in the staff break room. Now that all the others had left, she knew Mamm would want answers.

"I'm coming," she said, her bones weary and her mind buzzing with erratic emotions. "I had to help with a cleanup in the kitchen. Lemonade makes floors so sticky."

Mamm motioned to two high-backed white chairs.

Abigail sat down and met her *mamm*'s eyes.

"Abby, what were you thinking?"

"I don't understand," she said, stalling.

"Oh, I think you do understand, more than you are willing to admit." Mamm held her hands against her apron. Her beautiful face etched in worry and fear, she reached across the table, her fingers covering Abigail's hand. "I hope you are not falling for Jonah."

"I'm . . . I'm his friend."

"A friend who has spent hours creating a beautiful quilt that clearly depicts him and his life. What did you expect this afternoon, that none of us would notice?"

"I expected to have a few hours with my family and friends without being condemned for something I created. A quilt I had to create."

"*Ja*, but it's not our way. This beautiful quilt—and I do mean that—it's lovely and touching, but . . . my dear daughter, it is keenly obvious to me that you have strong feelings for Jonah. Feelings you can't have. Forbidden feelings, Abby. You must stop this before things go too far." Mamm shook her head. "We should have ended it the day we found him here."

Abigail dropped her head and lifted her eyes to her mother. "How do I stop what feels so natural to me, Mamm? It is like stopping my next breath. Impossible."

The back door opened and they both looked up.

Jonah stood there, his eyes wide with surprise before they shifted to Abigail. "I'm sorry. I didn't know anyone was in here."

Mamm looked at Abigail and then stood. "I have to go check on your *daed*. Would you walk with me, Abby?"

Abigail glanced from her *mamm* to Jonah before she answered. "Did you need something?"

"I had a few things to discuss," he said. "Work-related. We can talk later."

Mamm let out a sigh, clearly not happy. "I'll go ahead. Don't be long, Abby."

She sent Jonah a frown before she left the room.

Abigail's heart drummed with each breath she took. Her *mamm* was right. She cared for Jonah more now than ever. But she could not let him know that, and she certainly couldn't keep mooning after a man she could never have.

So she stood and smiled at him. "What else has gone wrong around here today?"

Jonah moved into the room, narrowing the space between them.

"You showed them the quilt, Abigail. You laid out what might be my life and my memories right there for all of them to see. Why did you do that?"

* * *

Abigail felt the chair behind her and sat back down to put her head between her hands. "I don't know. I wanted to show off, I think. My pride got the better of me. I'm so sorry, Jonah. I told you I might work on it today, but I never thought about how this would make you feel."

Jonah wished he hadn't snapped at her, but he had to know why she felt the need to make things even worse for herself. He'd stewed about it all afternoon. "I heard them talking when I was working on the leaky bathroom faucet. About me, Abigail, about pieces of my life, sewn together and then put on display."

Abigail lifted her head, the hurt in her eyes hitting him in his gut like a bullet.

"Abigail," he said, but she shook her head and pushed past him.

"I have to go," she called over her shoulder. "Your supper is on the stove." She ran out the door and didn't look back.

Before, she'd always looked back. Always.

Jonah wasn't hungry. He washed his hands and arms, then ran a wet hand through his hair. Tired and frustrated, he sat down at the big employee table, his mind whirling. He'd gone and done the one thing he'd tried to avoid doing—hurt Abigail.

Colette came in, carrying a small laundry basket full of dish towels, and glanced at him. "You look like a mule kicked you in the stomach," she said, her eyes missing nothing. "Wasn't Abigail just here?"

"She went home," he said, gruff and solemn.

"Hmm. Do you want to eat your supper here or take it with you?"

He stood. "It doesn't matter. I'm not hungry."

Colette, a spry little thing, blocked his way out the door. "You should take it for later, when your despair and anger calm down. You'll be starving and you'll wish you had some of that chicken casserole and fresh creamed corn. I think Abigail put in two cornbread muffins, too."

Ignoring her efforts to tempt him, Jonah asked, "How do you know I'm suffering despair and anger?"

"Because you look miserable. Want to tell me what happened?"

"I snapped at Abigail and hurt her feelings," he said, wondering how the King women managed to dig information out of him.

Colette didn't look happy. "Why would you do that?"

"It's the quilt. I . . . overheard everyone talking about it."

"Ah, that," Colette said, dropping the basket on a chair. "How did you happen to overhear us?"

He told her about being in the bathroom next door. "Hard not to hear. Your aunt grilled her in a loud way."

"*Ja*, you are right about that. Aenti Miriam has assigned herself as our moral compass, and the more self-righteous she becomes, the louder her voice. She has always been set on going beyond the strictness of the Ordnung."

"I hated hearing her ask Abigail all those questions."

Colette's expression softened with understanding. "Seems you're really angry on Abigail's behalf, but you took that anger out on her because she shared the quilt with everyone."

He let out a breath. "I guess so." He looked out the window and saw a couple with two small children. The guests here roamed the property at will. He tried to stay out of their way because he'd have a hard time explaining himself to anyone.

He watched as the little boy reached for his father's hand, his head turned up, a trusting smile on his face.

That image pierced Jonah's soul. He could almost feel the distant memories taunting him, always just out of his reach.

But he refused to give in to the headache today. Turning back to Colette, he said, "I think you're right. I was certainly caught off guard, hearing everyone go on and on about the patterns in that quilt. I recognized almost every one of them."

They matched the memory patterns carved in his head with bittersweet pain.

Colette poured him a glass of water from the container they kept ready for workers. "I'm sure it felt as if your privacy had been violated, but Abigail has worked on that quilt almost from the time she dragged you out of that water. It's her passion, a project that has her excited and full of hope."

"What kind of hope?" he asked. "It's impossible even to imagine."

"What *are* you imagining?" Colette asked. "You and Abigail can't be anything other than friends. But that quilt allows her to keep the memory of you . . . when you go away."

"She gets to keep my memories. What about me? What do I get to keep?"

Colette pointed to his head. "Your memories are in there, Jonah. You need to get them out. And you should do it before it's too late."

That stung, but she was right. He stood up. "I want to apologize to Abigail."

"Not now. Let her be." Colette lifted her basket again. "Later, you can do something special for her."

"What would that be?"

"She likes to walk on the beach early in the morning. That's how she found you."

"But we shouldn't meet up—alone, I mean."

"*Neh*, but you can show up and be quick about it. Keep to the left side of the inn, around the curve toward the cove and waterfall. That's where she usually walks. It's hard to see that path from the inn or from our cottage."

"Colette, why are you doing this?"

Colette gave him a long stare. "If you've upset her, you need to fix it. I think it would help her to hear a sincere apology, but you'll need privacy to be able to do that."

"Even though you don't approve of me?"

"It's not up to me to approve. You know what is right and what is wrong. But if you want to do something nice, meet her on the beach with flowers. Any woman would love that."

She walked out of the room and left him standing alone.

Jonah nodded, wondering why her sisters both seemed to push him away from Abigail, then turned around and encouraged him to spend time with her. But when he thought about it, Colette and Eliza both loved Abigail, and they always said she deserved something nice.

He could be the something nice in her life, or he could be too dangerous to stay here much longer.

Lately, everyone seemed to be trying to test his mettle

to see if he could resist taking things to the next level with Abigail.

He didn't know what anyone wanted, except for him to be gone. He couldn't understand the workings of their minds, maybe because he didn't understand his own mind.

He might be falling for Abigail. He could be married, even though he wore no ring. He might have a son, but he couldn't remember if he did. His heart tugged him toward Abigail, but he held back something to save for whoever he'd left behind.

Jonah got his food and hurried toward his tiny apartment, the image of that tree swing and that big front porch in his thoughts. Then the image of the couple he'd seen earlier came back to his mind.

He could almost see himself walking along, holding a child's hand. He stopped once he'd made it safely inside his place and put down the food, his hands shaking, his head throbbing.

"Stop it," he said, grabbing his head, his fingers digging into his damp hair. Slamming his fist against the wall, he welcomed the pain that trembled through his knuckles.

He decided to do what he should have done all along. He'd go into town and tell the local police what had happened. He'd give them his fingerprints to find out whether he was a criminal or not. He'd let them take his picture to pass around. He could be a missing person, a person of interest, or someone who'd gotten himself into a dangerous dilemma. That would explain his gut feeling that he hadn't wanted to involve the police. Because he might have been part of something illegal. Now, he had to know the truth, one way or another.

Who had shot him?

And why had he been stalling on this for so long?

Before he did all that, he'd get up early and pick Abigail some flowers so he could see her on the beach. At least one more time.

CHAPTER SEVENTEEN

"Why are you insisting I take a walk?"

Colette looked behind her and then back at Abigail. "Can't you do as I say?" she replied, her eyes wide while she pursed her lips. "Please."

Abigail shook her head. "The bread's almost ready and the muffins need to be iced. The breakfast casserole needs to cool for a few minutes. We have three couples for breakfast and a family of four—two of them younger than five—so put out the booster seats."

"I've got all that. Go. Now. To the beach where you always walk."

Abigail glanced around. "Edith will wonder where I've gone."

"Edith is shucking corn for corn pudding. I talked Matthew into helping her. Go take a break."

Colette practically shoved her out the door. Glad that Mamm had gone to visit a sick friend this morning, Abigail hoped her *daed* would behave and take it easy doing a few tasks around the cottage.

She should go check on him, but she hadn't had a

minute to herself lately. A walk would help her get over Jonah's harsh words to her after the frolic. She'd gone all morning without seeing him. Actually, she'd purposely avoided him.

She made her way down to the beach, thinking she hadn't been down in a few days, and then it had been just a quick early morning walk to watch the sun come up over the trees to the east.

Today, the lake waters shimmered in a blue haze that looked like a blanket full of diamonds. Abigail held her *kapp* and glanced at the curve where heavy oak limbs leaned out over the brown sand. A flock of seagulls lifted out over the water. Their cries always gave her a sense of peace. She stopped and breathed deeply, closing her eyes in a silent prayer.

She had not slept well. She'd hurt Jonah by displaying that quilt and she hadn't meant to do that. She'd meant to keep the quilt to herself, showing it only to her sisters. Why had she felt the need to display it so boldly, and with Aenti Miriam and Nan Zook there at that? Pure pride, or more. Perhaps she'd wanted to test the quilt, to see if she'd put too much of her heart in it.

Mamm had seen that right away. Jonah had heard it, too. She'd made a big mistake.

She opened her eyes and looked ahead, remembering the day she'd found Jonah here on the beach. Her heart had gone from calm to a fast beat when she'd spotted a man lying just out of the water.

And then, there he was, walking toward her, carrying a bouquet of wildflowers.

Abigail blinked. She must be dreaming or seeing things.

But he was real. Jonah hurried toward her, his eyes on her, his gait full of intention. "Abigail."

"Jonah, I didn't know." She stopped. "No wonder Colette almost forced me down the hill. She knew you'd be here, ain't so?"

He smiled a tight, intense smile while he kept his eyes on Abigail. "I have to be quick. We both need to get to work. I only wanted to say I'm sorry for . . . the other day."

"I'm sorry, too," she said, touched when he handed her the flowers. "Jonah, you didn't have to go to all this trouble. I'm the one who made a horrible mistake."

"I shouldn't have overreacted," he said. "Can we walk a bit and get back to being friends?"

"We'll always be friends," she said, holding the flowers to her nose.

The bouquet held one perfect magnolia blossom surrounded by yellow daylilies, daisies, and peonies, with a trail of jasmine blossoms. The flowers smelled divine. She loved the scent of magnolias and always enjoyed this time of year, when the one tree they had on the property produced lush, fragile blooms.

"*Denke*," she said, her voice wobbling.

He nodded, his eyes shining. "I wanted to give you these and tell you I had another memory. Me, walking and holding a child's hand. We were near a huge magnolia tree."

"Oh." She almost said she'd add it to the quilt, but she didn't want to ruin this fragile truce. "Did you get that awful pain in your head?"

"I did, but I forced it away and it wasn't as severe."

"That's wunderbar *gut*, Jonah."

She thought about what this new memory meant. It only solidified her suspicion that he had to have a child waiting for him somewhere. Bittersweet thoughts.

They stood staring, at a loss for words.

He finally tugged at his shaggy hair. "Abigail, I'm going to get my chores done and then I'm going into town."

"Oh, do you need supplies? Colette can pick them up."

He gave her an apologetic gaze, his eyes full of regret. "No, I . . . I've decided I need to go to the police station again. I'm going to tell them what happened and let them take my fingerprints and a headshot. To see if they can find out who I am, no matter who I am."

Abigail studied his face, the face she'd memorized and now knew so well. She saw the scar by his left eye, a scar so tiny it would be hard to notice. But she'd noticed. She saw the craggy, rugged jawline and the fuzz of a never-quite-full beard. She saw the deep blue of his eyes, bluer than the deepest part of the lake.

And she saw the fear and the dread and the apprehension that swirled in those deep eyes.

"You're leaving."

"No, not yet. I won't until I hear back, and I figure that will take weeks. It's a slow process."

"But you'll wait here and then you'll leave?"

She shouldn't keep repeating that, but for some reason she'd thought he might stay. Forever. Which was ridiculous, of course.

"Whatever they find or don't find, I have to get on with my life. I'm afraid I'm causing you too much trouble. I don't want to do that."

He looked into her eyes, and then his gaze moved down to her lips. "It's too tempting. You're too tempting."

Abigail felt a rush of warmth moving through her veins. "I don't mean to tempt you, Jonah."

He moved so close, the flowers were crushed against her apron. "You are so innocent. I don't want to ruin that innocence."

"But you'll go, just like that?"

"I'll go, but it won't be easy. It will take every fiber of my being to walk away. If I have a family out there, I need to find them." Giving her a beseeching gaze, he said, "If I'm married, I'd bring shame to you, the worst kind of shame."

She backed up, the flowers too fragrant now, his nearness breaking away her defenses. She held the flower stems tightly, their rough edges digging into her palms. "I must go. I have work to do."

"Abigail, please."

She kept walking, the tug of him like a magnet pulling her back with a force that almost brought her to her knees.

He didn't want to be here, and she couldn't blame him. She couldn't force him to stay. It wouldn't be fair. They could never be together in any way, and they both knew it.

And yet she held the flowers he'd given her and treasured the sweet feel of a hundred emotions. She could not watch him walk away.

Jonah went into the police station and stood at the front desk, waiting while the desk sergeant calmed down someone on the phone. He recognized the smells of stale coffee and hard-earned sweat, and he knew the familiar sounds of phones ringing, officers stomping through, someone being processed in or out.

He had lived this life, and while this place suffocated him with its smallness, he could see himself sitting at an old desk in the corner of a much larger precinct. A precinct. He'd been in one.

His head ached, his heart pumped, and his mind whirled between that scene and the sight of Abigail walking away from him this morning. His grand gesture had failed. Big-time. Now she was more confused and hurt than ever.

But in the end, he couldn't stop her hurt and he couldn't stay on here, thinking the thoughts he did about her, dreaming of her at night, being near her during the day. Not when he couldn't do anything more. Even if he were free and clear, he didn't know if he wanted to let go of this world to stay in hers.

"Can I help you, sir?" The desk sergeant had finished his call. A different one from the last time he'd tried to do this.

"Yes," Jonah said. "I need to speak to someone about . . . about helping me find out who I am."

"Come again?" The officer, gray-haired and haggard, looked up with a skeptical frown on his face.

Jonah tried again. "About three months ago, I woke up on the lakeshore, near the Shadow Lake Inn. I couldn't remember who I was. I had a head injury and I'd been shot. I've spent the last few weeks getting well and helping out around the inn."

"You work for the King family?"

He nodded. "They gave me a job, hoping I'd get my memory back. I haven't. I need help—official help."

"Uh-huh." The officer studied him. "I heard a man came in and claimed he had amnesia, but he left before we could talk to him. He looked Amish, they told me. You don't really look Amish."

Impatient, Jonah tried again. "I didn't have many clothes when a young woman found me on the shore. These were given to me—by the Amish family that took me in."

The sergeant glanced around. "Are you turning yourself in?"

"No. I'm hoping you can take my prints, send my photo around, and find out who I am."

Sergeant Garrison, Jonah saw from his name tag, looked as if he would either burst out laughing or call someone to take Jonah to the psych ward. "I'll find someone to help you."

Jonah's head throbbed; his pulse jumped and sputtered. Matthew sat waiting outside with the buggy, and Jonah almost bolted again. He could turn around and forget his past.

No. He had to do this. Abigail deserved the truth.

He held on to the counter until his knuckles were white.

Finally, the desk clerk came back. "Sir, Captain Sherman will see you now."

Jonah glanced outside, and then he followed the desk clerk to a small cubicle in the corner of a large, cluttered room.

It was now or never for Jonah.

* * *

Abigail walked into the cottage and glanced around. "Mamm?"

Daed walked in from the hallway. "She's out. The Weaver girl has gone into labor."

"Leah?" Abigail smiled at that. "Mamm might be a while." They'd known the Weavers all of their life.

"*Ja*." Daed sat down in his favorite chair. "I can have soup for dinner."

Abigail checked her father over. "Have you rested today?"

"I'm tired of resting," he admitted. "I've fixed everything around the cottage I can find to fix. I could start back helping Jonah with the chickens. That won't hinder me."

Abigail didn't want to think about Jonah. "We'll have to check with Mamm on that." She started gathering plates. "Colette is bringing over a squash casserole and some cucumber salad. The garden is producing a *gut* crop this year."

"That will bring nourishment," Daed said. "Jonah has taken good care of the vegetable garden."

At the mention of his name, Abigail stopped and sighed. She didn't even realize she'd done it until she looked over at Daed.

Her father's expression told her all she needed to know.

"You have feelings for our Jonah, *ja*?"

Abigail went over and sat on the stool by his chair. "I will not dishonor this family. I care about Jonah and I worry for him. I can't help my feelings, Daed."

Daed looked into her eyes. "I can see that, *Dochder*.

This man, as *gut* as he is around here, can bring you no happiness. You know that, *ja*?"

She bobbed her head. "He knows that, too. He went into town this afternoon to talk to the police. This time he's serious."

Daed's expression changed from pragmatic to shocked, but he quickly squelched his surprise. He nodded, and then he took her hand. "It had to be done."

Abigail fought back the tears. "I believe so."

"But you would rather he stay?"

"I can't ask that of him. I can only pray that he finds his way home."

"I am proud that you have taken the best path, Abby. It's the only way."

"But you like him?"

"I have grown to care about Jonah," Daed admitted. "He works hard and stays to himself. He is a troubled man with a big heart." Daed sank back against his chair, his fatigue obvious. "Jonah and I have held many interesting conversations. He's a strong person, stubborn and determined, but he is also a decent sort. I don't believe he came from a bad batch of people."

Abigail wanted to hug her father tight, but he would frown on such a demonstrative gesture. But in her heart, she felt joy that her *daed* could see what she saw in Jonah. It had to be enough.

"He can continue his work here until he hears," Daed said. "That is still our agreement. But if he *is* a criminal, they will find out and they will have to take him in. Will you abide by that, Abby?"

"I don't have any other choice," she replied. Then she

stood and cupped her hands against her apron. "I'll get the table ready for supper."

Daed reached for her hand, his eyes holding no answers. "Abby, if things were different, if he were one of us . . ."

Abigail nodded and leaned down to kiss her *daed* on his forehead. "I know. *Denke*."

Eliza came in, with Colette behind her. After Abigail explained that Mamm would be late, they set down the food. Then Eliza whispered to Abigail, "Jonah is back and doing the evening feeding. He didn't tell us anything, but he's okay, Abby."

She put a hand to her lips but said nothing. Fear and dread clogged her throat and held her. Behind that, a keen sense of loss tightened her whole body. She would not have a crying fit. She had to remember *Gott* was in charge, not Abigail King.

They got supper on the table and after Daed sat down, so did they. Then they said their silent prayers.

Abigail's prayers were scattered and unsure at first, but the more she prayed, the calmer her heartbeat became. She had to let go of Jonah. He wasn't hers to have. If she were married to him, and he went missing, she'd want him to come back to her. He had to find out if he had a wife and child, and she had to accept that as *Gott*'s will.

She would take the morning they'd shared on the beach, and she'd treasure the flowers, and the man. She'd have to put that scene on her quilt, but it would be a telling scene, a scene that showed the quilt's true story, one of goodbye. She could keep the quilt and sleep underneath it each night after he left. But that quilt would be the closest she'd get to having Jonah in her dreams.

CHAPTER EIGHTEEN

Jonah looked at the clock for the fifteenth time. It was late, but he couldn't sleep. Too many emotions roiling through his head, and too much at stake every way he turned.

He longed for the truth. Longed for the rest of those shattered memories to return so he could figure out his life.

The not knowing had become the hardest part. The only life he knew now consisted of hard work and a simple, peaceful existence.

On the surface. But underneath, the memories swirled like a strong lake current, lapping against the walls in his soul, pushing at his subconscious.

The trip to the police station had drained him. Dark shadows had moved through his head on the way home. Memories, mocking him and teasing him, had hovered in the back of his mind. Repeating his story had only reinforced what he didn't know, what he couldn't see. Now he was even more aware of his repressed memories.

After listening with a skeptical frown, Captain Mac Sherman got his prints and took a photo of him. Then he jotted down notes and suggested Jonah should buy a burner phone, so the police could call him immediately if they learned anything. Matthew took him to a local store where he could buy the phone with some of the cash he'd made working at the inn. He called Captain Sherman right away and gave him the phone's number, telling him he was using the name Jonah King—for now. What else could he say?

Matthew tried to calm him on the ride home. "Did you find any answers, Jonah?"

"Not yet." Because he liked Matthew, Jonah didn't snap at the younger man. "It'll take time for them to send out the information I gave them. At least they didn't throw me in jail."

Matthew grinned at that. "I'm thankful for that. You've helped me a lot with the heavy lifting around the inn. It's nice to have another man around to help with the hard chores. Those sisters can get bossy."

Jonah smiled at that. "Really? I hadn't noticed."

Matthew shot him a sideways glance, his dark eyes full of mirth. Then he shook his head. "Colette only talks to me when she needs something."

The kid had it bad. "She'll need you one day, Matthew. I see the way she glances at you now and then."

Now that he was back in his apartment, he realized he'd started a process that would either help him or doom him even more. What if the police couldn't find out anything? What if he never fully recovered his memory? Could he be content, living out the rest of his life here, near Abigail? That might be all he'd ever have—just the nearness of her.

He'd hurt Abigail by telling her he wanted to go to the police.

She'd been happy with the flowers and his apology, so why did he have to go and ruin things? He should have put off the trip to town, or at least gone without telling her. But he wanted to be honest with her. Always.

A soft knock at his door startled Jonah out of his musings.

He got out of bed, grabbed a T-shirt and tossed it over his head.

When he opened the door, his heart took off.

Abigail stood there, her eyes wide, her expression pinched and determined. Her hair tried to escape the white *kapp*, and she gave him a breathless, tentative gaze, proving she'd probably run all the way from the cottage.

"Is something wrong?" he asked, wanting to tug her close.

"I had to see you," she replied. "I only have a few minutes. My sisters are in my room waiting to make sure I get back undetected."

He tugged her inside and shut the door. "You shouldn't risk it."

"I need to say something, Jonah. To apologize for being so selfish in wanting you to stay. And I want to know if the police found out anything."

Jonah stood staring at her, seeing the fear and worry on her pretty face. "I explained everything and they took my prints, but they had a hard time getting good ones. My fingers are worn and callused. I told them what little information I could provide. They took a picture of me, a mug shot."

Her puzzled expression made him smile. "A closeup of my face."

She nodded, held her hands tightly together. "When will you know?"

"We wait," he said. Then he showed her his new phone. Basic, with no fancy apps. "It could be a while because they have to send everything to the state lab. They don't have the latest technology around here." He wanted to shield her, but he didn't know much more than Abigail at this point. "They took my fingerprints, but we can't be sure I'm in AFIS."

"What is that?" she asked, her brow furrowing.

"Automated Fingerprint ID System—it's the finger-print database. It would show data immediately if I had a criminal record."

"Then you don't?"

"As far as I know, I don't, but as I said, they didn't get any good patterns on my prints either. My skin is too dry and damaged from all the work I do around here. They have other ways to search for missing people. They plan to check with other agencies and . . . possibly get in touch with the FBI. The feds have a database that can pinpoint anyone based on descriptions. I don't know if the locals even believe my story."

"You mean the story of your being spit out of the lake?"

He shook his head, marveling at her pragmatic sense of humor. "Yeah, that story." He explained that the police had tried several times to take his prints, but his fingers were dry, cracked, and battered. Had they been that way before he'd arrived at Shadow Lake? He hadn't really noticed, and because the local police department didn't have a digital fingerprinting machine, tracking his identity would be tricky. Nothing in a small town moved fast—that much he knew.

"Did you ask them whether you might be a law enforcement officer?"

He shook his head. "I didn't. I still can't bring myself to reveal that. They could find out—I'd have to be in the FBI database if I signed up to be in law enforcement."

"So, you still don't know much."

"I'm probably not a criminal, because they haven't had any reports of criminals matching my description. It will take them a while to hear back from AFIS. They'll have to examine what they got and compare those prints to others. Apparently, results can be delayed even with modern technology."

He didn't tell her how he'd felt the memories pressing in on him while they tried to get his prints and his information. How he'd felt that he'd witnessed this process over and over, that he understood the process and the slow route justice sometimes took. He didn't need to tell her that.

Abigail frowned up at him. "I should have gone with you."

"No, and you shouldn't be here now."

"I had to see you," she said, her voice low and husky. "I worry."

"All the more reason for me to leave," he said, inching closer. "You shouldn't be here."

"But I am here, Jonah." She pressed against the door, appearing both afraid and intrigued, her expressive eyes showing him her heart.

Jonah moved closer, overcome by the need to smell

her sweetness. He braced his left hand on the door and lifted his other hand to her cheek, his eyes on her. Tracing a finger down her beautiful, high cheekbone, he said it again. "You shouldn't be here."

She didn't speak. Instead, she stared back at him with defiance and a bit of a dare in her eyes. Her lips parted; her eyes flared in awareness.

Jonah didn't let her speak. Instead, he leaned close, his lips grazing hers. A feather touch, so soft, so sweet, so heartbreaking. "Abigail."

She gave him one last desperate look that told him so many things and then she turned, caught between him and the door, her back inches from his chest. He tugged her back, so she pressed against him.

She sighed and whispered, "I'm glad you are safe, and I hope you hear something soon."

For one sweet moment of torment, Jonah held her there, his hand going around her waist, his lips so close to her slender neck. "Go home, Abigail, before I do something I'll regret."

She stilled. "You'd regret . . . me?"

Jonah swallowed, prayed for strength. "I could never regret you, but I'd regret hurting you."

He stepped back and opened the door; then he gave her a gentle shove. "Good night."

She looked back once, then ran away into the moonlight, her long skirt lifting out around her like butterfly wings.

Jonah watched until she'd made it around the corner. Then he shut the door and leaned his forehead against the rough wood. He would have kissed her, but they both knew there'd be no going back once he did. And he had to go back out into the world he'd somehow managed to forget. He couldn't move forward until he knew what he'd left behind. Today, he'd opened up a whole new can of worms. But it had to be done, before it became too late for him to leave.

Abigail came through the kitchen and slowly took the back stairs up to her room, trying to avoid the squeaky boards in the old wood. After she made it safely inside, hoping her parents hadn't heard her, she turned and leaned against the door, out of breath.

Eliza and Colette stood staring at her, their eyes wide, their lips pursed. They didn't approve and yet they understood. She knew she'd do the same for either of them.

"Are you all right, Sister?" Eliza asked, her tone a low whisper.

Colette rushed across the room. "Abigail, you're flushed and out of breath. Did someone see you? Did Jonah upset you?"

She shook her head and touched her fingers to her mouth, the memory of Jonah's lips grazing hers making her weak at the knees.

"He kissed you, didn't he?" Colette asked, her own breath rushing out. "Abby, tell us."

Abigail sat down on the bed and sighed again; little jolts of awareness were still burning through her system. "He did not kiss me. Not really. Well, he almost kissed me. It was—" She stopped, wanting to hold Jonah's almost-kiss close. "It wasn't really a kiss."

Colette shot Eliza an inquisitive glance and then looked back at Abigail. "None of us have ever actually been *really* kissed. Who are we to even know what a true kiss is like?"

Abigail didn't tell her sisters, but she knew for certain sure a true kiss from Jonah would be wunderbar *gut*. She'd wanted that kiss tonight, but he'd backed away. He wanted his old life more than he wanted to kiss Abigail.

Colette took her hand and leaned close. "Abby, what are you going to do?"

Abigail shook her head. "There is nothing to be done. He said he needs to wait to hear. The fingerprints didn't show up in any criminal files yet, so I don't know what will happen next. It's all foreign and confusing to me. Machines that can find out and print a man's identification in a short time, questions without answers, pictures to be sent out and sources to contact." Pushing at her *kapp*, she tugged it off her head and ran a hand through her tumbled hair. "I'm almost glad I don't live in that world."

"You aren't considering that, are you?" Eliza asked. "Leaving us to follow Jonah?"

"*Neh*." Abigail looked down. "I only consider what it would be like if . . . if Jonah were Amish."

"He's not," Colette said, dropping her hand away. "You've known that since you brought him here. You must accept that he'll leave one day. Don't pin any hopes on a future with Jonah."

"I won't," she said. But she got up and went to the window to stare out toward the carriage house. She could see the stable and the barn, two hulking shadows that stood between her home and Jonah. He had two windows in his tiny space. She looked at the one located on the back side of the building but saw no light shining. She also caught glimpses of the water in the waning moonlight.

The lake, as timeless as the air she breathed, held all Jonah's secrets.

Then she turned and pulled out her memory quilt and held it tightly against her. She had new impressions in her mind, but she'd wait until her curious sisters went to bed before she tried to sketch the images of an almost-kiss. Abigail thought of butterflies and feathers and a longing that pierced through her soul. How did she capture that?

How could she put those feelings into a picture on a quilt?

CHAPTER NINETEEN

The first day of July had turned out to be a perfect summer day. Only three more days and then Jonah could take Abigail for a walk in the apple orchard out past the main yard.

Right now, however, he had gardening to do.

The scents of roses and magnolias, peonies, and lilies filled Jonah's soul with peace. Working in the gardens with Abe keeping an eye on him made him forget that unknown world outside this quiet cove. He liked digging in the dirt to redesign a flower bed or picking beans and corn from the vegetable patch.

Abe had taken to sitting in a lawn chair to watch Jonah work, or offer him advice when he needed to figure out a planting grid. He'd tell Jonah stories of how he and Sarah had met and fallen in love, stories of how the Amish village at Shadow Lake had begun.

"Not much has changed since our ancestors settled here over seventy years ago," Abe said now, while Jonah deadheaded a bright red geranium within reach of his shady spot.

An older *Englisch* couple walked by and waved. "You're

doing a great job," the woman said, her blond hair short and stiff, her sunglasses huge and dark. "I need to teach my Ernie how to grow such pretty flowers."

Jonah nodded and smiled, but he kept working. Abe strolled over to talk gardens with the couple. He always sensed when Jonah didn't feel comfortable.

Jonah tried to avoid people. The less he talked, the less he'd have to hide. Glancing toward the kitchen, he wondered how Abigail was doing. It had been two days since he'd almost kissed her, but she had managed to avoid him.

He didn't blame her. They were playing a dangerous game that could cause Abigail to lose her whole family and her community. Each time they were together, it got harder to stay apart.

Abe finished his conversation with the guests and came back to his chair. "Nice people." Glancing back at the cottage, he nonchalantly said, "I might need your help cleaning up around my house. We're holding a frolic here on Sunday afternoon."

"Oh, another quilting?" Jonah asked, wondering if Abigail had moved on to a new quilt to work on. She sure didn't need to show their quilt again.

"No, more a social gathering where the young people who are at courting age get together to sing and mingle. Some will walk out together. Chaperoned, of course."

Sunday was the Fourth. Would Abigail forget about their walk in the orchard?

Jonah looked around at Abe, figuring the old man was trying to give him a big hint. Abigail had explained how *walking out* meant a couple had become exclusive and were officially dating. "That sounds interesting."

"The girls aren't getting any younger," Abe said, his

tone neutral. "I won't be around forever. I'd like to see them settled with the men *Gott* has chosen for them."

Okay. Jonah knew a definite warning when he heard one. Deciding to test Abe on that, he turned from weeding the daylilies and wiped his brow. "How does God do that, Abe? Pick a man for each daughter. Isn't he really busy with other things?"

"*Gott* takes care of all things," Abe replied, as calm as always. "He's all knowing, all seeing, all the time."

"Do you think he knows I'm here, with no memory, no money, and no hope?"

Abe sat with his hands on the arms of his wooden chair, his dark eyes perusing Jonah's face in a strong, silent way. "I believe he knows the reason you came to us, Jonah. I think all will be revealed in due time."

"What if I don't have time to wait for that?"

Abe's smile told Jonah nothing. "Why are you impatient in the first place?"

"Good question. I guess because I had a life, and some of my memories indicate parts of that life. I need to find out what happened before I can move on." He shrugged. "I wish God would get to me a little quicker."

Abe stood and stretched, then gave Jonah a level stare. "Have you considered that *Gott* might be telling you to be still?"

Anger crested against the walls of his heart, and Jonah wiped his hands on an old rag, then shook his head. "No, I haven't considered that because we both know I don't belong here."

"Are you so sure about that?" Abe asked, clearly enjoying

this conversation. He managed to stay calm while Jonah wanted to rant.

"Right now, I'm not sure about anything," Jonah admitted. "You know I care about all of you and this place, Abe. But you also know I can't care about Abigail. I can't give her what she deserves. You've made that clear, and now you've driven it home by throwing a party to match her up with some man she might not like."

"I understand my attitude angers you," Abe said, his tone serious now. "But it's not that I disapprove of you. It is that you are an outsider, and we can't allow you and Abigail to become too close until *Gott* shows us his plan."

"Such as?"

"You could stay here and confess your sins, be baptized, accept our faith, and become one of us. You'd have to confess in front of our church family, and then your former life would be gone, never mentioned again. You could take a wife and become an important part of our lives. Even more so than you are now."

Jonah put his hands on his hips. "Are you offering me your daughter if I agree to stay here and become Amish, Abe?"

"Are you accepting?"

"Daed!"

They both turned to find Abigail glaring at them with a frown on her face, her eyes full of shock. "What are you doing?"

Abe glanced at Jonah and then looked over at his daughter. "Trying to figure out what to do with our Jonah . . . and you."

"I'm not something you can barter away, you know.

I have feelings, and I think I can pick my husband for myself."

Abe gave her a fatherly frown. "Are you so sure about that?"

She frowned back. "I'm certain sure Jonah doesn't want to be one of us, even if he's stuck with us for a while. You are contradicting your own rules, Daed."

Abe didn't seem concerned. "I'm offering a sure solution, but I have other ideas, too, if you think this one is not proper."

"Your father says there's a frolic this Sunday afternoon," Jonah replied, aggravation making him bold. "You might find someone there. I hear it's a social type thing."

Abigail's angry gaze moved from Jonah to her *daed*. "I haven't heard about this."

"Your mother planned the whole thing," Abe explained while he tried to look innocent. "I go along with what Mamm wants."

Abigail shook her head. "I'll check with her, then." She sent Jonah an apologetic glance. "I'm sorry my *daed* is trying to pass me off to you, Jonah. We all know you want to go back out into your world, and I for one won't stop you."

With that, she whirled and took off toward the cottage, probably to ask her mother what they'd cooked up.

Jonah shot Abe a knowing glance. "I think we made her mad."

"She'll get over that. A father has to do what is needed, and right now, I need to either send you packing or make sure you understand the stipulations of courting my daughter."

Jonah jabbed at the moist dirt with his hand shovel,

then glanced up at Abe. "Or could be a father needs to be still and wait on God to show him the answers, too."

Abe chuckled, but his gaze was steely. "Think about what I said, Jonah. Because it is the only way." Abe waved a hand and turned to head home, leaving Jonah's mind whirling with images of what it would be like to stay here and accept this life.

At least Abe had given him a way to do that, which meant Abe and Sarah had probably figured out the obvious.

He was falling for their daughter, a woman forbidden to him, unless he decided to join them and forget his former life. Abe was a smart man. He wanted Jonah to understand the sacrifice he'd have to make in order to love Abigail, truly love her.

Abe also knew that would be near impossible. This situation, as much as Jonah loved it here, had to end. He'd call the local police first thing Monday to see if they had stumbled on any clue as to his identity. The sooner the better.

Jonah finished his work and went to his lonely apartment to take a shower. He found a plate of food waiting for him. Fried chicken, fresh creamed corn, and peas. With a slice of pound cake for dessert.

He showered and then sat down to eat the food, imagining what it would be like to come home to Abigail every night. Wondering, now, if he'd even have that precious time in the orchard with her.

Closing his eyes, Jonah prayed in silence.

God, if you're listening and you do have a plan for me, I sure wish you'd share it with me. I'm confused and lonely and I'm afraid. My feelings for Abigail are real, but I might already have a wife and a child. How long should I wait, Lord?

Jonah opened his eyes and listened to the silence.

Would God show him the answers? That was the burning question that kept him tossing and turning all night. That and wondering if Abigail would find a nice Amish man at the frolic and forget all about Jonah.

"I'm too old for this."

Colette and Eliza glanced at each other and then looked back at Abigail. "Mamm wanted to have the frolic," Colette reminded her. "And you know when Mamm sets her mind on something happening, it happens."

Abigail paced her room, her light green dress clean and her apron a sparkling white. She'd planned on meeting Jonah in the apple orchard today, but how would she do that now? "I have one parent trying to bring Jonah into the fold and the other trying to force me to find someone else. I'm perfectly content on my own."

"For sure," Eliza said, her eyes full of mirth. "I can't believe Daed suggested that Jonah should become Amish. A big step. Or a really wise move on his part."

"He's testing Jonah," Abigail said, getting angry all over again. "Forcing him to see what he'd have to give up in order to have me. Jonah seemed as shocked as I was when I heard them talking."

"It seems you're not so much mad about this frolic as you are about how Jonah reacted to the suggestion," Colette said.

"I'm mad about both," Abigail replied. "Jonah doesn't

want to be here, so he cannot do what Daed suggested. He might already be married." Pacing and frowning, she whirled. "Jonah only wants to flirt with me and give me these wild thoughts. And Mamm is trying to force me to choose someone else—someone she and Aenti Miriam have probably handpicked."

Her sisters sent her sympathetic looks but smiled at each other. "What's so funny here?" Abigail asked.

"She has invited most of the eligible bachelors within twenty miles to this gathering," Colette replied while she straightened her hair. "I for one intend to take advantage of the situation. Your nightmare is our dream, ain't so, Eliza?"

Eliza didn't respond.

"Sister?" Colette walked to where Eliza sat in a chair. "Are you remembering a different time, another youth social?"

Eliza sighed. "I think I prefer horses to people, especially men."

Abigail stopped her pacing and went to her sister. "I'm sorry. How could I forget? Here I am, going on and on about this social while you must have mixed feelings about it, too. You don't have to be there today."

Eliza had a bad experience with a boy once at a youth social, a boy she'd loved. If Abigail and Colette hadn't come up on them, something awful might have happened. They'd heard Eliza giving him a piece of her mind. Since then, she'd shied away from letting any man get too close. She liked Jonah, but then, she knew Abigail had found him, so Abigail got to be the one to claim him. It was the sister code.

"Mamm wants us all there," Eliza said. "She plans to parade us out like we're piglets going to market."

"We aren't going to be slaughtered," Colette said, snorting. "Just showcased." Then she took Eliza's hand. "You don't talk about it much. It's been a while now."

"I'd like to forget that night," Eliza admitted. "I haven't been to many youth socials since then. None of us have, for that matter. We're always too busy to think about marriage. This place requires our time every day, every minute, it seems."

"Oh, we think about marriage and having a family," Abigail said. "But we can't *make* it happen, no matter who tries to force us. Love is something we can't force."

Not even if the man she was falling for seemed to think he wanted to be with her. Jonah had to be confused, bored, and longing for the same things she longed for—a home filled with love, and someone to share that home with. Someone to share a life with. They'd been drawn together through an unfortunate event, but that didn't mean they belonged together.

"It's time," Colette said. "I'm not that worried. I won't know many people there, so I don't plan to get too excited."

"Oh, right," Eliza said, coming out of her bad memories. "Mamm mentioned Mattie. Keep that in mind."

Colette opened her mouth and then snapped it shut. "Why does he have to be there?"

"So he can see you," Abigail said. "At least you know him. I think Mamm has brought in people from here to Spartansburg. I still can't believe they are making us do this."

"What if you meet someone today?" Eliza asked Abigail. "Someone who sweeps you off your feet. How would you feel about Jonah then?"

"Brooms are for sweeping," Abigail retorted. She didn't dare tell her sisters about her plans with Jonah. "Men have to stay on solid ground and so do I. No one will sweep me away. Stop comparing my life to one of your romantic stories."

"You didn't answer the question," Eliza pointed out. "And what's wrong with romantic stories?"

Abigail wanted to hug her sister. Eliza and Colette had both loved reading and now they loved romance, too. But Eliza had lost some of her hope when a boy she loved had treated her cruelly. Colette hadn't had time to see what was right in front of her face—a boy who would grow into a good match for her.

"There is no question, and you know the answer," Abigail admitted. "There will never be another Jonah, but then, he and I cannot be together. He belongs in the outside world. Any romance for us will not have a happy ending."

She didn't believe for a minute Jonah would consider changing his status. Especially if he was still married and already a father. Perhaps she should make the most of this get-together to prove to herself and Jonah that they must go their own ways.

Jonah sat on his favorite rock taking a break from helping Maggie with the last of the departing guests, his back turned from the laughter that echoed out over the beautiful late afternoon. He'd offered to help in the kitchen and restaurant on the weekends because the Amish preferred not to work on Sundays. Maggie only worked because she needed the money, because she and her husband, David, had a child on the way.

A child. Jonah's heart burned each time he heard that phrase. Did he have a child? Had he known someone with a baby? He couldn't help but doubt his vague memories. He hated being in limbo, caught between two worlds.

He could hear the sound of buggies and horse hooves clomping along the old road. Gritting his teeth, Jonah tried not to think of Abigail. He had to get back to help Maggie; the two English girls would be leaving soon. His plans to spend time with Abigail in the orchard would have to be put on hold until he could sneak away.

The youth social had started around four o'clock and would last until sunset, a couple of hours away. Then the fireworks would begin. While he imagined Abigail spotting a man across the way and smiling at him, Jonah reminded himself he had no hold over her. She'd be better off finding a good Amish man to love her and cherish her. Someone who could help her with the burden of this inn and property.

But Jonah couldn't help picturing himself as that man. If he already had a family waiting for him, it would be impossible. Until his memories came back, or the officials could help him find his true identity, he had to believe she would be better off without him.

He stood and turned toward the cottage. The get-together was being held underneath the towering oak trees. Tables were set up, food carried out, and benches set about. When he heard singing, his heart surged. The voices blended nicely as they carried the old hymns out over the trees.

Abigail would be there, singing with her sisters.

He peeked around a tree, trying to see.

The high shrubbery and ancient oaks partially blocked his view of the house.

A traumatic event and his own fear of returning to the past blocked his memories.

Jonah pivoted and headed down the secret path to the lake. He'd go back to the inn from the other direction. He couldn't take any more of the laughter, or of imagining Abigail smiling at another man.

Not today.

CHAPTER TWENTY

Abigail stood with a few other unmarried women, her heart aching because she'd already found a man who could be perfect for her. She didn't need to be here, parading around as if she wanted to make a match.

Except Jonah wasn't perfect. He had flaws and torments and hidden memories. An outsider who'd come here washed up and world-weary, he didn't belong. Why did she feel so strongly for him?

"Hi." She turned to find Benjamin Meissner smiling at her.

Abigail knew Ben. A true bachelor and a couple of years older than she, he wasn't a bad-looking man. His dark blond hair was clean and curly, and he made sure he dressed in fresh clothes for church and frolics. But Ben seemed desperate for a wife. He'd been engaged once, but the girl had balked and left the community. She married another Amish man from a community in Eastern Pennsylvania.

"You look nice today, Abby," he said, his feet moving nervously in the lush grass underneath the trees. "It's been a while since we've visited."

Figuring Aenti Miriam had sent him, she smiled back. "*Ja*, you know I'm always busy since Mamm and Daed are partly retired. So much to do in order to keep this place running."

"You could use some help," he said, bobbing his head. "This is a big parcel for three women to run."

Ben also had a problem with women who worked. The Amish tenets had changed on that issue over the years, out of necessity. But some men still frowned on women working. No wonder that other girl had left.

"You need more manpower around here," Ben went on, a hopeful squeak in his voice.

"I have no choice," she said, trying to keep her tone neutral. "We love this place, and we enjoy our visitors."

"If you had a *gut*, strong man to help, might be better, ain't so?"

Abigail gave him a sharp glance. "We're doing okay, but yes, I suppose one day we'll hire more people."

"You could sell out, move somewhere else. Start a new life."

Abigail saw the hope in his pale gray eyes. But she had no desire to sell out and go away with Benjamin. She didn't want to hurt his feelings either.

"I suppose one day that will happen." Looking past his disappointed face, she said, "I think Mamm is motioning to me. It was *gut* to see you, Ben."

She moved away as quickly as possible. Why did anyone think this was a great idea? Her parents had her best interests at heart. But Abigail, well past her teen years, was too old for this. She'd been content with her life.

Well, she'd *tried* to be content. If she'd never gone for

that walk on that particular morning, where would Jonah be right now? Abigail didn't want to think about him out there alone, wandering around with a wound and no memory. *Gott* had sent him here for a reason. She only wished that reason would be revealed one day.

After she took some dishes into the cottage kitchen, she stood at the sink and looked out over the yard. People were mingling and laughing, even her two picky sisters. Colette was actually talking to Matthew with a smile on her face. Eliza stood with a group of young men and women, laughing.

Then she looked down the way and saw Jonah running toward the cottage.

What on earth was wrong with him? Had he seen her with Benjamin and now become angry because they were supposed to meet in the orchard? Surely he could see she hadn't been able to get away.

Then she heard him screaming, "Sarah, come quick."

Someone must be hurt if he needed Mamm.

Abigail dashed out the door and hurried toward where he stood talking to Mamm.

"Maggie," he said, his eyes wild with fear. "I found her in the inn kitchen, on the floor. Something's happened with the baby and she's in a lot of pain."

Mamm nodded. "Abby, get my bag. Colette, clean up and tell everyone it's time to go home. Where is Eliza?"

Eliza came running with her cell phone. "Should I call for help, Mamm?"

"*Ja.* And send word to David, too. Her husband needs to get here." Mamm turned back to Jonah. "Run back, Jonah, and stay with her. I can't run, but I'll get there. I don't want her to be alone."

Jonah turned and took off. Abigail started to follow, but everyone was watching. "Mamm, do you want help?"

"Get everyone on their way and tell them *denke* for coming. Make sure Daed is in his favorite chair, resting. Then you can be of help with Maggie. She'll be scared."

Abigail watched as Jonah disappeared into the kitchen. Maggie and the two weekend girls were watching the inn today. While the restaurant wasn't open on Sundays, they still had guests staying at the inn. They used a weekend crew of mostly *Englisch*. She'd forgotten that Jonah had offered to help out with things today.

She took a breath and said a silent prayer for Maggie and the *bobbeli*. Then she rushed to get Daed settled inside. She made sure everyone had left and then checked to see if the food needed to be put away in the kitchen. She hoped Maggie and the baby would be all right.

She also hoped Jonah would be okay. This could trigger another memory for him, a memory that could only bring him more pain if it didn't give him any answers.

Jonah held Maggie's hand and tried to soothe her cries.

"It's not time. I have another three weeks," she said, her eyes glazed with fear and pain. "Help me, Jonah. The *bobbeli* is coming. I think I'm having contractions—too close together."

Jonah pushed away his own panic. He couldn't stand seeing her in pain. Maggie was a sweet girl, and this was her first child. Jonah's gut burned with a feeling of elation coupled with a deep fear. Raising a child had to be both a joy and a challenge. Instinct told him he'd had firsthand knowledge of that.

His head boomed. Shadows danced across his mind, images of sirens and screams and a child. A little boy.

Maggie's moans brought him back. "You need to breathe," he said, his voice raw with pain. "Take deep breaths and hold on until Sarah gets here. She knows what to do."

Minutes had passed, but to Jonah it seemed like hours. Sarah came bustling in with her midwife bag. "Jonah, *denke*. Abigail will be here soon to take over. But it looks like you've done a fine job of helping our Maggie."

Jonah nodded, unable to speak. He'd moved Maggie from the cold kitchen floor to a rug in the employee dining room. He'd found an old tablecloth to cover her, and he'd grabbed a pillow from the linen closet.

"I told her to breathe," he said. "I think she's having contractions."

"Have you delivered a *bobbeli* before?" Sarah asked as she began to examine Maggie. "You seemed to know what needed to be done."

He looked at Sarah and shook his head, the shadows lurking like hulking giants against the walls of his mind. "I don't know."

Sarah only smiled as she removed things from her bag—a box of sterilized gloves, what looked like surgical instruments, and a stethoscope, a bottle of oil and some sort of cleansing wipes.

She had other supplies on the way, she explained to Maggie. "We've sent word to David. He'll be here soon. We called an ambulance, too. Your contractions are coming too early and too close together, so I think you'll need to go to a hospital."

"But I wanted you to deliver my baby," Maggie wailed. "At home. That's the way it's supposed to be."

"I wanted that, too," Sarah said in a soothing voice, her manner telling Jonah nothing. "But the main thing is to have a healthy *bobbeli*, ain't so?"

Maggie nodded and screamed as another contraction hit her. Jonah held her hand, surprised by the strong grip of this tiny woman.

He had a flash of a similar feeling, like déjà vu. How could he know what that word meant and yet he couldn't remember if he'd become a father or not?

The door flew open and Abigail stood there with towels and blankets. She glanced at Maggie and then Jonah, taking in the scene. "Mamm?"

Sarah gave Abigail a smile and a nod. "We're doing okay, but she'll need to go to the hospital in Lake City. I can't be certain why the baby is coming early."

Abigail sank down by the mother-to-be and wiped at her brow with a clean cloth. "We're here, Maggie. The ambulance is on its way."

Maggie wailed again, her dark eyes full of anguish. "I don't think I can make it. I did everything right. Why is this happening?"

"We'll have to figure that out. For now, try to stay calm. If you're upset, the baby can feel it." Sarah held the stethoscope to Maggie's stomach. "I hear a heartbeat. That's wunderbar *gut*."

Tears rolled down Maggie's face. Her brown bun, usually so neat, had come loose and strings of hair circled her pale face. "Alive. My *bobbeli* is still alive. Sarah, don't let anything bad happen."

Jonah looked at Sarah. She kept her smile intact, but he saw the apprehension in her eyes. Then he lifted his gaze to Abigail, hating the tears in her pretty eyes. She was afraid for her friend. She gave him a worried stare.

They heard sirens in the distance. The door burst open again and Maggie's husband, David, rushed into the room.

"Maggie." He sank down on his knees and took Maggie's hand. "Is she okay, Sarah? Is my wife okay? Will my baby be all right?"

Jonah stood, disoriented and sweating. Abigail took one look at him and ushered him out of the room. "Mamm has things under control now and help is here, Jonah. Let me get you some water."

He sank into a chair, tears in his eyes. "I remembered this, Abigail."

Abigail's hand shook as she poured water from the kitchen sink and handed it to him. "You've delivered a *bobbeli*?"

"No," he said, taking a long sip of water. "I remember being in a hospital room when a baby was born."

"Your baby?" she asked, her heart accepting that this man would never truly be hers. He had a past that had left him traumatized and confused, a time he wanted to get back, a family he had to find.

Jonah set the glass down on the table and took her hand. "I think so. In my heart, I know so."

His big hand burned warm in hers, the tug of his fingers like the ties in a rope, frayed but sturdy. "Do you remember anything else?"

Shaking his head, he took a deep breath. "No. I wanted to, tried so hard, but Maggie needed me to keep her calm. I lost the rest of the memories, but I know I witnessed a baby being born. A boy, Abigail."

Abigail held his hand and saw a tear moving down his face. Her heart, so open and yielding to this man, tore in half. Until this moment in time, she'd never thought too much about having a child. That was a someday notion. Now, sitting here with Jonah, she ached for a child. She saw a love so deep in his blue eyes, it hurt to witness it. While it hurt, it also made Abigail realize she'd been living a false life.

She wanted so many things now that she'd never dreamed of a few months ago. Reaching out, she put a finger to Jonah's face and traced the single teardrop.

"Then you should go out there and find your son, Jonah."

He looked up at her with wild eyes. "I should, I know I should. I have to do this, don't I?"

"*Ja*." She pulled away, wiped at her own tears. "It is the only way to ease that pain inside your heart."

But it would leave a deep gash in *her* broken heart, and it would leave a deep need inside her soul that she didn't think could ever be filled.

They sat off to the side while the paramedics came in and checked Maggie over. Abigail heard them talking, lifting Maggie onto a stretcher, telling her to hold on. David, begging them not to let his wife or child die. Mamm, assuring them everything would be all right.

Abigail's heart went out to Maggie and David. They were

a happy couple, so in love. She sat silent and respectful, watching as they left.

The whole while, Jonah held Abigail's hand, and he held his gaze on her long after the commotion had died down.

CHAPTER TWENTY-ONE

"Maggie and the *bobbeli* are doing fine."

Abigail saw the fatigue in Mamm's eyes. Her mother had stayed at the hospital all night. She'd arrived home just as the sun peeked up over the lake. She'd promised Maggie she wouldn't leave until she knew they were both all right. She also helped David stay calm while he waited to hear. Mamm was that way—she nurtured everyone in her calm, gentle way. David and Maggie were like family, and because their parents lived in another county on the other side of the state, Abigail and her family looked out for them.

"So kind of you to be there with them," Abigail said. She brought Mamm buttered toast and scrambled eggs, then placed a steaming cup of black tea by her plate. "Now eat this and then you are to rest all day."

"I think I'll do that." Mamm nibbled at her food. "It was touch-and-go for a while, but the babe's early arrival became a blessing. The umbilical cord was wrapped around little Samuel's neck. When that happens, it's called a nuchal cord. I couldn't be sure, but the babe's erratic heartbeat suggested some stress. I was concerned it might be that or a breach birth. Maggie and the baby both were in trouble. We got her there just in time for the ER doctor to clamp and cut the cord before little Samuel came into the world."

"I'm so glad we called for help," Abigail replied. She could tell yesterday when she walked into the room that her *mamm* was worried. Mamm could have tried to cut the cord—she had all the proper surgical instruments— but she must have realized it would be risky. Maggie hadn't needed to know that yesterday, however.

"Young Samuel is a fighter. He'll be fine and hearty soon enough."

A boy. Maggie and David had a little boy. Samuel.

Remembering how Jonah had finally stood after they'd taken Maggie away, Abigail said a silent prayer for the baby. Jonah had looked into her eyes, the torment in his heart flashing across his face. "I need to go."

Then he hurried back to the carriage *haus*. Soon after, she'd tidied up the inn's kitchen and left for the day. She hadn't talked to him yet today. He needed time to absorb all his new memories.

Abigail had watched the distant fireworks and wished she'd had that walk in the orchard with Jonah. That should have been their celebration, but after the events of yesterday, he hadn't been in a mood for walking out together.

Now Abigail sat down at the table with her mother, her gaze moving over the bay windows out to the garden. As if on cue, she saw Jonah hoeing away at the ever-present weeds in the vegetable garden behind one of the storage sheds. "What's it like, delivering a child?"

Mamm's gaze swept over the yard and then back to Abigail. "It's a miracle, birthing of any kind. To see that tiny being coming into the world. So precious and so fragile, but with strength built on love and family."

Abigail smiled at her mother, but her thoughts were with the man in the garden. A child. What would it be like to have a child to hold and love, someone who reminded you of your own love? Someone made from your own love?

"Are you dreaming of having children then, *Dochder*?"

Abigail looked up to find her mother's keen gaze studying her face. "Why did you plan the singing frolic, Mamm?"

"I think you know the answer to that, Abby."

"Did you know Daed talked to Jonah . . . about becoming one of us?"

"He what?" Mamm glanced around, but Daed was still asleep. "Why would he suggest such a thing?"

"You did not know?" Abigail's surprise matched her mother's. Daed always discussed decisions with Mamm before he proceeded. Why hadn't he told her about this one?

"I did not know anything about it." Mamm pushed away her plate and took a sip of tea. "I know my Abe likes Jonah, but this is unusual. What did Jonah say?"

Abigail told her mother about walking up on them in the garden. "He asked if Daed was trying to offer me to him in return for Jonah's staying here and becoming Amish."

"Do you mean my Abe tried to bribe Jonah to stay here?"

"I wouldn't call it a bribe," Abigail said. "It sounded more like an option."

Shaking her head, Mamm whispered, "Your *daed* has

softened in his old age. I think he worries that his daughters are too independent. But to push you off on—"

Mamm stopped and put a hand to her mouth. "Abe knows you have feelings for Jonah, ain't so? Perhaps he wanted to test those feelings, on both sides."

Abigail tried to stay neutral, but Jonah kept walking across the yard between the cottage and the inn, distracting her. "I care for him. It's hard not to care when he has such heartbreaking memories, and he is all alone in the world. Yesterday, he remembered being in a room when a baby was born. He became upset."

Mamm stood and carried her dishes to the sink. "Poor Jonah. Such a big comfort to Maggie, and to me. And all that time, him remembering another birth, in another world." She turned at the sink and faced Abigail, a plea in her words. "You must see that he belongs in that world, Abby. Not ours. I don't think Jonah will take your *daed* up on that offer, no matter how he feels about you."

Abigail lifted her head. "Do you think Jonah cares for me?"

Mamm glanced out the window. "I think he cares deeply for you, and that he likes it here, where it's quiet and safe. Still, he has a right to try to find the pieces of the puzzle in his mind. He's using the serenity of our ways to keep from facing the truth of what happened to him. Who would want to live like that? And what *Englisch* would ever give up that world to stay in ours?"

Abigail couldn't dispute her *mamm*'s words, even though sometimes *Englisch* did choose to become Amish, in rare cases. But in this case, it would do no good to dream of things that could not be. And yet, when she turned toward the window again and saw Jonah standing there with a rake, staring at the cottage, her heart melted with an unimaginable hope.

What if Jonah could one day take her *daed* up on his offer?

Abigail went about her chores. She had to make sure they had someone to fill in for Maggie. She found Henry in the lobby, perched on his check-in stool.

"Hey, there, Abigail," Henry said, standing in his gentlemanly fashion. "How are you today?"

"Hi, Henry. I'm tired, but we must get things done."

"No rest for the weary," he quipped. "I'm sure you're all tired today."

"It is Monday," Abigail replied, thinking this weariness came from many sources.

"I heard about Maggie," he said, his silver hair perfectly combed. He wore a blue shirt over dark slacks. "I'm so thankful mother and baby are okay."

Henry always dressed in nice clothes. He had been a military man, so his manner was respectful. The guests loved to talk to him because he knew the history of the inn and everything about the Amish who had become a part of it and the Shadow Lake Township community. He ran the front desk with a precision that Abigail admired, and he usually remembered returning guests by name.

"Quite an ordeal," Abigail said. "I hope the extra hours Maggie worked didn't bring this on. But I'm so happy that she and the baby are both healthy and *gut*."

"I am, too. My wife is cooking up a storm to take to

their place later. And I am going to help David clear some land. He hopes to add on to their home, making room for that big family he talks about when he comes to lunch here to check on Maggie."

"He always loves being with Maggie," Abigail said. "Especially if he gets fed in the process. Henry, do you know anyone who might help in Maggie's absence? She won't be back for a few months, and we weren't expecting the baby to come early. Something I overlooked with everything else happening around here."

Henry squinted and tapped his chin. "I could round someone up, but what about Jonah? He's familiar with the kitchen and he can take orders and wait on customers. Matthew does it when we're in a pinch."

"Jonah?" Abigail hoped her expression didn't show shock. "I hadn't considered him because he works mostly in the gardens and barns."

"He has off time in between," Henry replied. "Sometimes he comes by to visit me if it's a slow day. I think he likes to stay busy since . . . you know . . . he can't remember things."

Abigail had had no idea Jonah visited Henry, or that Henry knew Jonah's real reason for being there.

Henry leaned close. "He talks to me because we're both English and . . . he asks if I've heard anything regarding a missing man. I haven't, but I don't mind him visiting me. The poor man looks lost a lot of the time." Shrugging, he went on. "You know how gossip flies around here. I told him he could talk to me anytime; maybe in the process he'd remember what he's searching for."

Hearing that made Abigail see things in a new light. Jonah might think he cared for her, but in his heart, in that place where he'd shuttered the past, he still loved another woman. He had to find that woman. Working in the kitchen and inside the inn would make him feel less lonely but could bring him in contact with someone who might recognize him.

Did she dare risk that?

She couldn't hold him back.

"I'm glad you two got to know each other. I'll consider this and talk to Jonah about it."

"He'll do great," Henry said. "He's a hard worker. Of course, he might not stop and chatter with the guests the way Maggie does."

"You are for certain sure right on that, Henry."

She turned to go back toward the kitchen, her heartbeat thumping a new warning. How could she bear seeing more of Jonah each day when simply passing by him set her whole system on alert?

She'd have to discuss it with Eliza and Colette, and probably her parents, too. Mamm might not agree because she was in such a tizzy about Daed's absurd suggestion that Jonah stay here and become one of them. Giving him more work could encourage him to stay or make him even more skittish.

Jonah had a family, and she must accept that. Soon, her memory quilt would be finished.

Soon, Jonah would be gone away forever.

She did not expect him to spend a minute longer here than he needed, once he got his memory back or once he heard from the police that they'd matched his fingerprints to a name and a face.

Abigail had dueling prayers in that regard. *Yes, Lord, help him remember. No, please, let him stay, and start a new life with us.*

With her.

But that wouldn't be fair or morally correct.

She rounded a corner, her mind in turmoil, and saw Colette talking to Matthew. They were laughing and definitely flirting. Her sister looked happy and young, and Matthew beamed like a flashlight.

Well, at least one match seemed to have come out of Mamm's elaborate plan.

Abigail left them alone together. She wanted both of her sisters to find happiness, even if she might never have it herself.

"You are making more panels for the quilt?"

Abigail nodded in response to Eliza's question. They had gathered in her room to discuss the youth frolic, Maggie's new *bobbeli*, and life in general. "I'm adding a picnic scene, a beach scene, Jonah with Old Red—"

"You're including that terrible rooster on the quilt?" Eliza asked, giggling. "Now he will think he rules the roost."

"Old Red and Jonah have bonded," Abigail replied with a grin. "That rooster *kumms* running when he sees Jonah."

"He *kumms* running because he knows he's about to

be fed," Colette said with a giggle. "And Jonah named him that, so he knows his name when he hears it now."

Abigail glanced at the quilt. "I also want to add a square showing Daed and Jonah together."

"Sure seems as if they've bonded, too," Colette whispered. "Since Daed has practically asked him to join the family."

Abigail had filled them in on that new development the minute they came into her room. "Well, Mamm wants me to make a match with Benjamin." She almost shuddered. "I can't love Benjamin and I won't marry a man I don't love."

"Benjamin wants a woman to take care of Benjamin," Eliza pointed out, rolling her eyes. "We know Amish women take care of a lot of the work—the house, the food, the garden, the wash, the children."

"I'm tired already," Colette retorted. "That shouldn't mean we can't have our own lives and identities."

"Don't let Mamm and Daed hear you speaking of such," Abigail warned. "I do like taking care of the inn, even if there are those who frown on it." Then she said, "Henry mentioned asking Jonah to work in the kitchen, while Maggie will be on leave. What do you think?"

Eliza glanced at Abigail and then Colette. "We need every person we can get. Maggie was so *gut* with the guests. Jonah is not that friendly, but I think he would work out."

"And we have to consider Edith," Abigail said. "She might not want another man in her way."

"Jonah won't be in the way," Colette replied. "He's helped me some with the laundry and cleanup. I think it could work. He doesn't have to take food orders, but he can refill the drink containers and clean tables. There's always something to do, taking care of the lunch crowd."

Eliza squinted, her eyebrows furrowing. "We'd really only need him from eleven until two. He'd be finished with his morning chores by then, and he'd have plenty of time to tend to the animals after."

"He is able-bodied," Abigail said, causing her sisters to snicker.

"How would you have noticed?" Colette teased.

"Probably the reason Daed is desperate to keep Jonah around." Eliza shrugged. "He could be your front man."

"What are you talking about?" Colette asked.

"A man who looks like he's in charge," Eliza explained. "And Jonah sure looks like that kind of man, whether he can remember anything or not."

"I don't need a man to front me," Abigail said with a mock frown. "But if I did, Jonah would for certain sure be that man."

Eliza gave her a smug stare. "See, I told you."

Her sister spoke truth on that matter. Jonah was the protective kind, a man who made her feel safe, no matter the situation. Each time she thought about him tugging her back against his chest, his lips grazing her neck and his arms embracing her like a shield, Abigail wanted to be in that spot forever, with Jonah as her protector.

But who was protecting him?

Abigail pulled out the quilt and spread it on the bed so her sisters could see her latest work. She didn't want to think of Jonah not being here with her. This quilt would be her shield against heartbreak.

Colette and Eliza passed their hands over the bright, colorful panels. Then Colette asked, "Who is the woman alone on the shore, Sister?"

Abigail looked across at her sisters. "Me," she replied.

Then she turned and went to the window to stare down at the faint light shining from the carriage *haus*, her heart feeling another jagged cut.

Chapter Twenty-Two

Eliza had agreed to bring up Henry's suggestion at supper the next night. Abigail would talk to Jonah sometime during the day, hopefully in private. If he didn't like the idea, she'd find someone else, and Mamm and Daed would be none the wiser.

This morning, she watched for an opportunity to run into him without it looking obvious. People seemed to be keeping an eye on them, so she had to be extra careful. Then Eliza came into the hallway near the inn's kitchen, fresh from checking on the horses.

She went to the sink and washed her hands and arms, then scrubbed down her face. "I told Jonah to *kumm* and get a slice of fresh apple bread. He's on his way." She gave Abigail a pointed glance and then scooted away.

Abigail watched for him as she worked, wishing she didn't have to be so covert about trying to talk to a man. A forbidden man.

Those three words always played through her head, warring with the way he made her feel so alive and needed. She had to consider that Jonah had only attached himself to her because she'd been his rescuer, his nurse, his maid, and now, his supervisor. His infatuation would disappear once he became himself again. While her infatuation with him would linger for a long time to come.

He walked in, filling the small back entryway like a giant, his hair a tousled mess, his hands dirty, his clothes old and worn. The blue shirt strained across his broad chest. He'd taken to wearing a straw hat to keep the sun off his face, but now he flung it onto the high back of a corner chair.

Abigail clenched her hands into fists, her nails biting her palms so she wouldn't look anxious or lovelorn in front of so many curious coworkers.

"Hi, Jonah," Edith said from where she stood frosting a cake. Giving Abigail a soft smile, she said, "I heard you like apple bread. Abigail can cut you a piece."

Silently thanking the usually curt Edith, Abigail guessed Jonah had won over the prickly cook, too. Edith noticed everything and everyone, but she never gossiped, and she rarely made quick judgments.

"I'll get you some *kaffe* and a slice," Abigail said to Jonah. "Go wash up and I'll meet you in the employee room."

He nodded and hurried into the washroom.

Abigail cut a generous slice of the still-warm bread and slathered it with fresh butter, then poured a mug of steaming *kaffe*. Putting both on a tray, she added a tall glass of icy water. Then she took the tray into the employee room and waited for Jonah, her nerves jangling.

He walked in five minutes later, smelling like goat's milk almond soap, his hair now damp and finger-combed off his forehead. After drinking down most of the water she handed him, he finally smiled.

"This is nice," he said as he sat down and took a big bite of the apple-and-walnut bread.

"I needed to talk to you anyway," she replied, "so this worked out perfectly."

"Oh, okay." He took a sip of *kaffe*, his gaze intent on her. "Is this about us not having our walk in the orchard?"

"*Neh*." She tried not to show her disappointment. "I understand why it wasn't possible that day."

"I don't," he replied, his gaze moving over her face. "I don't understand why we can't still do that, and soon. I miss our private times."

Praying for strength, Abigail went right to business. "We need help in the kitchen while Maggie's out on maternity leave. Henry suggested you."

Jonah lowered his head, then lifted his gaze back to her. "Henry, huh?"

"*Ja*. I didn't know you two had become acquainted, but he likes you a lot. I told him I'd talk to you. I'd have to clear it with Mamm and Daed, of course."

"That should go over well."

"I've talked to Eliza and Colette, because Eliza runs the stable and Colette thinks she runs the kitchen."

He grinned at that. "I've noticed all three of you can be bossy."

"You'd be wise to remember that."

He smiled big this time. Abigail's world lit up. She smiled back.

For a moment, they sat like that, smiling. Abigail had begun to learn the art of flirting. And sometimes, she decided, silence was the most wonderful form of flirtation.

"What do you think?" he asked, bringing her back to earth.

She took in a breath and got herself refocused. "We need help and you're here. You have free time between your morning and evening chores."

"All of that is true, but what do *you* think, Abigail?"

She had to be honest. "I think it's the best solution for the next couple of months. Maggie needs time to heal and be with her baby, and we can give her that time. She'll bring the *bobbeli* here with her once he's older. Mamm has offered to help watch him, and Maggie can check on him and feed him at the cottage. Until then, you will help with any chores in the kitchen. Colette and Edith will let you know what needs to be done, I can assure you of that."

"I'm sure they will."

"You wouldn't have to interact with the lunch crowd too much."

"So, I'd work in the background, helping out as needed, and someone else can do the out-front work that Maggie normally does?"

"*Ja.* Would that be all right with you?"

He nodded, and then he leaned close. "You have to know, I'd do anything to spend more time near you, Abigail. So yes, I'll do this. Until Maggie comes back or . . . until I find out something about myself from the authorities."

"Or until your memory completely returns," she replied as she stood.

Jonah looked up at her with eyes full of both regret and anticipation. "There is that, too."

The silence surrounded them again, their eyes holding for a second too long. "I'll talk to Mamm and Daed tonight," she said. "I wanted to check with you first."

"All right. Thank Edith for the coffee cake. I need to get back out to the garden." He turned at the door. "Should I tell Edith I like to cook?"

"*Neh*." Abigail shook her head. "That would be *dummkopf*. Edith barely lets *us* cook in her kitchen."

"Well, I'm no dummy," he retorted. "Even if I can't remember my real name."

Abigail laughed. "Of course Mamm and Daed might not approve, but we can always use the help. And I'm not in the kitchen much, so I need someone I can trust to help out."

"So, you're saying you'll avoid me as much as possible?"

She glanced around and then back to him. "*Ja*. I have to avoid you. You are such a distraction."

"A good distraction or a bad one?"

"Both." She gave him one last glance and stood, needing to get far away from him. Why did she feel the urge to reach up and push that one clump of rebellious hair off his forehead? "I have to get back."

"So . . . you'll let me know tomorrow?"

She nodded and turned toward the door.

"Abigail?"

Abigail took a breath and turned back. "*Ja?*"

"What if I could come back here? What if there's nothing left out there for me?"

Abigail didn't want to hope, even though her heart leaped to answer for her. "I don't know. I think that would have to be up to you, Jonah. First, we have a lot to get through. So many things remain to be seen."

He stood and stared across at her, the distance between them only a few feet. But there was a wide chasm to cross before they could become more to each other. "I'll find out the truth," he said. "But no matter what, I will never forget you. Do you understand that?"

She bobbed her head. "Better than you'll ever know."

Then she hurried away before she gave in to temptation and touched him.

Jonah couldn't sleep. He'd heard nothing from the local police regarding his real identity. They hadn't found a match for his fingerprints or his face yet. They were running through the system—that's what they'd told him. Millions of fingerprints and sometimes they got only partial matches. Hard to say what they'd find. They had limited resources and such a small staff. Maybe he'd never been fingerprinted; there hadn't yet been a hit in the main criminal database. But if he'd worked in law enforcement, they should have his prints on file somewhere.

The FBI would have them. His prints would have been taken as part of standard procedure when he'd signed on to go through training.

Jonah sat up in bed. How had he known that?

Raking a hand through his hair, he stood and paced, then finally went to the notepad and wrote *FBI* with a question mark. If he'd been a dangerous, wanted criminal and they'd gotten a hit on his prints, they would have come for him by now. If he'd been in law enforcement, wouldn't they let him know that, too?

Possibly.

What if he'd gone rogue, gone to ground, changed his whole identity? Witness protection? Or deep into an undercover operation? Or perhaps he'd hidden himself from someone he knew? Could the authorities possibly be looking for him, but for different reasons than what he thought?

His mind got that buzz. The dizziness caused him to grab the closest wall. He fell against the little window frame's cool firmness, then settled his forehead on the glass.

Jonah forced his head up so he could look outside, so the panic wouldn't overtake him. He focused on the second floor of the cottage, knowing Abigail should be sleeping there. Blinking, he saw a silhouette against the glow of soft lamplight.

Abigail standing at the window. He couldn't see her face, but he knew she was there and hoped she could see him.

Jonah straightened, his hands grasping the sill, his knuckles going white as he held on. Abigail, his anchor to reality, his tether to a dream, his only hope. The pain in his head subsided as he breathed deeply and focused on that distant shadow.

Knowing Abigail was there, watching over him, made him feel as if he'd found a buoy, something to which he could cling. He didn't want to let go. He didn't want to fall into the black, choppy waters of his memories, because if he did so, he might not ever come back.

His mind wasn't ready for the truth. Not yet.

She'd asked him to help out more around the inn. He couldn't decide if that meant she wanted him to stay or if she really just needed the extra help. He didn't mind, but things could change in a heartbeat. If he only knew what lay out there in the other world, the world he'd left. But his mind wouldn't open that door.

He'd read the story of Jonah in the Bible Abigail had given him. Jonah didn't want to be a prophet, but he had emerged from that whale after three days to become a better man, a man who trusted God. He had accepted his mission.

This Jonah wanted to honor whatever God had in store for him. Could he do that here? Or back out there? Had he believed in God before? If not, he sure did now.

What was his mission?

The word seemed to strike a bell. *Mission.*

If he'd been undercover on a mission, maybe Jonah was supposed to finish it. Finish his work and then return to Abigail.

But that could also mean his being here had put her and her family in danger. Someone had tried to end his life. What if they came looking for him?

Jonah touched a hand to the glass, his mind recoiling from the shadows that tried to tug him back. Finally, the light in the room on the second floor went out.

He turned and went back to his bed, but he couldn't stop the one question that nagged at his conflicted brain.

Had he been working on a dangerous undercover mission?

CHAPTER TWENTY-THREE

Abigail didn't sleep. She'd seen a light shining through Jonah's window, and she'd seen the shadow of broad shoulders. Had he been staring at her room? Her feelings for him ruled her mind these days, always there. She burned for something she couldn't define, couldn't reach. A longing that scared her with its intensity. It wasn't fair that her father had suggested Jonah stay and become Amish. But then, Daed didn't know the whole story. She hadn't informed her parents that Jonah might be married, although they probably suspected it. That would only complicate matters more.

He wanted to leave. He should leave, go searching for his identity and his family. Abigail knew she didn't have the right to hold him back, but oh how she wanted to do that very thing.

Just the suggestion that he might want to stay and gain her parents' blessing, go through the proper steps to be baptized and accepted . . . and then marry her . . . had her heart racing.

This morning, she planned to tell her parents Jonah

would be working in the kitchen, along with the gardens and outbuildings. She prayed Mamm and Daed would let it go at that because the inn was short-staffed. But she knew they'd have concerns. Mostly about how she must avoid Jonah—and look how that had worked out. She'd done anything but avoid the man.

"Hard to do," she mumbled as she hurried downstairs.

"Talking to yourself again," Eliza said, right on her heels. "I'm late to tend to the horses."

"Well, don't run over me in your impatience," Abigail said as she grabbed the stair rail so her sister wouldn't push her down the last few steps. "What's the hurry?"

"Samson was acting strange yesterday," Eliza said. "As if there was someone he didn't know around. I never saw a soul, but he seemed fidgety. You know he's picky about who comes into the stable."

Abigail barely heard her sister lamenting about the horse. "Samson is a horse. He's always acting up."

Eliza shrugged. "He was extra-peculiar late yesterday."

Abigail stayed focused on what she needed to tell her parents. "I'm going to talk to Mamm and Daed at breakfast. Be ready to back me up."

"I'm ready," Eliza said. "I wonder if you are, though."

"I can handle it," Abigail said, trying to reassure herself as well as her sister. "I always handle things, ain't so?"

Colette came bouncing into the kitchen. "I slept like a rock."

"You are a rock," Eliza replied. "A cute, confused, lost-in-romance kind of rock."

Colette grinned. "I think Mattie has a crush on me."

"You're just now figuring that out?" Abigail said as

she brought the egg bowl to the stove, then turned up a burner.

Colette's dark eyebrows lifted. "What do you mean?"

"Never mind," Abigail retorted. "Let's get breakfast going."

Soon they had biscuits in the oven, ham frying, and eggs cooking. Daed ate oatmeal now, too, for his heart. Abigail made sure he had fresh fruit and only one cup of *kaffe*, which he complained about.

Mamm bustled into the kitchen and smiled. "You three make a *gut* team."

Abigail poured juice and fresh *kaffe*. "We need to discuss some things this morning, Mamm."

Mamm put her hands on her hips. "Ah, that explains the big breakfast and the nice smiles. What have you three been up to now?"

Daed walked in and stopped in his tracks when he saw the full meal on the table. "Is today a special day? Did I miss something?"

"Your daughters need to have a discussion with us," Mamm said, still showing she wasn't pleased with any of them. "And I have a strong feeling that it involves our Jonah."

Daed let out a breath. "Then I'd better eat while the food's still hot."

Abigail shot her sisters a glance, warning them to let her do the talking. When she sat down, and their silent prayers were over, she opened her eyes to find all of them waiting for her to speak.

Why was she so nervous about this?

"We need Jonah in the kitchen," Eliza blurted out when Abigail didn't speak. "Maggie will be home for several months, and it's the high season. Henry suggested Jonah could help with the dishwashing and background work, so one of us can wait on customers and guests. Colette already does her part, but she needs one more waitress out front."

Mamm glanced from Eliza to Abigail. "Did you suggest this?"

"*Neh*," she replied, silently both thanking and chastising her overeager sister. "Henry and Jonah have grown close, and Henry thought Jonah might be able to help in the kitchen. He also thinks if Jonah is around more *Englisch*, he might get his memory back."

Colette passed the oatmeal and biscuits. "Eliza baked the biscuits—so fluffy and good." Then she threw in, "Jonah would be great in the kitchen. He works very efficiently in the stable and barn. Keeps them clean and fresh every day—we could hold church in there."

"Stop." Daed held up a hand. "No one has to convince me that Jonah is capable. He's proven that over and over. My concern is having him in close quarters with all of you. Especially Abigail."

Abigail dropped her fork. "I'll do my work as always. I have rooms to clean and food to cook and plates to distribute, either in the suites or out to the restaurant, and a lot of to-go bags for workers around the community. I can take over serving our guests and customers. The days go fast when I'm out front. I won't have time to visit with Jonah."

She sputtered to a stop and waited, her head down while she watched the butter melting on her biscuit.

"But we did ask him how he'd feel about the extra

work," Colette added, bobbing her head. "I mean—Abigail talked to him yesterday when he came in on a break."

Mamm glanced back and forth from her oldest daughter to her husband. "I don't like this idea. The more we tell you that Jonah needs to go, the more it seems we give him reasons to stay."

Mamm got up to bring the coffeepot over to the table. She topped off Daed's brew and then poured from the percolator-style pot into her own cup. "I don't like it at all."

"You should have consulted us before you talked to Jonah, Abby," Daed said in that quiet voice that held more power than any shouting.

Everyone went quiet. Abigail didn't know what to say. She couldn't go against her parents' wishes any more than she already had. She'd pushed back and broken too many rules lately. Sometimes, she wished she'd never found Jonah there on the shore.

Daed glanced from Mamm to Abigail. Mamm sat down, aware that he'd have the final word.

"I will first talk to Henry. He is innocent in suggesting Jonah. He knows Jonah, and I gather they talk about *Englisch* life a lot. That could help jar Jonah's memories. And being around our guests could also help Jonah. Or it could make things worse. He tends to avoid the public."

Abigail and her sisters refrained from arguing. They would listen to Daed. They would also make their case. She did not, however, have a *gut* feeling about that.

"What did Jonah say?" Mamm asked, clearly hoping he'd declined.

Abigail chose her words carefully. "He only wants to do what he can to help us, all of us."

"Then he said he's willing to work in the inn, as well

as doing yard and stable maintenance?" Mamm pursed her lips.

Abigail nodded and looked toward her parents.

Her *daed* sat silent for a few moments. "After I discuss this with Henry, I will also talk to Jonah. He knows our ways by now, and while he and Abigail are close, he has tried to abide by our stipulations."

Mamm's cool gaze skimmed each daughter for deception. Abigail tried to look neutral, but her heart beat so fast, her apron bib shook with each breath. Did Mamm notice that? Mamm never missed anything.

"And what will you do, Abe?" she asked. "You can't allow this. You said yourself—Abigail and Jonah are close. It is not right for them to be so close. We all know this, and yet here is another example of allowing the rules to be broken. The bishop will be on this sooner or later."

"I will make a decision after I talk to all involved," Daed said. "Including you, Abigail. I have to know I can trust you on this."

Abigail took a breath and tried to compose her thoughts. "I will do what I need to do to keep the inn running. That's what I do—I make it all work. Extra hands are always needed around here, and I can find someone else, but that is a slow process. Most who want to work have already started their summer jobs. We need someone right now."

Mamm studied Abigail's face. "I tend to forget and take for granted what all you three do to make the inn run so smoothly. That doesn't mean I'm condoning this new work schedule, however."

"Jonah does have downtime in the middle of the day, which is our busiest time in the restaurant," Eliza chimed in, trying her best to look tired. "It would give all of us peace of mind to know a *gut*, strong man is willing to help."

Colette snorted, and then covered it with a laugh. "When have we—I mean, my sister is correct. We do need extra hands. Strong, sturdy extra hands."

Daed stood, meaning an end of the discussion. "I will find Jonah, and he, Henry, and I will talk about this."

They watched him head to the door. After tugging on his hat, he left to find the two men.

"Why do the men always get to decide such things?" Colette asked in a mumble. "We have working brains in our heads."

"What makes you think they make all the decisions?" Mamm countered. "I still have a say in my own household." Then she stood and started clearing the table. "But I will warn all of you—it's a balancing act, knowing how to get things done, follow your faith, and listen to your husband."

Eliza grinned. "Is that what you do, Mamm? You get the decisions you want for certain sure, but you make sure Daed officially makes the decision."

"All you need to remember is *Gott* knows all and plans all." Mamm shook her head and wagged her finger in the air. "You'll only hear the rest of my solution when you are about to be married, my daughters."

Abigail felt her mother's scrutiny on her, so she grabbed cups, took them to the sink, and pumped water to wash the dishes. Then she heated more water in the kettle to warm the sink full of dishes. The busywork kept her from running out the door to scream a warning to Jonah. Daed liked Jonah, despite the problems he'd created by being here. That gave her hope.

But she had to wonder—how could she get what she wanted when everyone around here except her sisters didn't want her to have it?

She couldn't have Jonah. Ever. There was no solution for that.

Jonah looked up to find Henry and Abe walking into the stable. Samson was still jittery today, but the big Percheron had finally calmed down after Jonah had given him an apple and a good run in the corral. Jonah didn't want the animal to get all riled up again, so he stroked Samson's nose and walked toward the two men, meeting them at the other end of the stable.

He knew why they were there.

"Jonah," Henry called, lifting his hand. "There you are."

"Hello," Jonah replied, his gaze hitting on Henry before settling on Abe. "What brings you two out this far from the inn?"

Abe chuckled. "Ain't that far, even for an old man."

Henry looked nervous and sent Jonah an apologetic smile. "We wanted to discuss something with you."

Jonah wouldn't make it easy, though he liked both of them. "What's up?" He hadn't decided whether he wanted to work inside the big inn after all.

Abe placed a hand on an empty stall door. "My daughters—those three are always plotting. But they do have the responsibility of taking care of this vast property. I can only do so much, and Sarah has her mid-wife duties and taking care of me."

"All of that's to say," Henry said in a rush, "we need you to help in the house more, if you want to do it."

Jonah took off his hat and shook straw out of his hair. "Abigail did mention that yesterday. I told her I'd do what needs to be done. I don't mind the extra work and I appreciate the pay you've given me, Abe. But I won't do anything to dishonor Abigail or this family. If that means I stay out of sight and out of the house, then that's what I'll do."

"There is no dishonor in hard work," Abe replied, a note of admiration in his tone. "I believe you to be an honorable man, Jonah. Maybe in your past, you were the same. We can't know that for now. If you can abide by our tenets as I've stated before—and if you and Abby remain friends and coworkers only—then you have my permission to work anywhere on this property, from the inn to the outer banks. We need more able-bodied men, and you happen to need work and a temporary place to live."

Temporary.

That word grabbed Jonah, tugged him into the black hole of his memories. He grabbed for something to hold on to, his mind remembering a woman's tears, a woman's voice, cracking, losing control.

"It's only temporary. That's what you always say."

"I'll be back as soon as I can."

"That's what you always say, too."

"Jonah?"

He looked up at Abe and Henry, his head filled with agony, his knuckles white against the post he'd grabbed hold of. "I'm fine. I need some water."

Abe held a hand on his arm while Henry hurried to the tack room for a water bottle. "Jonah, did I say something wrong?"

Jonah fought the fog, tried to grasp the woman and her words. Lost.

"No. Nothing. A vague memory." He glanced around, remembered where he was now. Henry shoved a bottle of water at him.

After gulping down the water, he said, "I can do the work, Abe. And I won't do anything to upset your daughters or you."

Abe gave him a studious, concerned stare. "Let's go up to the kitchen and get some lemonade. You need a break, and we can go over your new schedule and maybe steal a cookie or two."

Jonah nodded, seeing the confused glance Henry shot him. "Yes, lemonade sounds good. I'll start my new hours tomorrow."

The three of them slowly made their way toward the inn. It bustled now, no vacancies and plenty of cars in the side parking lot underneath the tall oaks and pines.

Jonah took a long breath and counted to ten, then reminded himself he stood on solid ground. Abigail had taught him how to deal with his anxiety. She'd looked it up on the Internet and printed it all out for him. Deep breaths, count to ten, study your surroundings, hold your feet to the ground. Use the five senses to calm and soothe yourself. Name things and see their colors.

Right now, he saw red geraniums in clay pots, smelled lilies and roses mixed with the scent of baking bread, and

Edith's macaroni and cheese. The inn. The inn would protect him and keep him on solid ground, not shifting sand.

He'd be around so many more people, working inside the house. What if he saw someone he remembered? Or . . . what if someone remembered him?

CHAPTER TWENTY-FOUR

Abigail didn't know if she should be thankful or full of regret. Jonah now worked wherever he was needed, and that seemed to be everywhere she had to be. It was unnerving how she could feel his presence before she turned to find him glancing at her. He was subtle, she'd give him that. If he hadn't been in law enforcement, he would have made a great policeman. *Stealth*, that was the word that came to mind. Good at moving about unnoticed.

But Abigail remained acutely aware of his presence.

She'd run smack into him yesterday morning. In a hurry to get the tablecloths back on before the guests showed up, she'd grabbed him by the arm to help out, not saying a word in greeting.

"Each table needs one of these," she'd explained as she scooted around like a mad hen. "Make sure you smooth them, so they aren't puckered anywhere."

"Yes, ma'am," he'd said in that quiet, studious way. Then he'd gone to work, and in no time he had the round cloths on and straightened to perfection.

At least they were too busy to stop and chat, even if

he did look at her in that way that made her feel all warm and dreamy.

After Daed had told her about the talk he and Henry had had with Jonah, she'd worked herself into a frenzy, trying to pray Jonah out of her head.

"I'm counting on you, Abby, to be an example to your sisters. Jonah has been a big help around here, but he is still a stranger, not one of us. You must abide by that. Do not give him false encouragement."

No false encouragement.

But a lot of real feelings that were almost impossible to hide. Her family would never understand the many hours she'd sat with Jonah, praying for him to live. They'd never understand how he'd talked to her, listened to her, and asked for her advice. His real need for her made her want to protect Jonah. But she knew he needed no protection physically. Emotionally, yes. More than most. He must have suffered a great trauma out there in the water.

Jonah somehow knew the part of her heart she kept sealed away, the part that dreamed of a life she shouldn't covet. A life of travel in which she could learn more about the world and her own heart.

Jonah had brought change to her door, offered her a new perspective on the world outside this quiet cove.

Now she wanted nothing to do with the outside world. She wanted to stay here, safe and cocooned with Jonah.

Dear Lord, take this longing away from my soul.

She heard Jonah's laughter, a rare thing.

Craning her neck, Abigail peeked out the office door and saw him helping Matthew move some tables so they could sweep the kitchen floor. Edith demanded a clean kitchen from top to bottom.

She took in the sight of Jonah's broad shoulders and hefty biceps. How could she wipe him from her mind?

If you're trying to test me, Lord, it for certain sure is working.

"You're going to have a crick in that neck," Eliza said as she rounded the corner, her expression torn between *I told you so* and *I understand your dilemma*.

Abigail slid the desk chair back into place and pretended to study the accounting books spread before her. "I only wanted to check up on my workers."

"Matthew knows what to do, and he's been showing Jonah his daily tasks around the kitchen and dining room. I do believe Jonah is giving him advice regarding our little sister. There, you are all caught up."

Ignoring her sister's smart report, Abigail frowned. "Colette? What advice would help with her?"

They both grinned at that.

"She's actually taking notice of Mattie lately, so whatever Jonah said to him must have worked."

Abigail thought about Jonah tugging her back against his chest, his hands circling her waist, his lips moving like a soft feather down her neck. She had to swallow and close her eyes.

"Abby?"

She sat up and stared at Eliza. "What?"

"Are you okay, Sister?"

Abigail knew she could be honest with Eliza. "I'm as okay as I can be, under the circumstances. I get annoyed when everyone asks me if I'm okay. I'm here, I'm functioning, I'm doing my job. It seems, however, that Jonah and I are pushed together at every turn. It makes me think our loving parents are trying to torment me or test me. Maybe *Gott* is, too."

"Will you pass the test?"

"I will do what I have to do. I won't bring shame to my family. Jonah won't start anything he'd regret."

"That's all we can ask for," Eliza replied in a calm tone that only added to Abigail's irritation. "Right now, I need Jonah in the stable. I know it's not his official time to be there. May I borrow him?"

Abigail gave her sister an eye roll. "Only if you bring him back in one piece."

Eliza giggled. "What if I don't?"

"I'll *kumm* and find him."

"He is handy and well-liked," Eliza admitted. "If only—"

"Don't say it."

Abigail watched her impish sister hurrying away and wondered how the family would react if Jonah up and left one day.

She did not want that day to come. Everyone liked him, even her *daed*. Mamm held back, but Abigail had seen the sympathy in her eyes.

I need to keep praying on this subject.

She listened as her sister told Jonah she needed help with one of the buggy wheels. Eliza had taught Jonah all about the buggies they used, and how each season had a different one, ranging from open air in the summer to a black- or brown-enclosed family buggy for when they all went to church together in the winter. He'd even helped some children yesterday with Peaches and the pony buggy, his smile bittersweet and his eyes distant. The man would probably never forget what he'd learned about horses and buggies.

Nor would they ever forget what they'd learned from having him around. His quiet strength and banked frustration made Abigail wish she could help him find some peace.

She glanced up as he passed by, following Eliza. He smiled, his shaggy, dark hair falling across his forehead in a way that only endeared him to her more. Then he winked at her.

She put her hand to her mouth. A man had winked at her!

She didn't think that would be allowed under her father's rules. But she couldn't stop the silly grin that spread across her face or the warmth she felt, knowing that Jonah was a special friend.

But that was all he could ever be.

"Aenti Miriam keeps asking about your quilt."

"When have you seen her?" Abigail asked Colette. She wondered if her aunt could be sneaking around the inn, watching. She had a habit of showing up out of the blue, and always with a critical attitude. Sometimes, Abigail couldn't believe her sweet *mamm* and Aenti Miriam could be related.

"I usually run into her at the market in town. I think she waits around there to get all the gossip. And a lot of canned goods, from what I see in her basket."

Abigail sat on the bed in her room, staring at Colette. "And what did you tell her about my quilt?"

"That it's your quilt and I am leaving you alone to

create it. She wants you to move in with her, to keep you away from 'that evil *Englisch.*' Her words, not mine."

Their aunt didn't even know Jonah, yet she had already judged him as an outsider.

"He is not evil."

"I don't think so," Colette replied. "He works as hard as two men at times and even Edith has a soft spot for him. She sneaks him apple pie and brownies."

"He does love his sweets."

"I think he loves being here, too," Eliza said from where she sat in the rocking chair near the bed. "He is content and safe here, so why would he be in a hurry to leave? He is great with the horses. Samson adores him, and even that ornery pony Peaches has taken to him."

Abigail tugged at the quilt, thinking that all this praise and adoration did not help her get Jonah out of her head.

Nor did this quilt.

She'd added a panel that showed a small table with a slice of apple pie and a cup of *kaffe* centered on it. Then across from that panel, the apple orchard where Henry and Jonah, along with Abigail and her sisters, had gone the other day to see the first tiny apples of the season. Summer had begun to flow by like the stream that poured into the lake, lazy at times and swift-moving at others. The spring blossoms of azaleas and magnolias had come and gone, and the fresh lushness of that season had been replaced with green trees and shrubs, fields filled with produce, along with Gerbera daisies and old roses, sunflowers and hardy camellia bushes that would bloom in the fall.

Though they'd been in a group, Jonah had still watched her in that quiet way of his. She'd look up and he'd give her a long glance, his smile so hidden, no one noticed it. But she'd noticed. He caught up with her by a big tree full of green apples. "So, this is our walk, I guess."

"As close as we'll come," she whispered. "Does it bother you, being out here?"

"Not as long as I have you to look at," he replied. He might have her to calm him, but she could see that far-away darkness in his eyes.

Time kept moving when she wanted it to be still. She wanted to be back in the apple orchard, watching Jonah with covert eyes as he experienced the falling blossoms and the tiny green apples bursting through. She'd watched as he closed his eyes and held on to a tree's firm trunk. Had he remembered another time, in another orchard?

Colette touched her fingers to the quilt, jarring Abigail back to the present. "Has he told you all his memories?"

Abigail stopped working on the magnolia she planned to put in the middle of the quilt. "*Neh*, only those that involve people or places, scenes that come into his head. I'm sure he's remembering little bits and pieces that won't fit on this quilt."

She wouldn't tell her sisters how she longed to hear all Jonah's memories.

"You haven't added the woman," Eliza pointed out. "Maybe near the house and the little boy in the swing?"

"I can't bring myself to do that," Abigail admitted. "It seems too personal to add the woman he could have married—might still be married to. I think it would confuse him and upset him."

Her sisters looked at each other and then back to her. "But you're the woman walking on the beach, ain't so?"

She had no answer for that. "I am a part of this quilt.

I've stitched it and studied it and even exposed it to ridicule. I found him. I brought him here. I have a right to be on this quilt." She touched a hand to the little boy. "It might be the only place I'll ever have in Jonah's life."

Colette put her arm across Abigail's back. "What is next then, Sister? With your quilt?"

Abigail's mind drifted back to the way Jonah had held her and kissed her neck. He hadn't touched her since then, but she knew he remembered that scene, too. How could she capture what they'd felt that night? That interaction remained too personal, too special to try to stitch into any fabric. But it would remain stitched to the walls of her heart for a long, long time.

"I don't know what's next," she admitted. "And maybe that's why I'm so fascinated with Jonah."

"A dangerous fascination," Colette said, standing to straighten her apron. "One that can only lead to heartache." Shrugging, she went on. "I'm beginning to see romance doesn't always have a happy ending."

Eliza stood, too. "Abby, are you all right, truly?"

She nodded, her fingers clutching her creation. "I will be. I have to be. We all know how this will end."

Her sisters hugged her good night and went to their rooms. Abigail sat staring at her work, finding mistakes and finding the beauty in this story. Then she went to the window and stared out, searching for the light that seemed to appear every night.

The light in Jonah's room. For now, this was the only way they had of communicating with each other. She dreaded the night she'd find that room dark and vacant again.

Chapter Twenty-Five

Jonah dreamed of the apple orchard.

Of the woman and the child, laughing. The woman had light-colored hair that shimmered like gold. The boy's hair was darker and thick.

"Like your daddy," she'd said to the child, her smile radiant and loving.

They moved ahead of him, always too far away. The light shone so brightly on them as they danced through the trees, their laughter floating in the air.

Jonah watched as they slipped into the mist. He tried to reach them, but his feet felt like lead. He tried to call out, but his voice only whispered into the wind.

"Wait," he called. "Turn toward me. I need to see you."

They kept going, running and laughing underneath the apple blossoms.

Why couldn't they hear him and turn so he could see their faces?

Then the woman did pivot, but she had changed. The blond woman and the child were gone. Abigail walked alone on the beach, coming toward him, her eyes like the sky on an early spring morning. She wore the blue wool dress and a black shawl, her hair flowing out beneath her *kapp*.

An angel coming to take him to a place of peace and quiet, where there was no more pain. *Dear God, no more pain.*

He woke with a start, his body drenched in sweat, his mind roiling. His head banged and clattered with memories he couldn't accept, memories he'd sent to the bottom of the lake. They emerged like flotsam, hitting against his skull but refusing to enter his mind. Still, he felt them there, tapping with an urgent need.

Jonah grabbed at his hair and tried to silence the pulse that throbbed with a painful, tormenting beat.

After each nightmare, he always had to remind himself of the here and now. Of how he'd gotten here and how long he'd been here. August was halfway gone, but the routine of the long days had helped steady his mind. He liked the hard work that made him so tired, he could get a few hours of sleep.

But he still had a restlessness about him that wouldn't be hushed. He needed to leave Shadow Lake and never look back. He could get up in the middle of the night and go. Find a place to sleep and get a job of some kind, search for his identity. Or he could become Jonah King.

That would be so easy—to slip into this persona and never return to the world out there. He could stay here and work in the garden, chase the chickens, be with Abigail. If he could hold her in his arms, he knew he'd sleep better. He'd have peace and calm in his life.

But . . . would he ever get over the not knowing of what had happened to him?

Jonah got up and took a shower. Then he sat and

studied the list of scant memories he'd uncovered. A tree swing, an old oak, and a woman and a boy. The apple trees. The scent of magnolias. His brain still couldn't follow the path back. Did he know these people? Had he been a family man?

A baby. He'd held that baby as sure as he breathed. He could almost smell the scent of baby lotion and lemons.

His heart accepted what his brain refused.

He was married. The woman and child were his family. How could he find them?

Then he thought of Abigail. She had sketched everything she'd put on that quilt, each pattern, each panel. If he described these faces in detail, and she sketched them, maybe that would help the police find his real identity.

It could be another way to find the truth. Because he'd run out of ideas, and the police had been unable to give him any help. The memories of police stations and interrogations still came and went.

He'd helped Abe after his heart attack, helped Maggie when she was about to have her baby. How did he know the appropriate way to react in those situations? He had to have some sort of training. Then why hadn't the police found his prints and his identity? Fall would come soon enough, and still he had no idea what he'd been doing before he arrived here.

He sat at the little table and stared out the window to the lake. Moonlight glistened on the water in the distance. He blinked. Had he just seen a white boat passing like a ghost through the night?

A big, white boat.

The same kind of boat he'd seen in his nightmares.

* * *

Three days later, Abigail waited for the staff to gather around the big table in the employee room. Her sisters passed out lemonade and water and placed fresh tea cakes on the table. She went over her notes, her mind distracted by knowing Jonah would need to attend this meeting.

Matthew and Jonah came in together, laughing and talking, Henry right behind them. Since Matthew had been hanging out with Jonah more, he'd picked up some pointers on flirting. He smiled big at Colette and made her blush.

Eliza rolled her eyes and then grinned at Abigail.

Jonah glanced at her and lifted his chin, careful not to be so obvious, even while his eyes went a deep blue that tugged at her soul. Abigail felt his presence like a ray of hot sun hitting her skin. She hoped *she* wasn't blushing, but she seemed to break out in a sweat whenever she saw him.

A few more employees came in. Now that the lunch rush had ended, they had to discuss the upcoming Shadow Lake Fall Festival. The inn had always been a part of the festival.

Edith marched in. "Whew, I'm tired. We're getting busier every day. My feet hurt."

"Have a seat," Matthew said, offering Edith a chair. He'd learned if he was polite, she'd save him a cookie or a piece of chocolate cake.

"*Denke*, Matthew," Edith said. "And pass me some lemonade."

Matthew obliged and then found his own seat.

Jonah shot Abigail a soft smile, then grabbed a cookie.

"Okay, let's get started," she said, her notebook and calendar ready. "The festival is in three weeks. We'll do the usual—spruce up the inn, get the gardens ready to sell produce and potted plants, especially mums. We'll have the pumpkins delivered that week for the pumpkin patch. We need to have the pony corral cleaned up so the *kinder* can pay for rides."

"Festival?" Jonah asked, his chin going up. "What kind of festival?"

Matthew glanced at Jonah. "The Shadow Lake Fall Festival is the biggest event of the season. We give part of the money we make to needy families in the Township." Turning serious, he said, "Most are Amish, but some *Englisch* around here are out of work. We raise a lot of money for the whole community."

"We try to hold it after the mayflies have swarmed and are gone," Colette added, her grimace showing her distaste for the black-winged little bugs. "No one wants to be at a festival when they come through."

Henry nodded. "The festival is for a good cause, and holding it in early fall brings in some of the leaf-lookers, too. People love buying handmade quilts and freshly baked food when they know it's to help the community. We have all kinds of food—breads and casseroles, jellies and jams, and desserts, and we cook a lot of good meals to sell in our booth between the kitchen and the gardens."

Abigail glanced at Jonah. "We have the proper permits needed to rent tents out to different businesses. The Township maintenance crew helps us set up the tent covers, and people rent booths to sell their wares. Like a spring mud sale without the mud."

Jonah nodded, but she could see the confusion and

apprehension in his expression. He'd been a great help all summer, but he tended to stay in the background. The festival would force him out into the public eye.

"Don't forget the Amish furniture makers who line up. They create all kinds of unique furniture and the tourists love buying it," Eliza explained. "Mamm always buys something, big or small, to support them."

Jonah sent a glance toward Abigail. "What can I do to help?"

"Just about everything," Henry said before she could speak.

Everyone laughed at that, but Abigail could see the uncertainty and fatigue in Jonah's eyes. He'd been avoiding her lately, and she'd tried to stay busy so she wouldn't think about him. They hadn't had much time to talk. Did he miss their quiet times as much as she did?

"Jonah, how do you feel about being part of the festival?" Colette asked, giving Abigail a knowing smile.

"I said I'd do whatever needs to be done," he replied, his expression stony and hard to read. "Push me in the right direction."

"Okay, Jonah can be our emergency backup," Eliza said. "That means if something goes wrong, you're in charge of fixing it."

"What could go wrong?" he asked, his gaze scanning the room.

"A fire in one of the hamburger grills," Henry said. "It happens."

They all laughed. "Henry accidentally set a grill on fire one year," Abigail explained.

"Or a goat chasing a woman who had on a flowered

skirt," Eliza called out. "So much fun, but not for the poor goat or that frightened woman."

"A horse running away," Matthew said, his head down. "My first year and my one task—to watch out for the horses."

"He came back," Abigail said. "I mean, the horse and Mattie both came back. They were hungry."

Jonah smiled at that. "I think I can handle it," he said, his eyes on Abigail. "I'll stay in the background and do the heavy lifting, same as always."

"You'd be good with the pony rides," Eliza said. "The animals seem to like you."

"You do what you feel comfortable doing," Henry replied. "You're a big help around here, Jonah."

Jonah nodded, his alert gaze hitting on Henry and moving back to Abigail. She knew him well enough to see he had something on his mind. What was bothering him? She'd have to corner him and find out if he truly could handle a big crowd of strangers.

They moved on to the date for the festival, which always fell the last week of September, when the inn would be booked solid with early fall travelers. The men talked about setting up booths and getting the yard pretty and pristine. Abigail and Mamm would handle the potted plants and flower decorations.

"We'll have picnic tables set out underneath the great oaks on the bluff," she said, remembering how she and Jonah had gone off on the secret path near that area. "It's always shady and not as hot out there."

"You mean the bluff where that big rock juts out?"

Jonah asked. "I like to sit on that rock and watch the water."

"*Ja*," Eliza replied. "It's a peaceful spot."

Abigail tried to breathe. Was he sending her a message? She'd sat on that very rock herself, and she knew he liked to go there and stroll down to the old path she'd shown him. She thought her heart might burst with a need to know that contradicted her determination to stay away from him.

"We'll have to set up lots of big trash bins," Matthew told Jonah. "And we have to empty the big bags and put them out by the entryway on the main road so the garbage crew can remove them."

Again, he looked at Abigail. "I can do that. As I said, I'll do whatever is needed."

Sensing he'd had enough, Abigail checked the clock. "Okay, we have a plan and we'll all help out. We'll start cooking and preparing food to freeze for the limited menu to feed people on festival day. Let's finish getting cleanup done before the supper guests come in tonight. There's an art walk in town all day, so we might get a few extras for supper tonight."

Everyone scattered except Jonah. Hovering near the door, he glanced around. "I need to talk to you."

Abigail held her hands together against her apron. "If it's about the festival, you don't have to do anything that makes you uncomfortable."

"It's not the festival, Abigail."

Her heart hit her chest. "What is it, then?"

"I called Captain Sherman early this morning."

"The police captain?" She held a hand to her mouth. "You heard news?"

"No, that's just it. They're still trying to find me—the real me. A slow process, or so he says. I don't know if I believe him. It's been almost two months since I went in, but he seems determined to keep looking." He shrugged. "Or they already know and they're not telling me for some strange reason."

"I'm sorry you didn't receive *gut* news, Jonah."

"Nothing about this is good," he replied. "Except you, Abigail."

She couldn't speak. His eyes held the truth. He wanted to find the family he'd left behind, but he also wanted her. He couldn't have both, and really, she could not hold out hope. She had to remain firm in her faith and call him a friend.

"Jonah . . ."

He held up a hand. "I know I'm wrong to say that when nothing can come of it, but it's the truth."

"I'm glad you are safe here and that we are close," she replied on a whisper, light-headed from the heat in his eyes. "I have to be careful, and you need to keep your distance. I hope you know I care."

"That's why I need your help," he said. "We care about each other and that will never change, but we both need to find out the truth."

"The truth, *ja*. But how can I help any more than I already have?"

"I need you to sketch my face," he said. "And I also need to describe the woman and child I see in my dreams."

"What?" She had to catch hold of the table. His firm, serious tone made the request seem so final. "You never wanted that before—not your face sketched." And certainly not the woman or child.

"I do now," he replied, the plea in his eyes telling her she would lose him soon. "I've waited, I've gone to the authorities, but I'm in limbo. They claim they haven't found a hit on the partial prints they got on me. I think they know something, but they're not saying what. They could be watching me, waiting to make a move." Pushing a hand through his hair, he shook his head. "No one should have to live like this. I can't continue to be a nuisance around here—a threat to your beliefs."

"You are no threat." Except to her heart.

"I can't trust the police, so I have to try to get answers myself."

"Why would the police lie to you? Why do you feel you can't trust them?"

"If I was one of them and . . . I turned bad, they could be biding their time while they gather evidence and put together all the pieces. I don't want them to show up here, especially with a big festival coming up."

"So, what will you do with my sketches?"

"I'm going to take them to the locals, and I'll make copies to post everywhere I can. It's a beginning."

"Or an ending," she said, not even realizing she'd blurted out her thought. "This could be dangerous for you."

"It's already dangerous," he said. "I need to know what I've done, good or bad."

"I'll sketch you," she said. "I'll need to explain to my parents. We can do it at the cottage, out on the porch. Plenty of chaperones that way."

"Probably wise," he said, moving closer. "I know it's a lot to ask, but I trust you. Only you."

Abigail swallowed the emotions tearing at her throat,

the fear, the longing that could never be fulfilled. She must accept that he had to find the life he'd left behind.

"I'll let you know when," she said, wiping her hands down her apron. "Maybe later, with the sun soft on the horizon."

"Thank you, Abigail."

She could only nod, knowing her sketches were the last resort for a desperate man. A man she cared about, and would always care about, a man who could be lost to her forever.

CHAPTER TWENTY-SIX

"He's coming!" Colette turned from the window and nodded at Abigail. "Jonah's walking toward our house."

"Go and tell Daed," Mamm said, her gaze on Abigail. "And once Jonah is here, he can have supper with us before you draw his face."

Abigail could only nod, thinking her parents were being so understanding and cooperative about her drawing Jonah's face.

"That's kind of you, Mamm," Eliza said. "He sometimes eats all alone in his room."

Abigail's heart bumped and her nerves tingled. When she'd asked her parents if it would be okay for her to bring Jonah here and sketch him so he could put up copies of it around town, she'd been sure they'd say no. But to her surprise, Daed had nodded and agreed. Mamm reluctantly had gone along with the plan, too.

That showed how eager they were to help Jonah find himself again.

She didn't know if she'd even be able to hold a pencil or a bit of charcoal, her hands were shaking so badly. Although her parents tolerated Jonah and liked him well enough, they had to wonder if he'd ever go away. While she could only wonder if he'd stay.

She knew they worried about her marrying and settling down, but she'd visited with Ben twice here in the parlor since the day of the frolic and nothing had come of that. She'd had to tell him in a gentle tone that she wasn't ready for marriage.

Ben had given her a surprised, confused stare. "But you're not getting any younger, Abigail. We could have a *gut* life together."

Not exactly the best of proposals. She'd sent Ben back to his farm.

Mamm and Aenti Miriam had finally given up.

"You girls are too stubborn," Aenti Miriam had blurted out the last time they'd held church here. "I've run out of eligible bachelors. I'm washing my hands of this burden."

"They do have minds of their own," Mamm had answered. "We raised them to be independent and educated, but also to stay true to our ways." Then she'd taken her sister's hand. "They are *our* burden, and one we cherish. You don't need to worry on that account."

"And that's the problem," Miriam had replied, oblivious to any hints or reprimands. "Too much time on their own, forming their own views. You've ruined them, Sister."

Abigail had to bite her tongue when her aunt lamented about them. Her aunt's two boys had married women she'd picked for them and had several children between them, but their *fraas* for certain sure always looked tired and weary. Not happy.

No one in her aunt's family seemed happy, for that matter. As if laughter was a sin in that house. Thankful for her own loving, considerate parents, she knew they'd done the best they could for their three girls.

Jonah knocked on the screen door, looking apprehensive. Daed motioned him inside.

"*Gut* evening, Jonah," he said with a slight smile. He and Jonah had grown close, but they kept things more formal when they were around the women. Abigail often heard them discussing everything from the spring crops to the proper way to bait a hook. They'd even gone fishing together several times.

An almost natural, normal friendship.

"We'll eat a bite before our Abby draws your image," Daed said, making sure that came out as a statement. "We're having meat loaf, fresh potatoes, corn, and lima beans with corn bread."

"Mamm made an oatmeal pie," Eliza said.

Jonah nodded, his gaze casting about until he found Abigail. "I wasn't expecting supper."

Abigail couldn't find her voice. It seemed odd, having him here with her whole family around. "You have to eat," she finally managed.

"We insist," Mamm said. "You've been so busy helping with tents and such for the festival, I wanted to feed you properly." Then she gave him a glance full of hope. "It's a brave thing you're doing, having our Abby sketch you so you can see if anyone recognizes you. It's easy to fall into this simple life, so I know you did not make that decision lightly."

He looked overwhelmed, his eyes moving from Mamm to Abigail. "It has to be done, one way or another."

Abigail had cautioned him not to mention the wife and child. She'd sketch those two later, after she'd been able to talk to him when they were alone. Somehow, she'd find a way.

"*Kumm* and sit with me," Daed told him. "They will tell us when supper is ready."

Colette laughed at that. "It takes all of us, *ja*?"

Abigail didn't think she'd be able to eat. Seeing Jonah in her home for the first time proved to be bittersweet. He was here, laughing with her *daed*. But soon he might leave all of them.

And her sketches might be the catalyst that took him away from them for *gut*.

Ignoring the enormous ache in her heart, she served tea and set out steaming plates of potatoes, corn, and beans. Then she sliced chunks of corn bread and lined them up on a plate. Colette cut and plated the juicy meat loaf.

Jonah listened to her father explaining the fall vegetable garden while the women worked in the kitchen, but his gaze drifted back and forth to her. Eliza poked her in the ribs, giving her a warning eye, while Colette chatted to keep Mamm from noticing too much.

But Abigail felt like an open book being read by her family. She'd tried so hard to stay away from Jonah. She hadn't walked on the beach for weeks now, afraid she'd run into him. They only talked when they were with others and sometimes, if he caught her alone, they'd walk a bit but always with care, and spaced at a proper distance. The words they didn't speak to each other shouted the loudest, however.

Each night, after her sisters left her room, Abigail would hurry to the window and see the light on in his apartment. She'd stand until her legs grew weary and her eyes begged for sleep. She was always the first one to turn out her light. Jonah waited, and then he did the same. He made her feel safe there in the shadows. But this longing in her heart felt dangerous and reckless. If they ever unleashed their feelings, she wasn't sure she could handle the intensity. She stood and imagined him as her own.

Easy to imagine things in the dark. Things such as the two of them walking freely together in the orchard or on the beach, the scene of a wedding taking place—their wedding. Children running near the waterfall—their children.

The nightly routine was not nearly enough of a connection, but it stayed between them. She'd already sketched a cabin with a light shining through the window. That image would make it to the quilt she'd almost finished.

Almost, but not quite. She had to see how the final pattern would turn out.

"Time for prayer."

Abe's words brought Jonah out of his daze. He couldn't stop glancing at Abigail, but he had to be careful. Abe and Sarah both kept a sharp eye on their girls. Especially Abigail. He looked down, but lifted his gaze to watch her. Their eyes met and held until she lowered her head and silently prayed.

Jonah knew enough to do the same. His prayers were ragged and raw. How did a man talk to God when that man wasn't sure about his own life or his soul? But he did talk to God. He asked God to help, please help, with this situation, and to protect Abigail and her family.

Jonah finished and lifted his head. Silence, and then everyone started talking at once as they passed the food around. It felt different, being here with the family. He could almost imagine this as his life—a new life. If he could get to the point where he was free and clear, he'd have a lot to consider.

Living here in her world?

Or leaving her behind to go back to his world?

"Jonah, would you like some bread?"

Jonah looked at Eliza and saw the warning in her eyes. He had to get it together. "Yes, thank you." He took the bread plate and grabbed a warm square of corn bread. "This looks so good. It's nice to have a meal with all of you."

Abe nodded and began to eat. Sarah took the plate and passed it on, her smile warm even if her expression remained cautious.

"Do you think these sketches will help identify you, Jonah?" Sarah asked. "I don't know much about the police and how they operate, but Abby says they use sketch artists to help them find people."

Jonah finished his first bite of meat loaf and nodded. "Yes, they have experienced sketch artists who work for larger police departments. The Shadow Lake Township doesn't have a lot of resources to help them solve missing persons cases. They took my photo, but so far, I've heard nothing. I'm taking action on my own."

"And you decided our Abby could do the job?" Abe's soft smile was indulgent, but not quite approving.

"If you don't mind," he said. After eating a few more bites of the wonderful meal, Jonah put down his fork. "I trust Abigail. I trust all of you. You've been nothing but kind and patient with me. But we know I can't stay here forever."

Abigail gave him a speaking glance, but then she looked away and toyed with her fork, moving it over the food she'd hardly touched.

"Then we must get on with it before the sun goes down," Abe replied, his expression serene.

"Let's finish our meal," Sarah suggested. "Abby, you can sketch what you need and then we'll have dessert out on the porch. It's going to be a nice, pleasant night, ain't so?"

Jonah nodded and went back to the food he'd piled on his plate. The food tasted great, homemade and fresh. But his appetite took a dive each time he glanced at Abigail.

He shouldn't have led her on—not even a little bit. He should have kept his feelings to himself. Did she truly care about him, or just the idea of him? Jonah couldn't be sure. He felt so many things with Abigail, but had he only fixated on her because she'd saved his life?

He could be sure of one thing, however. If he didn't leave this place soon, he'd never want to go.

And that wouldn't be fair to anyone. Especially the family he might already have. He needed to talk to Abigail and make her understand. This had to be the way. The only way.

They talked a little more, mostly about the upcoming Fall Festival and all the work entailed. But he had to wonder if everyone here could feel the tension that seemed to tighten around them. He'd brought this tension to their world. He'd have to be the one to lighten it and end this, one way or another.

* * *

Abigail lifted her tote bag full of sketchpads and pencils. She couldn't remember a time when she didn't doodle or draw. It was in her blood, and for a long time she'd tried to fight it. But when Lydia Marshall, the previous owner of the inn, had spotted Abigail drawing one day when she was ten years old, she'd said, "You are talented, Abby. You're an artist."

Abby had beamed, but she shook her head. "Daed says I shouldn't spend my time doodling."

"Art is as important as any hard work," Lydia had said. "But you have to follow your papa's suggestion. That doesn't mean you can't use your art for a good purpose. Find a way that won't dishonor your beliefs. I know you love to sew with your mother. Maybe you can create some pretty quilts with your designs."

That was the beginning of an idea that had sustained Abigail for years. She'd continued to draw, but she'd never used her images on any quilt until Jonah. Now, her talent might help a man who needed to find out who he had been before he arrived here.

"Are you nervous?"

She turned from the stool she'd placed on the porch, in the best light. Jonah stood with his hands tucked against his suspenders, his hair long and shiny, his face rugged and tan from working outside so much. He shaved with a kit Henry had given him, but he had a shadow of darkness on his jaw. A five-o'clock shadow, he'd told her once. He looked Amish, but he still had an edge about him, a hardness that covered him and made him even more intriguing to her.

Somehow, she had to capture that. Somehow, she had to study him, sketch him, catch the essence of him, so he'd be able to use this sketch to find his way home.

Her heart fought against her head as she sat down, took a deep breath, and started sketching.

Mamm and Daed sat at the other end of the long porch, in matching, hickory wood rocking chairs. She could feel their presence, but instead of irritating her or making her nervous, having them nearby soothed Abigail. They loved her enough to trust her, so she would earn that trust.

She worked with a steady hand, her eyes on Jonah. He sat, at first uncomfortable and fidgety; then, when he finally looked into her eyes, she heard him take a deep breath and he settled back, keeping his eyes on her.

She worked quickly and concentrated on what she had to do, but when she finished, Abigail let out a sigh and realized she'd been holding her breath. Working with Jonah gazing directly at her seemed like a precious, decadent gift. One she now had on paper.

"I'm done," she said on a whisper.

Jonah still sat staring at her, the look in his eyes telling her what he couldn't voice: his need, his longing, his wanting.

Oh, the wanting. He'd looked inside her soul, and in return, she'd captured his essence on paper. When she looked at the sketch of Jonah, she knew what her heart had been hiding.

She was in love with this man.

From the way he'd sat watching her, and from what

she'd captured on the paper, she could tell that he felt the same about her.

Jonah loved her.

But he would have to leave her one day soon, and Abigail would need to let him go, even knowing that he loved her.

She stood and handed him the sketch.

"It's done, Jonah."

Then she gathered her paper and pencils, and with one last glance, she turned and went into the house.

CHAPTER TWENTY-SEVEN

The next time they met, Abigail prepared to sketch the images he had in his head. She'd made copies of the sketch she'd done of Jonah, using the printer in the inn's office. She kept the original for herself. She'd earned that much at least.

Colette had followed Abigail inside the other night, urging her to come back out onto the porch. Abigail had forced herself to do so, but only because her parents had been wary of her sketching Jonah to begin with. If she acted emotional or weepy, they'd assume the worst.

They sat and had dessert that no one really wanted after her grand exit. Jonah tried not to look at her, but she'd felt him staring at her. He'd gotten up after eating some of his dessert and smiled at all of them.

"*Denke*," he'd said. "I appreciate all of you."

Abigail had never wanted to run after a man so badly.

But she'd sat there, frozen inside the truth. She had fallen for a man she could never have.

Now, three days later, with Mamm sitting in the corner of the employee dining area knitting, she sat down with a sketchpad and turned to Jonah. "I haven't told my parents what I'm sketching today," she said on a low note. "Just to warn you."

He gave her a Jonah look, his eyes holding her in the same way he'd held her in his arms that one time. "I'm not sure I'm ready for this."

She knew she wasn't ready for this. She'd avoided him for as long as possible. "Do you want to stop?"

He sat down across from her, looking tired and unsure. "No, I can't do that. I've already taken the copies of the sketch you made into town. The newspaper took some, and the police station reluctantly took one to post, but who knows what they actually did with it. Of course, they reminded me they have my photo on file."

"And yet they give you no answers."

"I have to try, Abigail. I have to know."

She nodded, settled the sketchpad against the table and slanted it onto her lap. "Then let's get started." Steadying her emotions, she asked, "What do you remember? Tell me about the woman."

Her mother's head shot up, but Abigail didn't flinch. Best that Mamm heard it in increments, rather than Abigail blurting everything out at once. Mamm and Daed had both been giving her concerned glances since supper the other night.

Jonah swallowed, looked down at his callused hands. "Blond, laughing, happy." Shrugging, he said, "I don't know the color of her eyes, but she was—she is pretty."

Abigail lifted her pencil, lowered her head, and tried to form an image. "Why do you want me to sketch some-one we can't see?"

"So I can see that someone better," he said, his tone almost apologetic.

She went on, her pencil moving like a lead weight. "Long hair or short?"

"Long. Shoulder-length, wavy, windblown."

Each word jabbed like a knife in her heart, but she created an empty face and added hair. "What do you think her face would look like?"

He sat with his hands together, his booted feet braced on the floor. "An oval, freckles across her nose. Dimples."

He lifted his head, his eyes lighting with a new fire. He seemed to be really remembering this woman.

Mamm stopped knitting and watched him for a moment before gazing at Abigail.

Abigail's charcoal pencil fell out of her hand and hit the tiled floor. Jonah stood and stooped to pick it up. "Abigail?"

"I'm all right," she said, glancing at her surprised mother. "Clumsy me."

She settled back into the chair, her face hot with humiliation. She went back to work, silently bringing an image to life. "Anything else you can remember?"

Jonah watched her with a cautious intensity. "She turned once in my dreams and I caught a glimpse, but then the image changed."

"Changed? How?"

Jonah looked toward her mother and then back to Abigail. "To another woman," he said, so low she had to strain to hear his words.

Another woman.

Abigail looked into his eyes. The brightness stayed there.

"A woman on the beach," he said, giving her a focused,

determined stare that washed her with both longing and regret.

She didn't dare ask who that woman was. She knew within her heart. Jonah had dreamed about her.

"Abby, finish this," Mamm called. "We have much to do this week."

Abigail blinked and finished the sketch. Then she turned the page so Jonah could see it. "How does this look?"

Jonah inhaled and pushed at his hair. "Close. So close," he said on a raw whisper. Then he stood. "This was a bad idea. I have to go."

With that, he rushed out of the room, the back door slamming behind him.

Abigail stared down at the face she'd hastily sketched. Had he recognized the woman? Or had the attempt caused him to remember?

Mamm stood and came to look over her shoulder. "Abby, did Jonah tell you about this woman before?"

Abigail nodded. "He dreams about her and . . . a child."

Mamm nodded and let out a sigh. "I suspected as much the day Maggie went into labor. Does he have a family, Abby?"

She looked up at her mother's understanding eyes. "I believe so."

Mamm touched a hand to her shoulder. "That is enough for today. You've done all you can for him."

"He wants a sketch of the little boy, too," Abigail said with what sounded like a sob.

"He is putting you through too much. More than you should have to handle. I'm afraid you are taking his actions in the wrong way. You know *Englischers* like to tease and flirt, and if he is that kind of man, you'd best let this go."

"Jonah is not that kind of man," she said, remembering the few times he'd held her. "I have to help him. He's trapped here, and he wants to go home. That would be the best thing for both of us."

"And where will that leave you? When he has gone back to this woman and their child?"

"Right where I've always been," Abigail replied, her heart sinking. "Right here, Mamm."

Jonah sat on his rock, staring out at the lake. Boats motored by, their occupants happy and laughing. Those people had no idea how a body of water could hold a vast secret. The seagulls cawed and floated effortlessly on the wind, while herons walked with methodical grace along the shallows. Trees swayed and clouds moved by.

While he sat in limbo, caught between two worlds.

Caught between two women.

The pretty, smiling blonde he'd almost remembered earlier and Abigail. He pictured her sweet, wholesome face, a face he could never forget.

Dear God, what have I done? How can I make this right? Who am I? Where do I belong?

Jonah remembered that the Amish believed everything in life happened because of God's will. Jonah wanted to believe that, to let nature take its course, to meet fate with faith.

But he needed proof, needed answers, had to see something to believe it.

He lowered his head and closed his eyes, his prayers broken and edged with distrust and doubt. But oh, how he wanted to feel something, anything, in his heart that would free him from whatever shadows were chasing him.

"Jonah?"

At first, he thought the voice called inside his head, coming from his past. But when he opened his eyes, he saw her standing there, the same way she'd been standing there in his dreams.

Abigail.

She stood with her hands together, her heart in her misty eyes. "I had to find you."

"I know," he said, his heart racing. "I know."

She didn't move toward him. Instead, she clutched her hands against her chest. "What are we to do?"

Jonah shook his head, wiped at his own eyes. "I don't know."

"Did you remember her?"

"No, not all of her. I remembered her face, Abigail. For a moment, I could see her face, but I still don't know who she is, or even her name. Then . . . I also saw your face."

"I am in your dreams?"

"You've been in my dreams since the day I opened my eyes and saw you there on the beach," he admitted. "Like an angel. I thought I'd died because, you see, I'm pretty sure I'd been trying to die."

She moved forward. "I don't understand."

"I think I had what we call a death wish." She looked so innocent and confused. "It's like I wanted something to happen to me, something that would kill me."

"Did you try to take your own life?" she asked, horror on her face.

"No. But I don't think I would have minded if someone else had."

"Was that why you were on that boat?"

"I think it might have been. If I worked in law enforcement, I might have taken on some sort of dangerous assignment, knowing I could be killed."

She moved another step, anger flaring in her eyes like heat lightning. "So, are you angry at me, Jonah? Angry that you managed to live?"

He stood and moved toward her. "How could I be angry with you? You saved my life, in so many ways. You nursed me back to health, both physically and mentally, you gave me shelter—me, a stranger. You are everything good there is in the world, Abigail. And I'm afraid I'm the opposite. I could be everything bad in the world."

"Jonah, you are not bad. I can see your heart in everything you do."

He stood, putting the slanted rock between them. "Then you know that a good man would want to find his family, the family he sees in his dreams."

She nodded, tears forming in her eyes. "I do know that. A bad man would have taken what he wanted without any qualms, before he left to find his family. Or maybe he would have left, not worrying about his family . . . or the woman he hurt."

"I don't want to hurt you."

"I don't want you to die."

They met, but stood apart. "You've taught me how to live, Abigail."

Tears spilled from her eyes. "And you've taught me about how I might live."

He'd never wanted to hold and kiss a woman more, but it was too dangerous, too much of a risk. He lifted his hands and then dropped them by his side, a feeling of raw defeat making his bones ache. "I wish . . . I could make this right."

She wiped at her eyes. "Do you still want me to try to sketch the child?"

His own eyes burning, he shook his head. "I can't. I'm not ready to go there. It hurts too much. I don't know what's holding me back, but it's something very dark."

"You'll have to face that darkness, one day."

"I'm getting close. I can feel it. But . . . as I said, I don't want to hurt you, Abigail."

Abigail started to move closer when they heard a noise along the secret lake path. Footsteps.

She stepped away. "I must go."

Jonah whirled, his whole system on alert. "Hurry," he told her in a whisper. "We'll talk later."

She turned and rushed away, but she looked back at him with fear in her eyes.

Jonah listened, that feeling of being watched coming over him again, the way it had the day in the stable, when Samson had gotten agitated. He could be imagining things, but his instincts were still intact, even if his brain wasn't.

Who was out there and what did they want?

Had someone finally come to finish him off?

CHAPTER TWENTY-EIGHT

Abigail felt a headache coming on. The festival started next week, and even though it only lasted one day, it took weeks to prepare for it. Today, one of the ovens had stopped working, and the trailer full of pumpkins that a local Amish farmer usually delivered had turned over on the main highway; half of the pumpkins were cracked and crushed. Now she had to find a second source for pumpkins. The farmer, a friend of her family, had apologized and offered to give her back the down payment.

"*Neh*," she'd told John Weaver when he'd brought her the news. "If you can help me find enough pumpkins for the festival, I'll be thankful. And if you can get them to lower the wholesale price, I'll save you a chocolate cake."

"*Denke*, Abigail," John had replied. "I know a man."

John needed every bit of the pumpkin crop money she'd paid him. He was Leah Weaver's brother-in-law and had four boys and two girls to feed.

Now, she stumbled into the office and sank down on the cushioned chair that had been here for as long as she could remember. She hadn't slept after she and Jonah had talked by the rock yesterday. How could two people feel so much and yet seem to hurt each other with every word they spoke?

Because he is the wrong man for you, and you are not the woman in his life. His other life.

She'd tried to convince herself of that most of the night and all day long. Jonah had avoided her as assiduously as she'd tried to avoid him. If someone had seen them together and almost in each other's arms, she'd be in serious trouble. She felt sure Mamm and Daed would have questioned her by now if they'd heard anything.

Abigail didn't want to live her life like this. Always looking over her shoulder and outright fibbing to her parents. She knew better. She'd been caught up in a dream that could never come true. She stood and headed out to find some fresh *kaffe*, but when she reached the hallway she ran straight into Jonah.

He grabbed her arms to keep from colliding with her. "Abigail?"

For a few heartbeats, they stood staring into each other's eyes. He let her go when he heard someone coming.

"Are you all right?" he asked, pushing at his hair.

Her breath caught. "I'm fine. I need *kaffe*."

"That sounds good," he said. "I didn't sleep very well."

"Me either." She turned toward the big kitchen, knowing it should be empty until the night crew took over. Knowing she should tell him to come back later.

Hurrying ahead, she let out a breath when he grabbed her hand. "Abigail?"

"Do not *Abigail* me," she said, tearing her hand away. "We almost got caught yesterday."

"We weren't doing anything," he whispered close to her ear.

"But we were thinking things."

Now he pushed in front of her, his eyes demanding her attention. "What were you thinking?"

"That I can't do this anymore," she said, lowering her head so he wouldn't see the truth in her eyes.

Jonah started to say something, but then looked past her. "Excuse me?"

"You are not excused! Get out of this kitchen."

Abigail whirled. "Aenti Miriam, what are you doing?"

Miriam advanced toward them, a raging fire of disapproval in her eyes. "Finding you two huddled up, I do believe."

Her aunt glared at Jonah. "What is he doing here—that is the question!"

"I work here," Jonah said, his tone calm. Too calm. "Abigail is my boss. We were discussing the festival."

"That didn't look like a business discussion," Aenti Miriam replied, her hands on her hips. "I came to help out and a *gut* thing I decided to check the kitchen first. Abigail, you are above such behavior."

Jonah tried to move past Abigail, but she held up her hand. "We were about to have some *kaffe,* Aenti. Would you like to join us?"

"*Neh.*" Her aunt huffed and turned to go out the side door. "I'm going to find your *mamm* and tell her this has to stop."

"It is going to stop," Jonah said, his tone conversational. "I'll be leaving soon. But I want you to know, Abigail has done nothing wrong. I'm a big flirt and she knows that. She told me to stop. I shouldn't flirt with the woman who saved my life, took me in, and gave me honest work. Ain't so?"

Abigail had never seen her aunt speechless, but the woman opened her mouth and then closed it again, her brown eyes bulging with indignation. Then she finally spouted, "I appreciate your taking responsibility for your inappropriate actions. You need to pray on that account."

"I will," Jonah said. "Abigail also gave me a Bible. Sure are a lot of sinners in there who managed to become saints. I've learned all about forgiveness. Judge not, lest you be judged."

Again, an openmouthed silence. If Abigail hadn't been so embarrassed and scared, her reaction would have been comical.

"I'm still going to have a word with my sister," her aunt finally said. "And you, whoever you are, better keep your word."

"I plan to do that," he replied. Then he shrugged. "I think I'd better get back to work, Abigail. But you both can rest assured I'll be leaving after the festival is over."

Abigail tried not to flinch, but her aunt gave her a shrewd glance that told her she'd failed. She watched as her aunt went in one direction and Jonah went the other way.

She wasn't sure which way *she* should turn.

"Are we ready?"

Abigail glanced around the inn's dining room, where the entire staff and her parents had gathered. The last few days had flown by, and she'd been too busy to worry about her aunt's interference. But she did fret about Jonah's words. Would he really leave, just like that?

Mamm hadn't said a word to her, making her hope that

Aenti Miriam was finally minding her own business. Abigail accepted that her aunt was right to call her out. She'd changed over the summer, and not in a good way. The adventure she'd always craved had come to her door, and now she was thankful for her home.

Thankful for Jonah, for his kindness and his hard work, she accepted that they'd changed each other.

Keeping busy had made it possible to avoid him. Her heart hurt with a gentle piercing each time she thought of Jonah no longer being here.

So she breathed in and focused, trying not to look directly at him. They had to get through this big, busy event before she could collapse in a heap and cry like a *bobbeli*.

"It's time. We open in one hour. All the booths are set up and ready, all the vendors anxious to sell their wares and products. You each have assignments, so let's get to it. And remember, we are kind and considerate. We are the ones who leave an impression about Shadow Lake Inn, and about our Amish community."

"And it has to be a *gut* one," Eliza said, grinning. "No goats attacking people and no more fires on the grills."

Everyone laughed at that and then scattered. The kitchen staff scurried to get things out to the cooking tent while Abigail went over her long list again.

Matthew hurried by. "I'll be working the outside tables with Colette," he reminded Abigail for the fifth time. Smitten.

Henry gave Abigail a big smile. "I've got things under control at the front desk and lobby, don't you worry. Anybody who isn't registered here won't make it upstairs."

"*Denke*, Henry," Abigail replied. "The café will be

busy enough without people wandering the hallways upstairs."

Edith called out, "We have enough pies for the second coming."

Maggie, back and with her younger sister Ruth Ann to watch little Samuel, rushed by. "It's nice being here in time for the festival."

"Don't do too much," Mamm said to Maggie. "You can rest and feed Samuel whenever need be."

Jonah stood back, but finally moved in front of Abigail. "I'll be helping with the pony rides and . . . wherever else you need me, Abigail."

I will always need you, she thought.

"*Denke*," she replied, using her professional tone, her eyes downcast.

"I'm not leaving after this," he whispered. "But soon, Abigail. We can talk before I go."

Was that supposed to make her feel better?

He gave her one last glance, his eyes wistful, then walked away.

Mamm came to stand beside her while Daed walked out with Jonah. "Abby, you look tired. I'm concerned about you. Your *aenti* is worried, too."

"I'm sure she's told you horrible things about me," Abigail said, her tone curt.

Mamm frowned, her brow furrowing. "Not really. She only told me you were working too hard. Is there something more I should know?"

What, her aunt hadn't rushed to tell everyone about her sins?

"I'm sorry, Mamm," Abigail said. "I am tired, but I'll rest when I can. We're in for a big crowd."

"I'll help where I can," Mamm said. "Miriam is out in the pie booth, thankfully."

Still nothing about her aunt catching her with Jonah the other day. Abigail nodded, wondering who'd been on the secret path when she and Jonah were talking. Maybe her mind had been playing tricks on her, and her guilty conscience had caught up with her.

"I'll start in here and come around to check on everyone."

Mamm nodded, then took her hand. "I love you, Abby. You are a *gut dochder*."

"I love you, too." Abigail hugged her mother close; then they parted and Mamm hurried away. Could her mother be protecting her, getting her through this event before she said anything more?

"I don't think we've ever been this busy," Abigail told Eliza that afternoon. They were in the café, serving plates of fried chicken, chicken salad, beef stew, and pork chops and gravy. They had side dishes of macaroni and cheese, greens, salads, and potato casseroles. Tourists loved home-cooked Amish food. Edith had been right about the pies. She'd cooked rows and rows of chocolate, apple, pecan, and sweet potato, along with shoofly and schnitz pie, and apple dumplings. Now, half of them were gone and Edith and Mamm were working away on the next round.

She rushed to the pass-through window and noticed a couple waiting at the café's entry. Abigail grabbed a pad and went out to seat them. "*Kumm*," she said, a smile on her face. "I'm sorry you had to wait."

The man was burly, with leathery skin, his eyes dark and darting. The woman was overmade, as Aenti Miriam would say, and her hair looked artificial. But they were hungry, and she had plenty of food, so Abigail would serve them.

"The special today is the roast beef," she said, glancing around to find Jonah standing near the kitchen. Probably waiting for pies to take out to the tent. Giving him a quick smile, she turned back around.

The man looked from her to Jonah. "Does he work here?"

Abigail's smile cracked, but she managed to stay calm. "*Ja*."

The man gave her a smirking stare. "He looks familiar. I think I know him. What's his name?"

She didn't know how to answer. This man had obviously seen some of the sketches they'd passed around.

"I have to hurry," she said to change the subject. "What would you like to drink?"

"Water for me and unsweetened tea for Stephanie."

"I'll be right back. You can look over the menu while I'm gone." She glanced back toward the door by the kitchen, relieved to see that Jonah wasn't there now. Maybe he'd gone back outside. She'd have to find him and warn him.

The man held a hand on her arm. "I said I think I recognize that guy. He looks a lot like a man I saw on the news months ago. What was his name, Stephanie?"

The blonde tossed her puffed hair. "Ken, Kevin. No,

Kent Dixon." Her brown eyes widened. "Wasn't he the one who planned to testify against that Mob boss in Chicago?"

"That's him," the man said, snapping his thick fingers. "Except . . . he went missing."

Abigail dropped her pad and pen. Hurrying to pick it up, she felt the man's hand over hers, his black eyes devoid of any emotion. "Let me get that." When she managed to hold on to the pad, he said, "We'll have the roast beef."

The blonde giggled. "He'll eat most of it."

Abigail nodded and twisted toward the kitchen. She quickly gave the order to one of the extra cooks. Then, still shaking, she grabbed Colette. "I have to go outside for a moment. I'll be right back."

Colette's eyebrows shot up. "What's wrong?"

"I'll explain later. If anyone asks, please cover for me."

Colette looked confused and then let out a sigh. "Abby, be careful."

Abigail nodded and hurried away. She had to find Jonah. Because she didn't trust the man who'd questioned her. She'd seen the evil in his dark eyes.

Jonah had never worked so much and so hard, but it felt good to get out some of his restlessness. He would leave this week, no matter what. He couldn't stay here with his feelings for Abigail eating away at him. He'd start by going to the FBI; the locals were either way behind or stonewalling him for some reason.

He'd tell Abigail that he loved her, that he'd never

forget her. But he had to find out about the woman and the child.

Right now, he headed toward the stable to help Eliza. The pony and buggy rides for the kids were a big hit. Despite his worry that he'd panic or have a memory flash, Jonah had managed to enjoy helping the little ones. Eliza kept him moving, but the crowds kept him on edge. Too many people milling around, staring at the Amish, making comments. He must never have liked crowds before because he sure didn't like them now.

He'd barely reached the open doors to the stable when he heard someone call his name. "Jonah!"

He turned and saw Abigail running toward him, fear on her face. He met her near the buggy rides, dodging running children and balloons as he hurried. Eliza saw them but was busy with the children. Jonah could see the concern on her face.

"What is it?" he asked Abigail.

She was out of breath, but she kept waving her hand back toward the inn. "A man, a big man with dark eyes. He says he recognizes you, Jonah."

Jonah's heart raced like a runaway train. "What else did he say?"

"He told me you were on the news a few months back. You were going to testify against a . . . Mob syndicate. Your name is Kent Dixon. You went missing." Grabbing his hand, she said, "Jonah, he's not a *gut* man."

Jonah stood still, his heart dropping to his feet, the breath leaving his body in a gut-wrenching rush. His head exploded with a pain so intense he almost doubled over. Abigail held his arm, guiding him to a bench. He looked up at her, then toward the inn, the anguish in his heart burning with a heat that scorched his soul. He looked up, glancing around, knowing he had to hide.

Abigail gasped. "That's him. The man and that awful woman with him."

The man and woman were walking together toward the stable, smiling, laughing. Until the man looked up and into Jonah's eyes.

Then Jonah knew. He knew who he used to be, what he used to be, saw the past in a flash, remembered what had happened to him. And to his wife and child.

Jonah stood and grabbed Abigail by the hand. "We have to hide. Now, Abigail."

The man hurried across the grounds, pulled out a gun, and aimed it straight at them. Jonah shoved Abigail into the barn and held her behind him. He heard a swish of air as a bullet hit the barn door two inches from his head. A silencer. The man knew what he was doing all right.

Eliza called out, "What's wrong?" She couldn't leave the children, so she stood watching them.

Abigail shook her head and gave her sister a warning stare, then Jonah grabbed her hand and said, "Run. Now."

"Jonah, what's going on?" she asked as he tugged her through the stable to the open doors on the other side. "Jonah?"

"I know, Abigail. I know that man and I know what happened. I remember." He stopped only long enough to touch his hands to her face. "He's a hit man, and he's here to kill me."

CHAPTER TWENTY-NINE

Abigail's heart hammered warnings, her hand still in Jonah's. "What are you saying?"

"I remember," he replied, glancing back once they'd escaped through the back of the stable. His breath came in huffs as he tried to speak, but his words were shaky and his voice husky. "We have to get out of here. He saw you with me."

Dragging her past the big rock, he stumbled over saplings and undergrowth, until they were hidden in a bluff full of trees with changing leaves. Off in the distance, he could hear the waterfall splashing and gurgling.

She tugged him to a stop after he'd turned her toward the secret path to the lake. "You remember *everything*?"

His expression told her the answer to that question. A tormented expression etched his face. "Jonah?"

He took in air, shook his head, nodded, and then held her hands in his. "I'm not Kent Dixon or even your Jonah. I'm Kane Dawson. I'm a detective with the Atlanta police."

"Atlanta? Georgia?" Abigail couldn't believe this day

had come. "How did you . . . what were you doing on Lake Erie?"

They heard footfalls running in the grass near the rock.

"Let's get out of here," he said, not waiting for her to agree. Then he tugged her down the treacherous path. Dodging shrubs and slippery fallen leaves, he kept hold of her as he zigzagged across the bluffs. Below them, the water rushed and crashed against the shore in a choppy, dark mood.

"Jonah, we should call for help," she whispered, frightened by the way his whole countenance had changed. This, she guessed, was the way he used to look. "My family will be worried. I have to do something to let them know."

He kept dragging her, lifting her when the path became too narrow. "We'll do that once I know you're safe."

"Why wouldn't I be safe?"

"Because, Abigail, I told you—he's seen you with me. He won't leave any witnesses."

"A hit man? What does that mean?"

Jonah guided her down another incline. "It means someone is paying that man to find me and end my life. He won't like that you came to warn me. You're in a lot of danger, Abigail. And . . . it's all my fault."

Abigail held the fear caused by his words at bay. "I have my phone. We can call nine-one-one."

They made it down to the beach and he looked around. "We will, but not yet," he said. "We need a place, Abigail. A quiet place, before you call anyone. I need to tell you something."

She heard the catch in his voice. He remembered

everything, which meant he remembered the woman and the child, too.

"The waterfall," she said. "We'll be safe there until you decide what to do."

He nodded, and then he looked into her eyes, his hands reaching for hers. "I know what I have to do, but first I need to be honest about the man I used to be, and what happened to that man."

Jonah listened to the sound of the falling water, his mind whirling with so much information he felt like a computer about to overheat. *Dear God, why did I have to remember this? Why?*

They needed to hurry and find a way out. Abigail didn't deserve to be in danger, but he had to tell her the truth.

"Here," she said, guiding him to a low rock that made a perfect bench. "I'm going to text Eliza that I have an emergency."

"No," he said. "Just give me a few minutes before . . . before we go back."

He knew he'd be leaving now. He had no choice. But first, no matter what, he had to be honest with Abigail.

She put her phone away and stared at him. "You said you remembered everything?"

He nodded, the adrenaline now draining away to leave him exhausted and full of a grief he'd tried to bury. Taking her hand, he marveled at the beauty of it. Her fingers were slender with clean, groomed nails, her skin like pale, blushing porcelain, her touch so soft, so tentative.

"I remember them," he said, his throat husky with tears he'd held back for years now. "I remember both of them."

Abigail took in a breath. "You are married, then. You have a family."

He saw the tears in her eyes. Then he said on a shaky whisper, "I *was* married. A dad. Happy, but my work took on a life of its own and . . . we had troubles. We loved each other, though, I can tell you that."

Abigail wiped at her eyes. "What happened?"

"They're gone now," he said, a sob shuddering through his body. "Dead. My beautiful Dani and my sweet Ethan. Gone."

Abigail put a hand to her mouth, tears rolling down her cheeks. "Jonah, I'm so sorry. Jonah . . ."

"They murdered my wife and my sweet boy, Abigail. Rigged the brakes on her car and she lost control, went into a ditch, a ravine." He let go of her and bent his head over his hands. "I figured things out, knew Dani was on her way home. I tried to call her to warn her, but she didn't answer. She didn't answer."

"Jonah." Abigail moved closer to him and took him into her arms. "I'm so sorry."

He reached for her and held her close, clinging to her because she'd saved him. "I got there as soon as I could, and it was horrible. The police and an ambulance came right after I found them. I tried to save my wife. I tried to save Dani, but Ethan, he was already gone. My little, four-year-old boy who used to love the tire swing on the old oak in our front yard—gone. He lay there, asleep. Just gone to sleep. I kept telling myself that. He's only asleep. He'll wake up. I even told the paramedics that, didn't want them to move him out of my arms. They made me give him up. They took Dani and Ethan away."

He stopped, the tears too much, the pain as unbearable now as it had been back then. He held Abigail while he cried the tears he'd kept sealed away, cried for the family he'd lost and for his soul, his lost, angry, reckless soul. Before he'd cried with rage and anger and a deep determination to seek revenge. A death wish. In a way, he'd gone to ground because he wanted to end his torment, one way or another.

Lifting his head, he felt Abigail's soft touch on his damp hair, on his jawline, her eyes full of understanding. But she had to know the whole story.

So, he told her the truth.

"And then I set out to kill all of them."

"The day I buried my family, I vowed I'd kill all of them. I came so close, Abigail, so close."

Abigail sat in shock, her heart heavy with what he'd told her. His family had died, murdered by horrible people. No wonder he didn't want anyone to find him. He was running from his memories, and he'd had a need for vengeance that had overcome him and almost killed him.

"You told me once you wanted to die," she said, her emotions crashing along with the waterfall beside them. "You almost did."

"My soul died," he said. "My heart died." He took her hand, his tears spent now. "You brought me back to life."

Abigail didn't know what to say. He was the same, but different. That rugged, raw edge she'd caught glimpses of was now in full view. And the sadness. So much sadness.

"What should we do?" she asked, concerned for him and for her family. Her phone had been buzzing with calls from Eliza and Colette. Her sisters were obviously covering for her. She texted back, "I'm okay. Will explain later."

"They're worried," Jonah said. "I shouldn't have dragged you away. I didn't want anything to happen to you."

"I have to go back, Jonah. My whole family could be in danger, and we've got people everywhere." She'd fall apart later. Right now, she had to be practical.

He nodded and wiped at his face with a choppy, quick touch. "Call nine-one-one and find a spot for the police to pick me up. I'll ask them to send someone to the inn, to watch over all of you. They'll take you home."

She nodded, wondering if she'd ever see him again. Wondering if he knew how much she loved him.

She gave him the phone. "You need to make the call."

"Okay. How do we get back to the road?"

She told him about a walking trail. "It could be crowded today, but we can cut through the woods and make it to the road."

They started walking, hurrying now, while he made the call for help. She could feel Jonah slipping away from her, could see the apprehension and determination in his eyes, in the way he barked orders into the phone.

They reached the road and waited for someone to pick them up. "Why were you always so wary about the police?" she asked, still trying to accept what had happened today. "If you're one of them, didn't you trust them?"

"Because I left, Abigail. I left and I went undercover on my own. They couldn't protect my family and they can't protect me. But I can't hide forever. Now that I know what I need to do, nothing can stop me."

Not even me, she thought. *You won't give this up for me?* Then she realized how selfish that sounded. This man was hurting and had just remembered losing his family in a tragic car crash. She had no part in this. But her heart told her otherwise.

"Jonah," she said, taking his hand again. "You can't take on a vendetta, not another one. You almost got killed."

"I was so close, but someone tipped them off. They were trying to take me to Chicago, to the boss. I escaped, but they caught me in Pennsylvania and put me on a big yacht, brought me to Lake Erie to kill me and feed me to the fishes. I tried to get away again, to make it to Chicago on my own. They shot me and hit me over the head, thinking I'd drown."

"But you didn't," she said. "You were given another chance. Please, don't do this on your own. Jonah, please."

Before he could respond, a police cruiser arrived, and two officers jumped out. She listened while he told them about the man with the gun, and about him getting his memory back. Then he told the officers to take him to the station so he could call the FBI.

Within a matter of minutes, the patrol car had taken Abigail back to the inn. Before he let her out of the car, Jonah made sure they alerted the patrol car already at the festival to watch over the crowd, and to stay on guard until further notice.

Jonah touched her hand before she got out of the car. "I'll be back later to make sure you're okay." When she hesitated, he said, "Abigail, I mean it. I will be back."

She could only nod, her eyes tearing up again, but she felt in her heart that Jonah would never return.

Abigail made her way up to the porch and into the inn. Henry took one look at her and ran to grab her. "Abigail, what's happened? We realized you were missing and . . . then we found out someone had fired a shot. Eliza saw you and Jonah running toward the woods. Your parents are upset. Your aunt has them believing you ran away with Jonah."

"I know," she said. "I know. I need to get to the cottage."

"I'll call Matthew. He can bring the golf cart."

"*Neh*," she said. "Let one of my sisters bring the golf cart around. Matthew needs to stay out of this."

Henry nodded, worry clear on his face.

"I'll be in the ladies' room," she said.

Abigail hurried to the privacy of the women's bathroom. She washed her face and then leaned over the sink, her mind whirling with so many emotions she felt as if she were clinging to a buoy out in the middle of the vast lake. Jonah had his memories back, but what horrible, awful memories.

He'd lost his family to an evil organization.

He'd lost his soul to grief and revenge.

Now that she knew the truth, she wondered if she'd ever had a part of his heart at all. Or if he'd just been biding his time until he could seek that revenge again.

CHAPTER THIRTY

Eliza brought her a cup of hot tea. Colette tried to get her to eat. Her mother kept checking on her. Aenti Miriam stared at her.

Abigail couldn't move. She could hardly find her next breath. The numbness of what had happened had her shaking and frozen in time. She remembered the man lifting that strange-looking gun, the woman smirking as she watched. No one else had noticed, but Eliza had seen the whole thing. Jonah had shoved Abigail, and then she was running, running, Jonah's hand in hers.

"The girls and the staff have taken care of everything," Mamm said, her eyes full of uneasiness. "Your *daed* has talked to the police. They can't find the man with the gun, but Eliza saw him and the woman running away, and several people were able to describe both of them. That will back up what you saw."

"This is what happens when you play with fire," Aenti Miriam said, her tone full of a grating indignation. "I thought he would honor his word, but obviously he didn't. He could have taken you hostage, Abby."

"He would not do that," Abigail finally said. Standing,

she paced the kitchen. "He only wanted to protect me and this family, and he is living up to his word. He's leaving, probably today."

"*Ja*, because he brought this danger right into your home. The very thing we were all afraid of has happened."

"Miriam," Mamm said, her tone curt and clear, "do not make me regret letting you stay the night. We are okay, and that is all that matters now. I hope Jonah will find the peace he needs."

Aenti Miriam settled down. "He's dangerous. I could see that the first time I met him."

Mamm glared at her sister. "Remember when we were young and foolish, Sister? Remember that one summer during our Rumspringa?"

Her aunt's face turned pale, and her eyes dulled. Giving Mamm a shocked stare, she went quiet and got up and left the room.

Thankful for that, Abigail placed her hands around her teacup. "She's right. I was foolish, but this is not my running around season. I'm old enough to know better."

Mamm came to her and sat her back down. "You have a kind heart, Abby. It's not a bad trait to have, but it can cause you to care too much. We should have put our foot down from the beginning, but we thought it would work itself out. And it has. Awful, terrible what these evil people did to his family, but Jonah knows who he is now, and he's gone back to that other world. You must let this go, and you must let him go."

Abigail lifted her eyes to her mother. "How can I let him go when he's in my heart, Mamm? I know it's wrong. I shouldn't feel this way about a man who is not like us, but I saved him, brought him back to life—or at least showed him our way of life. He did okay here with us."

"*Ja*, but he does not belong with us," Mamm said, touching her hand to Abigail's cheek. "You should rest."

"I can't rest," Abigail said. "I'm going to walk the property and help with cleanup."

"*Neh*." Her mother's tone of voice told Abigail that couldn't happen. "It might not be safe for you."

Abigail stared out the window. The crowds had died down now. Eliza had told her that after the man with the gun ran away, several people had left the festival.

"Only a few saw the gun, but word got out, and little by little, people began to leave. We'll have to see how the grand tally goes, but I think over all we'll make enough to contribute as much as we usually do to the community."

Abigail would think about all that later. Thankful that no one had been hurt or killed, she knew she'd relive the horror of that moment when she'd looked up and seen that gun aimed at her and Jonah.

Now she watched the empty gardens for any sign of him. It had been hours and he still hadn't returned.

He said he'd be back.

She couldn't think beyond that, so she turned to help clean the kitchen and get ready for the night. She wouldn't sleep. How could she? But she glanced out the window one more time.

And saw Jonah walking across the yard.

Abigail rushed upstairs, not bothering to explain. She hurried to the big armoire where she kept the quilt, grabbed it, and hurried back downstairs, past her shocked mother and aunt, past her sisters, who were walking along the path between the inn and the cottage.

Jonah saw her coming and stopped.

"Abigail," he said, his voice husky and raw, his eyes red-rimmed and weary.

"I only wanted to give you this, Jonah."

She tried to hand him the folded quilt.

Jonah looked down at the soft materials. "Let's go to the rock."

She glanced at her sisters, who were now within earshot. "Tell Mamm I'll be right back."

They nodded, watched as she and Jonah walked away.

They made it to the rock, and he sat and motioned for her to do the same. "I came back to change clothes and gather what little I have. I need to go back to Atlanta to testify on what I know about these people—a big organization of gunrunners and drug dealers. We have enough evidence now to prosecute them."

"We? You've cleared things with the police, then?"

He looked up and into her eyes. "I did, after talking to the FBI. They were watching me, but only because they thought I might still be deep undercover. They had no idea about my memory loss. I wanted to blame the police back in Atlanta, but they didn't do this. I had suspicions someone on the inside had set me up, and I was correct. But that officer is dead now. These criminals killed him to keep him quiet. I told the FBI I'd infiltrated their organization. I have files hidden, files that can prove what they've done. I have to go back and finish my job."

"In the proper way?" she asked, her whole system

missing him already. "You won't go off on your own again—promise me?"

He took her hand. "*You're* the reason I *didn't* strike out on my own again."

Abigail didn't want to cry, but the tears slipped down her face. "I'm proud of you, Jonah . . . I mean, Kane."

He wiped at her tears, his touch soft, his callused fingers soothing her broken heart. "I'll always be your Jonah. Don't you know that?"

She wanted to believe him, but he seemed different now. "Will you take the quilt?"

He lifted it and opened it up, spreading it out on the soft grass. Then he looked at all the squares, his hand going to his mouth as a dry sob hit him. "The tree swing," he said, pointing to that scene. "My Ethan." He touched the boy's laughing face. "The house with the big magnolia tree in the backyard—the home I wound up selling because I couldn't live there alone."

Abigail sniffed and nodded. He touched his hand on the square with Samson. "I love this horse," he said. Then he touched the scene with the woman walking along the beach. "You," he said, moving his fingers down the stitching. "You—coming to me like an angel on earth."

"It's not finished," she said. "But you should take it."

He shook his head, breaking her heart all over again. "No. You keep it, because one day it will be finished."

Then he stood and lifted her up and into his arms. "I came back today for one more thing." Holding his hand on her neck, he tugged her close. "I want to be the first man to kiss you, Abigail."

His mouth covered hers as a soft gasp left her lips.

The kiss told her all she needed to know. He loved her.

He might not be able to stay here, but he loved her. His lips were tender and sweet, demanding and passionate, and full of love.

He finally lifted away and touched his hand to her cheek. "I'm coming back," he whispered. "I'm coming back for you." Giving her a feathery kiss, he said, "Keep our quilt and when I return, you can finish it."

Then he folded the quilt and handed it back to her. "Go now and be with your family. I've got people watching this place. So be safe until I return."

Abigail couldn't stop crying. She took the quilt and watched as he went toward the carriage *haus*. Then she turned and headed home, their quilt the only pieces of him she ever expected to have.

Over the next week, Abigail went about her business as usual. She gathered all the receipts and invoices from the festival, glad they'd managed to make a decent profit so they could give most of the extra funds to the community to help those in need.

But she didn't know if she'd ever be able to enjoy the Fall Festival again. Everywhere she turned, memories of Jonah followed her. She'd come with Eliza this morning to finally clean the apartment. She'd put if off all week, but the thought of Jonah not waiting there made her sit down in a chair and stare at the wall, a pillowcase clutched to her chest. She took in the fresh, clean smell mixed with Jonah's scent, her heart caught in the memory of their kiss. Until Eliza took her hand.

"Abby, I can finish this," Eliza said. "Why don't you

go for a walk on the beach? The police said we're safe now, since they located the man who tried to harm Jonah."

The beach.

She couldn't go back there right now.

"Abby, we all miss him, even Daed. Take a short break. Winter is coming, so use this time to enjoy your walk before it's too cold." Eliza motioned toward the door. "I know you've spent your free time adding to the quilt. Why don't you go to the place where it started, and let go of your pain?"

Abigail nodded and slowly made her way out into the gardens and down the path she'd taken the day she'd found Jonah. The open path. No more secrets. She'd had some quiet talks with her parents. They wanted her to consider Ben's offer.

Abigail had explained she'd rather be an *alte maidal* than marry a man she didn't love. Even Aenti Miriam gave a nod at her words.

"The girl does make a *gut* point," she'd said before she left yesterday. "I married quickly to a man I didn't love. I came to care for Joseph, but . . . we had a difficult marriage."

Abigail decided she'd misjudged her cantankerous aunt. She might wind up like her one day.

Now, as she stood on the beach and let the wind and water spray a cool mist over her, Abigail prayed to be cleansed and made new again, to be able to forget how much she loved Jonah. Today, with the mauve and orange leaves dancing in the crisp fall air, she knew she'd have to wait for the Lord to bring her healing.

Then she turned to go to the house and saw a strange

man approaching her. Sensing he wasn't friendly, she whirled to hurry away, but the man rushed toward her and caught her arm. Then he shoved her toward the water, a gun in his hand.

"What do you want?" she asked, trying to gather her wits to escape despite her deep fear.

"I came here for one reason," he hissed, his eyes dead and dark. "I've been ordered to kill you. Kane Dawson will have to live with another death on his conscience."

They'd sent another man—seeking revenge on Jonah yet again?

Abigail tried to breathe, tried to think of a way out. Jonah would never forgive himself. This would be the end for both of them.

The man shoved her toward the choppy waves. She pushed at him and tried to make a break for it, but he held her arm, his meaty hand pressing into her skin with a painful heaviness. "Don't run. I'll shoot you in the back."

Abigail went still and accepted there was no way out. She stared into the man's eyes without fear. "Then do what you must. I will forgive you."

That seemed to startle him. He stumbled and hesitated. "I appreciate that," he said. "But I still have to kill you."

Then she thought of Jonah and what might have been. She'd had the love of her life. That love would last through eternity.

She closed her eyes and waited, praying the bullet would kill her instantly. She focused on Jonah and how he'd kissed her. She concentrated on that feeling, that release, that peace.

But a shout down the beach caused her to open her eyes.

"Stop!"

The man shoved Abigail down into the ice-cold water and pivoted around. Gunshots pierced the quiet countryside, scaring birds from the bluffs. The panicked man turned the gun on her.

Abigail screamed and lifted herself out of the water, ready to fight.

Jonah came running toward her with several police officers.

"Drop the gun," Jonah called.

The man shook his head and pushed her into the water, his gun so close she could see into the barrel.

"Drop the gun," another officer called out. The man shoved her back down and aimed.

One of the officers lifted his gun and shot the stranger before he pulled the trigger. The man fell into the water, his blood marring the wavelets.

Jonah rushed to Abigail and lifted her out of the water, his eyes wild with fear. "Are you all right?"

She couldn't believe he was here. She managed to nod before she started shivering. He took off his jacket and wrapped it around her. "Abigail, Abigail."

"How did you know?" she asked, tears in her eyes.

"I was coming home to you," he said, holding the lapels of his jacket together to keep her warm. "I decided to walk the beach . . . I don't know why. But then I saw a man lurking on the road near the cove. I called the local officers for backup." He tugged the jacket over her and pulled her into his arms. "I could have killed him myself, but . . . God's will, Abigail. God's will."

Then he kissed her and whispered, "I love you. I told you I'd come back, and this time I'm here to stay."

While the officers called in the shooting and went about their business, Jonah held her there. "It's over, Abigail. My evidence was solid. I proved they killed my family, and I got word from the Chicago police that they've rounded up everyone who worked for this organization. This guy was the last holdout, obviously. I'll testify in court later, but they can't hurt us anymore. I promise that life I remembered is over. You're my life now."

Abigail smiled up at him. "So . . . you want to become Amish, Kane Dawson?"

"I want to become Amish. But I'm Jonah now. Jonah Kane. I'll change my name legally and . . . I can finally grow this beard because I plan on being a married man soon."

"Married? To me?"

"Who else would I marry?" he said, kissing her.

While the water lapped around them, Abigail cried tears of joy. "Nice to meet you, Jonah Kane. And . . . I love you, too."

The next spring . . .

Jonah finished dressing and looked at the quilt folded on the bed. He could never walk by it without touching it, moving his hands over the stitches, seeing the patterns and the squares that told a story. His story.

Abigail had finished it over Christmas, while he'd

finished his sessions with the bishop and several other elders of the community. He touched the big magnolia blossom in the middle of the quilt; then his fingers trailed over the image of a blond woman glancing back at him in an apple orchard. His Dani, with Ethan laughing at her side. He'd always love and miss them.

His hand stopped on the panel Abigail had finished last week.

The panel of a man and woman in Amish wedding clothes, holding hands as they stood by a big, jutting rock with the lake in the background.

His bride, their bedroom, in their new home not far from the cottage, their stories merged in this quilt. Their future merged together as they became man and wife.

"The memory quilt," Abigail had told him. "And we'll make new memories together."

"We're gonna need a bigger quilt," he'd whispered in her ear.

A knock at the door brought him around.

He opened it to find Matthew and Henry grinning at him. "Is it time?"

"Time," Henry said. "Your beautiful bride is waiting."

"Well, we can't have that. She's waited long enough."

Jonah made his way to the bluffs and the rock, decorated now with freshly cut flowers. Rows of benches lined the open aisle as friends and neighbors waited for them to speak their vows. He smiled and wiped at his eyes while he waited for Abigail, his bride, his life.

When he saw her walking toward him in a pretty, cream-colored dress, a bouquet of colorful flowers in her hands, her sisters with her in light blue dresses, he knew he was exactly where he was supposed to be.

Jonah smiled at her and she smiled back, tears in her eyes. Just as he'd seen in his dream, she came walking toward him. But this time, he knew they would always be together. He felt content and loved, here in this quiet place, with these Plain people.

Abigail loved him, and he loved her.

No more secrets. They were on the right path now.

Please read on for an excerpt from

THE FORGIVING QUILT

by Lenora Worth,
Book Two in the Shadow Lake Inn Series.

"Doc, will I ever be able to walk straight again?"

Eliza King gave Dr. Samuel Merrill a pleading stare, her heart as heavy as the cast on her left leg. She'd never get on a ladder again, that was for certain sure. "I miss my horses."

She missed her mobility, too. She'd been in the hospital for a few days now. Still remembering the excruciating pain of falling from a ladder onto the hard floor of the stable alley, she tried to block out the awful sound of her bones breaking and the shivering shock moving through her system.

That had been a week ago. She was ready to go home.

The Shadow Lake Inn, nestled in a cove near Lake Erie, Pennsylvania, always had a lot of visitors during the fall. The leaf-lookers would fill the woods and walkways and keep the inn's employees hopping as they served in the restaurant and cleaned the guest rooms. The inn would be so busy in the next few weeks. She had picked a bad time to get hurt.

But when was there a *gut* time?

The gray-haired *Englisch* doctor patted her arm and

smiled. "Eliza, you have been impatient since the day you were born. Even though I didn't deliver you, I've taken care of you most of your life. But this is serious. You shattered your leg with that fall, you had surgery to repair it. The bones will take time to heal."

"You know how things are at the inn," Eliza said, wondering how Abigail and Colette were handling things without her. Fall had come in vivid reds and golds—her favorite time of year. Jonah would take care of the horses, of course. Her brother-in-law was *gut* with the animals, but now that Daed had cut back the time he spent helping around the Shadow Lake Inn, Jonah had taken on even more responsibility in the second year of his marriage to her older sister, Abigail.

Eliza needed to be with her horses. "How long, Doc?"

Mamm sat in a chair by the window. "Eliza, you heard the doctor. Surgery is serious. Your bones were pinned back together. Healing will take time." Looking up at Dr. Merrill, Mamm said, "She will follow all your directions. I'll make sure of that."

Dr. Merrill nodded. "Your mother is highly qualified to take care of you. Being a trained midwife does come in handy, and Sarah, you go beyond just helping with births. I appreciate your keen interest in all things medical."

"And I appreciate all your *gut* advice through the years," Mamm replied with a smile. "So let's go over your instructions for Eliza."

"At least six to eight weeks in the cast, then a cane or a walker, and a lot of physical therapy."

Eliza let out a sigh. "That's the whole winter season."

"You can sit and read and rest, Eliza." Then he smiled again. "You will have other seasons."

Eliza knew the doctor had her best interests at heart. "I don't want to get an infection or cause more pain. I'm thankful you helped me and found a competent surgeon. I'll do my best to stay off my leg."

"You must," Mamm said. "You asked for over-the-counter medicine, but I'll mix up a batch of herbal ointment to ease the itching and dryness and soothe your muscles."

"And remember, Eliza," Dr. Merrill said, "if the pain increases, don't be brave. We can send you a prescription."

"Can you send me a helper?" she quipped, glancing at her mother's soft smile.

The doctor, so familiar with her family history and her love of books, sat down behind his desk. "I know a man who's good with horses. He's Amish, someone who recently returned to Shadow Lake. He's looking for work. He's also a farrier, so he can make sure Samson and his brood are happy and healthy. I've had him out to my farm to work with my horses."

"But I have a stable with spoiled, picky animals," she reminded him. "And unlike you, my place is not a fancy ranch with lots of helpers."

"I do have a great staff," he said with a grin. "They could use some advice from a taskmaster like you, however." Placing his hands on his desk pad, he chuckled. "Samson is a handful."

Samson was their big, gray draft horse—and her favorite. Rosebud, Sunshine, Pickles, and the pony, Peaches, they all needed her.

"I can't abandon my animals, Doc."

"You won't be abandoning them. You can visit the

stable as long as you keep this leg elevated as much as possible. I could arrange for a wheelchair."

"*Neh*," Eliza said, shaking her head so fast the ribbons on her *kapp* shook. "I'll rig up a small buggy. Pickles can give me free rides to the stable."

"That's my Eliza. Innovative and determined." He wrote out some orders and handed them to her. "Don't overdo it. If you do, your leg might not heal properly and then, yes, you could walk with a limp."

"Crippled?"

"We don't refer to it in those terms. And you wouldn't be completely disabled."

Eliza would get well. A lot of people depended on her, and she wouldn't let a broken leg get in the way of her responsibility to them. Meanwhile, she'd do what she had to do. "You can send that man over, Doc. We need the help." Then she tossed out, "But if I don't approve of him, we'll find help elsewhere."

Levi Lapp stopped at the end of the lane leading up to the Shadow Lake Inn. He'd never dreamed he'd return here one day, not after that terrible night six years ago.

The night he'd made the worst mistake of his life.

But when Dr. Merrill called him yesterday and told him he was needed, Levi couldn't say no. He'd come back to Shadow Lake for two reasons—to find work closer to home and to ask Eliza King to forgive him.

But he couldn't have imagined those two goals would merge into something he wasn't yet prepared to do—face his mistakes head-on.

His *mamm* always said, "*Gott* will find you, and he will redeem you."

Well, Mamm, *you were so right there.*

Gott seemed to have a sense of humor, too. Or a sense of justice.

Levi reckoned it was time to face his past, head-on.

After Dr. Merrill had called him, he'd asked his friend to let him make the introductions. The doctor had been too busy to argue with him. Now here Levi was, about to start working for the very family he'd dishonored in a foolish attempt to impress his friends during Rumspringa. His running around days were over and he'd returned to his faith. But he'd been away traveling for years, doing his work in various Amish communities. When his *mamm* had got word to him that Daed was ailing, Levi had hurried home. Now he'd stay for the rest of his life. His *daed* had died three days after he returned.

That was a month ago.

You need the work, he reminded himself. *Don't be a coward.*

Levi snapped the reins and sent Rudolph, the gentle, reddish-brown quarter horse he'd raised from a colt, back onto the gravel lane. Rudolph really did have a furry red nose, with a white streak of fur moving up that noble nose to shoot across the top of the gelding's head. Children loved him, and Rudolph loved humans. Maybe he would help Levi win over Eliza again. Dr. Merrill said he knew the Kings very well, and that they needed a hand right now. Not sure what had happened, Levi knew enough about medical privacy rules to keep from asking questions.

Rudolph was *gut* at dealing with hurting humans, but

Levi wondered if *he'd* be able to help Eliza, or if she'd send him packing.

He went on up the lane, taking in the canopy of fall trees in various colors, ranging from golden yellows and bursting oranges to russet, with burgundy splatters here and there. Fall, the air crisp with a freshness that sent away the hot winds of summer and replaced them with clean, fresh, cold rushes of air.

He guided Rudolph toward the stable, hoping to avoid the historic, Colonial-style inn where the three King sisters would surely be bossing everyone around. He smiled at that. Those girls were different, more independent and a little more progressive than most of the Amish girls he'd met.

Eliza had a mind of her own, and the one time he'd tried the wrong moves on her, she'd let him have it with a slap and a promise that she'd knock him out if he ever came near her again.

To calm his nerves, he took in the view of the lake below the bluffs, then turned to glance toward the inn. A huge, old place, steeped in history, and still thriving thanks to the King family, who'd taken it over after the *Englisch* couple who'd hired them had left it to Eliza's parents. He'd spent a lot of time here, at singings and frolics and during church, when he'd glance across the aisle to find Eliza's golden-brown hair and beautiful hazel eyes. Her eyes reminded him of the changing leaves—so many different facets and colors, depending on her mood.

He prayed she'd be in a *gut* mood today.

Levi pulled his custom-built buggy up close to the open barn doors. He didn't have a sign on his buggy, but it was equipped with whatever he'd need to take care of shoeing a horse or cleaning up an existing shoe.

After tying Rudolph's reins to a hitching post, he started toward the stable, his heart hammering, his hands sweaty with regret and apprehension and just a dash of anticipation. Maybe Eliza's hard feelings for him would have softened by now.

Then he heard her.

"I don't like this, Jonah. A stranger working with Samson. You know how Samson is, ain't so?"

The man answered her. "I was a stranger, and *Englisch* at that. You accepted me."

"But I trained you," she said. "I was able to watch you and help you and correct you." A pause, a sigh. "Besides, you were a fast learner, and I had to keep you away from Abigail."

"*Ja,* you sure did all those things."

Her laughter, like the sound of tiny bells chiming, hit Levi square in his midsection, somewhere in the vicinity of his heart. He remembered that laughter. He also remembered her tears.

He'd embarrassed her, hurt her feelings, and if she hadn't stopped him, he might have done something he would have regretted. He regretted even thinking of such a thing now.

He was going to need a lot of courage to go into that stable and face the woman he'd tried to seduce when she was seventeen. Eliza was no longer a child.

But he was no longer that kind of boy either. He'd changed and grown in ways that had left imprints on his heart. Eliza King had left a big imprint on his heart.

He would never be that stupid again.

Connect with Us

Visit us online at
KensingtonBooks.com
to read more from your favorite authors, see books
by series, view reading group guides, and more.

 Join us on social media

for sneak peeks, chances to win books and prize packs,
and to share your thoughts with other readers.

facebook.com/kensingtonpublishing
twitter.com/kensingtonbooks

Tell us what you think!

To share your thoughts, submit a review,
or sign up for our eNewsletters, please visit:
KensingtonBooks.com/TellUs.